Readers love the
Club Whisper series by Xenia Melzer

A Dom and His Writer

"The writing is vivid with all the best emotions and feels. This was a heartwarming and entertaining read with a bit of angst and hot chemistry. Highly recommended."

—Love Bytes

"It's been a long time since I've stayed up until the early hours of the morning reading a book, but this one had me hooked."

—Open Skye Book Reviews

A Dom and His Artist

"A really enjoyable read that brought home the fact that BDSM is not about a set of rules that cannot be broken, but about finding the right set of rules…."

—Two Chicks Obsessed

"Ms. Melzer does an amazing job of character creation…."

—The Romance Reviews

A Dom and His Warrior

"This is a great read, and I hope you all enjoy this as much as I. Happy reading."

—OptimuMM

By XENIA MELZER

Love Wins Anthology

CLUB WHISPER
A Dom and His Writer
A Dom and His Artist
A Dom and His Warrior
A Dom and His Gentleman

Published by DREAMSPINNER PRESS
www.dreamspinnerpress.com

A DOM AND AND HIS GENTLEMAN

XENIA MELZER

DREAMSPINNER PRESS

Published by

DREAMSPINNER PRESS

5032 Capital Circle SW, Suite 2, PMB# 279, Tallahassee, FL 32305-7886 USA
www.dreamspinnerpress.com

This is a work of fiction. Names, characters, places, and incidents either are the product of author imagination or are used fictitiously, and any resemblance to actual persons, living or dead, business establishments, events, or locales is entirely coincidental.

A Dom and His Gentleman
© 2019 Xenia Melzer

Cover Art
© 2019 Aaron Anderson
aaronbydesign55@gmail.com
Cover content is for illustrative purposes only and any person depicted on the cover is a model.

Digital ISBN: 978-1-64405-428-4
Trade Paperback ISBN: 978-1-64405-429-1
Library of Congress Control Number: 2019930017
Trade Paperback published June 2019
v. 1.0

Printed in the United States of America
∞
This paper meets the requirements of
ANSI/NISO Z39.48-1992 (Permanence of Paper).

For Aquamarin—you always help me find my calm.

ACKNOWLEDGMENTS

THANKING ALL the wonderful people who help me get my stories out never gets old. A very big thanks to Rose Archer, my new senior editor, who made the transition of editors perfectly smooth for me. Also thank you to Yv and Liz Bichmann, for finding all those pesky mistakes I generously read over or just blatantly ignore. You polished this story to perfection! Big hugs go to my husband, who had to put up with my (not so) temporary obsession with everything silver fox and British Gentleman. I swear I'll stop swooning over Anderson Cooper sometime soon. Also thank you to everybody at Dreamspinner working behind the scenes, and Aaron Anderson for the perfect cover. The biggest thanks go out to my readers, who keep telling me nice things about my stories, which I greatly appreciate!

CHAPTER 1

CURTIS MORRIS, renowned art dealer and agent for the famous and internationally sought-after artist and painter, Rainbow Snake, didn't know whether he should laugh or tear his hair out about his charge's latest idea. Collin, aka Rainbow Snake, would have his second BDSM exhibition at Club Whisper soon and had had some kind of artistic epiphany, something that happened quite regularly with him. It usually fell either to Curtis or Martin, Collin's fiancé and Dom, to guide the armada of Collin's wild ideas into calm waters.

"Collin, I like your idea, I really do. But don't forget, Doms are delicate people. Most of them wouldn't deal well with a sub wielding a chainsaw in front of them in an environment that—at least in theory—is designed solely to enhance their dominance."

There was silence at the other end of the line, and Curtis could practically see the gears shifting in Collin's head.

"Martin doesn't mind." Collin sounded a bit petulant. He was very proud of his skills with the chainsaw and rightfully so. Not everybody could turn a block of wood into a dragon so lifelike it seemed as if it would spread its wings at any moment. Curtis sighed. He hated making Collin sad. It always felt like kicking a puppy.

"That is because Martin is very secure in his masculinity and not easily threatened by anything."

"I know. He's so great, isn't he?"

Curtis closed his eyes for a moment to fight down the wave of sadness surging in his heart. Talking about Martin never failed to make Collin happy. It also reminded Curtis of everything he had lost—or had never had, considering what an asshole his ex had proven to be. Curtis steeled himself against those negative thoughts and focused on Collin again. Opening night for the exhibition would be in three days, and after talking Collin out of the chainsaw demonstration, he went over the timetable with him, which was kind of useless, since he would forget anyway, but Curtis always made a point of including Collin in everything regarding his art. It made Collin happy, and now and then he would surprise Curtis with a sudden burst of insight.

After telling Collin to have a wonderful day and hanging up, Curtis stared for some time at his favorite Rainbow Snake print. A beautifully drawn raven, shown from the back, with its wings spread from one side of the picture to the other, emerging from a field of brightly colored flowers and flying into an equally bright sun. The contrast between the raven's dark feathers and the vibrant hues was stunning enough, but when the onlooker took a closer look at the picture—which was always a good idea with Rainbow Snake's work—it revealed small details in the field of flowers. Like the green spider sucking out a fly in the blossom of a red poppy, or the hornet catching a butterfly in flight, or the small army of ant princesses getting ready for their maiden flight, or the bumblebees emerging from their nest in the ground. To Collin, all of it held beauty, and he made the spectator see it as well. The original, a personal gift from Collin to Curtis—*"Because you're always there for me, and you understand me even if I don't make sense, and mess things up, and change the subject too often, and never know the right things to say, even though the words always make sense in my head, which is kind of scary, come to think of it, the discrepancy between in and out, and me and the world, you know, and I guess I just want to say thank you for being my anchor, my connection."*—had a place of honor in Curtis's bedroom and was protected by a whole battery of motion sensors and alarms.

Looking at that picture always had a calming effect on Curtis, and contemplating the deeper meaning behind it helped him not to think about the desert his love life had been for the past three years. After Jasper had traded him in for a newer, younger model, Curtis had been too devastated to start dating right away. It had taken him more than eight months to return to Whisper, and since then, he'd only played a few times and never twice with the same partner. He was an experienced sub, and even though his once-flat abs now sported a slight paunch, he knew he was still attractive at forty-five. The problem was Curtis wasn't used to submitting without a personal attachment. When he did a scene just for the sake of the scene and to get rid of some of his sexual frustration, he could never completely let go. It wasn't fair to him or the Dom he was playing with. In addition, many of the Doms were intimidated by his wealth and academic and family background. Those were three things Curtis couldn't—and wouldn't—change. Sometimes he contemplated looking for a partner and Dom outside of Whisper, maybe on one of those dating sites, but if the Doms at Whisper, who were all on the upper end of the food chain moneywise, had problems with his social standing, how would somebody "normal" react? Somebody whose monthly income didn't have five figures or more? Curtis tried very hard not to become an arrogant, stuck-up snob who thought about people in terms of social classes, but it was hard when he himself got categorized and judged based on the way he dressed and talked every day. If he was honest, it was a good thing most of the time, because it got him special treatment, and he would be a liar if he said that wasn't nice, but when it came to finding a new partner, it sucked.

He sighed again. Sitting in his office and feeling sorry for himself wouldn't get any of his work done, and there was plenty before the exhibition started. At least being busy would keep him from moping, which wasn't that much fun to begin with.

CHAPTER 2

ANDREW STOOD at the back of the BDSM club he had chosen to check out tonight and seriously contemplated leaving right away. When he had moved to Miami from Colorado four months ago, it had taken him some time to get settled in—there were still unpacked boxes in one of the rooms in his apartment—and today was the first time he felt he could go out without leaving too much work undone. A thorough internet search had given him the websites of several BDSM clubs in Miami, and Club Submission had been his second choice. His first would have been Club Whisper, a gay BDSM club that had an excellent reputation, but one look at the annual fees and Andrew had known he wouldn't even go there for one free night as a guest. There was no reason why he should look at what he would never be able to afford. So he'd come to Club Submission instead. It was a mixed club and too big for Andrew's taste. He liked a bit of an audience, but not the two hundred people or more lingering in the huge hall that doubled as a dancing and demonstration area. He also didn't like that Club Submission was a hardcore club. Andrew had seen a few Doms and subs here, but most of the pairings were Masters and slaves, and the play he had witnessed so far was less *safe, sane, and consensual* and heavy on the *risk-aware consensual kink*. While Andrew knew there was nothing wrong with playing hard as long as all parties involved were of age and had consented, he didn't feel comfortable watching it and couldn't imagine doing it himself. For him, the pain was just a sometimes necessary part on his and his sub's journey to true submission, which was one of the reasons he never played with pain sluts. He found it fascinating how many different aspects there were to BDSM and what people saw in it, but he also knew he wouldn't come back to Club Submission. The scene on the stage, where a Dom and a Dominatrix were whipping a slave girl with a single tail bullwhip, turned him off big-time, and not because the sub had the wrong body parts for his preference.

"What a shit show, eh?" A deep, raspy voice startled Andrew out of his contemplation. He turned to look into a face where the nose was too prominent, the lips too thin, the jaw a bit too angular, and the brows too thick to fit the modern definition of beauty, especially in Miami. The eyes, though, and the broad, open smile more than made up for the lack of handsomeness. As did the build of the man, who was as big as Andrew—six three—but almost twice as broad. The stranger—clearly a Dom from the way he held himself—extended his hand. "Hi, I'm Tim. I'm only here for the second time, and judging from the look on your face, you're as excited about this demonstration as I am." Tim's voice was a bit too loud to be considered polite, and the sarcasm clearly dripping from every syllable was earning them a few dark looks from people standing nearby. Since Andrew had no intention of coming back here, he wasn't overly concerned, but he also didn't want to cause a scene. There was enough of that going on at the stage. With a polite smile, he took Tim's offered hand, shook it, and then started dragging him toward the exit. He had seen enough.

On the sidewalk in front of Club Submission, Andrew looked at his new acquaintance. The harsh light from the streetlamp above them didn't make Tim's looks any more endearing, but Andrew felt drawn to the man's open smile and sparkling eyes. Since his move here, he hadn't met anybody outside of work yet, and he wondered if Tim could become a friend.

"So, what do we do with the rest of our evening?"

Tim shrugged. "To be honest, I'm not in the mood to try another club, but I know a biker bar not far from here where we won't stand out in our clothes." He gestured at their black leather trousers. Andrew had opted for a black silk shirt for the evening, while Tim was wearing a red T-shirt. They both had black biker boots on their feet, and Andrew had to agree with Tim.

"I could do with a beer."

He followed Tim down the street to the next block. The biker bar was at a corner and well frequented, though they were lucky and managed to secure a small booth at the back when a couple left. Once the waiter had placed their beers in front of them, Tim raised his glass.

"To never going back to that club!"

Andrew smiled and clinked his own glass to Tim's. "To never going back." He took a swig of the beer before putting it back on the table. "Unfortunately, this means I have to keep searching for a club." He sighed.

Tim looked at him over the rim of his glass. "If it's any consolation, I'm looking as well."

"Are you new here too?"

Tim nodded. "Came to Miami five months ago. I'm originally from Denver, but I had a bad breakup there and needed a change of scenery. Since I do most of my work from home, moving wasn't too difficult. Though I have to admit, finding a BDSM club is beginning to seem like an impossible task."

"I'm from Colorado as well. Small-town boy, though. I come from a little village close to Lyons. Life there got too stifling, so I decided to move here. I have a bakery over at Thirty-First Street, close to Quincaya Lyovo."

"That's a nice area. Was today your first try?" The smile on Tim's face transformed his entire being. Andrew was fascinated.

"Yeah. Couldn't have gone worse. They really should put a warning on their website about it being a hardcore club."

"They probably think the name is warning enough. Don't get me wrong, I can understand, at least on an intellectual level, how it might be a kick for a sub to be at the mercy of somebody they don't know, to have to rely on the audience for their safety. And for a Dominant it must be heady to be given such responsibility, to gauge somebody else's reactions and make it good for them, but I have to admit, I like to be told immediately when I fuck up. Not find out a few hours or days later, while the police read me my rights."

Andrew snickered. As serious as the topic was, he liked Tim's openness, especially since they were of one opinion. "Yes, I like to know that too. Plus, I'm very firmly in the safe, sane, and consensual corner. I know it sounds strange, given where we met, but I'm a pretty conservative guy. I value clear consent above anything else."

Tim raised his glass again. "A man after my own heart. Are there any other clubs that have woken your interest?"

"Well, the one I'd definitely want to try, but won't because it's way above my financial possibilities, is Whisper. I've only heard the best things about that club, and if it's half as good as the website suggests, it's an absolute winner."

Tim sighed. "Yeah, I've looked at Whisper as well. I met somebody who's a member, and apparently the website doesn't do it justice at all, but like you, I don't see myself there."

"Which leaves us with...?"

"I don't know, man. I thought about checking out Club Eros. It seems tamer than Club Submission and has an okay reputation. Though I have to admit my sense for adventure has been dampened by tonight's events." Tim smiled ruefully.

Andrew could only nod in agreement. He hadn't expected to find the perfect club on his first night out, but he was disappointed about the outcome nevertheless. "How about we give it another try next week? I'd certainly prefer to have somebody like-minded at my side when I brave another club."

"Sounds like a plan. I've got lots of work anyway, so how about we try Club Eros next Saturday?"

"I'm in. Here, give me your contact info." Andrew held out his smartphone. Tim typed his information in, and Andrew sent him his own. "Thank you. I'm glad I finally met somebody outside of work, who shares my kink no less. It was getting lonely."

Tim gestured for the waiter to bring them another round of beer. "I'm glad too. I was getting desperate. Not everybody can handle my brand of humor, but you seem like a tough guy." He grinned, showing all his teeth, and Andrew was sure they would be getting along great.

"I like your humor. And I like men who don't have a problem saying what's on their mind. There's nothing I hate more than guess-the-problem games."

"Amen to that." The waiter brought them their new beers and they toasted.

"To new friendships and finding the perfect club." Andrew raised the glass to his mouth.

"To new friendships, finding the perfect club, *and* the perfect sub." Tim grinned. "I like to aim high."

"Then that's what we do."

CHAPTER 3

"AS STARTERS, we'd like the shrimp and octopus in lime, please. And your famous melon drinks, virgin. We don't need any wine."

Curtis handed the waitress their menus back. She took them with a polite smile before clearing their wineglasses. When she left the table, Collin started to talk immediately.

"Oooh, I just love it here. It always smells so good and everybody is so friendly, and I think you look really cool when you order, all self-confident and polite and knowing, as if there's nothing in the world you haven't seen or tasted yet, and is that actually possible, because I think there's always something new to discover, and you didn't know about peanut butter, jelly, and banana sandwiches—" Curtis couldn't suppress a shudder when Collin mentioned this special food from hell. "—and I'm sure Dean knows many more such things because Emily likes the funniest food, like pasta with eggs, sugar, and applesauce, and I never thought that could be good, but it totally is, and Richard said if Dean ever made that again when he's home, he's going to spank him so hard he won't be able to sit down for a *week*, so I think Dean is totally going to do it, because he loves getting spanked."

Curtis smiled at Collin, though the mention of pasta and sugar in one sentence had his stomach rolling. He was a delicate eater, and one of the reasons he was so glad to be living in the States now most of the time was that he didn't have to face "traditional" English food like bangers and mash or black pudding anymore. While he understood that everybody's tastes ran differently, the mere memory of evenings spent trying not to throw up his portion of black pudding while his parents happily nagged each other about anything and everything, was enough to have him shuddering. Americans had their share of doubtful foods as well, but Curtis had found out most things tasted okay when fried.

The waitress brought their drinks and Collin's smile broadened. He inhaled deeply, with his eyes closed, his way of assessing food. "This smells great, like summer and blue and green and orange and red all in one, warm and spicy, yet with a cool undertone. I wonder how that would look on a canvas or maybe in glass. I could try working with glass again—or wax. Wax is a good medium and it doesn't have to be so hot to work with it, so I'll have to order wax, and I only hope they still have the original beeswax tiles at the art supply, because the ones with paraffin just don't work the way I want them to, and they don't smell even half as good as the others."

Curtis gave a serious nod, knowing how hard it was for Collin to find the perfect mediums for his art sometimes. He raised his glass in a cheerful toast. "To a highly successful second BDSM exhibition. The pieces you created were stunning and our customers beyond happy to purchase them."

Collin beamed. "It went pretty well, didn't it, even though I didn't get to do the chainsaw demonstration, but you were right, most of the Doms there probably wouldn't have appreciated it, and I was so nervous, I was glad I didn't have to wield anything sharp, and I talked to Martin and he said it's up to me, because it's my money, so I wanted to give you this, because I don't really need it and I just can't express how happy I am that you're helping me and taking care of me and that you're my friend." With that, Collin put the glass down to retrieve something from the front pocket of his washed-out jeans. Curtis found it funny how Collin still wore mostly old and battered clothing, despite himself and his fiancé being so rich. It fitted him, though. Now Collin held out a piece of paper, and when Curtis took it to see what it was, he couldn't suppress a gasp. It was a check for over half a million dollars.

"Collin, you can't…."

"I can. Martin says it's my money and I wouldn't know what to do with it anyway, and you do so much for me, and there's no way I can ever thank you enough, and I know you have a lot of money yourself, but I thought maybe there's something you really want and haven't bought because it would just be an indulgence, and I know you try not to buy things just for the sake of buying, which I think is great, because many people just lose themselves in the rush of spending money, and that's scary, because money should be there to feed and clothe you, but not to eat your soul, and since this is money from me, you can spend it without feeling bad about it." Collin's smile was a bit anxious, and Curtis knew better than to reject his gift. He would talk to Martin later to figure out what they would do with the money.

"Thank you, Collin. That was very thoughtful of you." He put the check in his wallet. "I'll make sure to put it to good use. Now should we talk about the exhibition?"

Before Collin could answer, the waitress brought their shrimp and octopus salad. She served it with a polite smile and then refilled their water glasses. The excellent service was one of the reasons Curtis liked to come to OLA, the other being the fact that it was close to the botanical garden, which he loved at every time of the year. They both had their first mouthful of the salad, and it was as good as it looked. Collin moaned happily.

"This is wonderful. I have to tell Martin to come here with me. He loves seafood. He loves any kind of food, really, especially when he doesn't have to cook it himself, so coming here would be killing two birds with one stone, and have you never thought this expression is kind of odd, because I don't think it's possible, unless you hit the first bird and that one is so big, that when it hits the second one, it kills it with its sheer weight, and it's sad anyway, and Wilma and Fred only get one bird in one go, though Dean says they're mostly too lazy to hunt anyway because cats are like that."

Curtis nodded. He was by now so well acquainted with Collin's way of expressing himself, he sometimes got caught off guard when talking to other people and expecting them to go on and on. And since they had seen even more of each other before the exhibition, he was fully in tune with Collin's trains of thought. There was one thing, though, which they had to talk about.

"Collin, in regard to the exhibition, I wanted to talk to you about the two Doms who wanted to buy the *Sleeping Sub*."

A look of defiance appeared on Collin's face. "The sculpture was all wrong for them. They wouldn't have been happy with it, and then they would have sold it, and then it would have ended up somewhere terrible! I couldn't give it to them, Curtis. I just couldn't!"

"I understand, Collin, I do. And it's not that I want you to sell your work to people who won't be able to appreciate it or are unfit to own it. I wanted to talk to you about how to steer your customers in a way that leaves them feeling—let's call it superior, for lack of a better word."

The blank look on Collin's face was endearing, since it told Curtis the young man was still innocent enough to not get the meaning behind his diplomatically phrased meanness.

"What I want to say is that if you don't want a customer to buy a certain piece, you have to carefully steer them toward something more suitable for them while at the same time giving them the feeling they're doing this of their own free will. It's another form of art, I'd say."

Collin looked at him wide-eyed. "You mean like when Leeland or Dean want something, but they want Jonathan and Richard to think it was their idea to give it to them?"

Curtis grinned when he thought how easily their two friends were able to twist their Doms around their little fingers. "Yes, exactly like that. By offering them a commissioned piece, you distracted them wonderfully, though it would be preferable if you tried to get them to buy something you've already made next time."

"I'll try my best, Curtis, I promise. And if I'm unsure, I'll just tell them to talk to you instead." Collin looked at his almost empty plate. "Oh, what a shame! With all the talking, I didn't even realize I've eaten all the delicious octopus. Eating and talking don't go well together, don't you think? You can only really concentrate on one, while the other falls by the wayside, which probably is why you're not allowed to talk during mealtime in a monastery, or was that some Buddhist temple, I can't remember, but they have a point, and sometimes I wonder what would happen if people stopped talking altogether, and a few days ago I heard a wonderful song by a band called Disturbed on the radio, it was called the 'Sound of Silence,' and it made me think if silence really has a sound and what color it would be, and now I have this great idea for a glass sculpture, but I think I need to talk to somebody who knows a bit about statics, because I want it to be high and broad and there's going to be a lot of colors, and I have to get the swirls right, and do you think that nice woman would let me borrow her glassblower equipment again, and I'm going to need…."

Curtis kept listening to Collin's monologue while he made a mental note to talk to Sara Stanton, the glassblower who had allowed Collin to use her equipment before, and signaled the waitress to bring them another round of melon drinks and a plate with samples of the restaurant's seafood selection. After their meal, they decided to take a little walk in the neighborhood to enjoy the nice weather and walk some of the consumed calories off. When they headed onto Thirty-First Street, Collin suddenly started tugging on Curtis's sleeve. "Look, Curtis, that store they were renovating has finally opened! Let's see what's in there now!"

They walked a little faster, Curtis infected by Collin's excitement. When they stopped in front of the small shop, Collin clapped his hands wildly.

"Oh my God, it's a bakery! We have to try it out and tell the others about it. Come on, let's get in. We need to find out what they have."

Curtis glanced at the sign above the shop, telling them they were about to have a "Sweet Break," before he followed Collin inside.

CHAPTER 4

ANDREW LEFT the kitchen when he heard the shop bell chime. It was half past two, the usual after-lunch lull in full swing. He normally used this time of quiet to get his kitchen in order for the next day, which saved him from doing it after hours. That way he could retreat to his apartment sooner and take care of unpacking the last boxes from his move. It never ceased to amaze him how much stuff he still had even after throwing half of it away during packing. His sister was right; he was kind of a hoarder. When he entered the salesroom, Andrew stopped dead in his tracks. The most perfect man in existence stood at his counter, dressed in light gray linen slacks, a short-sleeved, blue shirt, and with a gorgeous smile on his lips. His blue gaze was settled on his companion with an expression of loving exasperation. That man was a lot younger than the hot silver fox and glued to the glass of the counter, behind which the macarons were on display. Or at least what was left of them. Andrew was about to greet his two customers, when the young man looked up at him and said in a voice tinged with awe: "You have the rainbow in your counter."

Again Andrew parted his lips, but the customer was faster. "That's so cool! I didn't know you could have the rainbow in sweets, or no, that's not true, you can have the rainbow in the smells and then it's in your mind, not for the eyes, and I just read a book about colors and did you know colors aren't really there, only in your mind, and other creatures, like bees and cats and dogs see them differently, so perhaps it really is all in our mind and I'm not sure if that's great or not, but I'll take two of each color, and can you tell me how you made them?"

Andrew was so overwhelmed by this avalanche of words, he looked at the silver fox for help. The knowing smile on the man's lips told him he was used to his companion's antics.

"Collin, I'm not sure if the gentleman can tell you how he makes those macarons. It's probably a secret. Otherwise, everybody could just bake their own."

Andrew felt his lips part into a beaming smile. The silver fox's voice was like liquid chocolate in his ears, all warm and soothing and with a distinct British accent that made his knees go weak. He only hoped the young man—Collin—wasn't his boyfriend. Only one way to find out.

"Your boyfriend is right. How I make my macarons is a secret. It took me some time to get all the ingredients just right."

Collin nodded his understanding, and then shook his head vigorously. "Oh no, Curtis isn't my boyfriend; he's my agent. Martin is my master and he keeps the bad people away from me. Curtis sees to it that people pay me for my work, which is nice, because now I have money to buy as many rainbow sweets as I want, look, I even have my own credit card, though Martin has put a limit on it, because sometimes I forget to keep track of what I bought, and nobody needs so many things, except for sweets, even though Martin pretends not to like them, but I know better, which is why I'm getting two of each."

Collin beamed at Andrew, whose confused brain had managed to latch on to two important things: that Curtis was *not* Collin's boyfriend and that Collin had a master, which meant Curtis at least knew about BDSM, which in turn eliminated the sometimes insurmountable hurdle of explaining to an outsider how a BDSM relationship worked. It could still be that Curtis wasn't interested in that type of sex, but at least he would probably know what he would be getting into with Andrew. Now all Andrew had to do was find the guts to ask the hot silver fox out.

While he carefully arranged the macarons in the bright yellow paper box with Sweet Break's logo on it, he wracked his brain for how to get the conversation with Curtis going again. He was nearing the last two types of macarons—purple and orange—and was getting desperate. Then, out of nowhere, inspiration hit him, and he closed the box before taking another pair of tongs to get two of the mini-éclairs that were his other specialty. He put them on a plate, which he offered to his two customers. "On the house."

Collin's eyes lit up and he grabbed both sweets, holding the slightly bigger one out to Curtis. When Curtis took it with a nod and a graceful "Thank you" in Andrew's direction, Collin put his éclair in his mouth, closed his eyes, and groaned in utter delight. Curtis followed suit, and Andrew got the great pleasure of watching how those beautiful lips parted to let the sweet in. Unbidden, but definitely not unpleasant pictures of those lips closing around his cock flooded his mind and made his jeans a tight fit. The things he wanted to do to Curtis! It had been a long time since Andrew had felt so strongly for somebody and he felt the urge to come around the counter and just kiss Curtis senseless.

"Why are you staring at Curtis like that?" The question poured the proverbial bucket of ice water over his erotic daydreams that were getting hotter by the second. He stared into Collin's eyes, which were of a stunning blue and filled with innocent curiosity. Andrew felt a flush creeping up from his neck. There was no plausible explanation for his behavior, but before he could come up with at least an attempt at veiling his true motives, Collin already went on, seemingly completely oblivious of Andrew's discomfort and, as a quick glance toward Curtis showed, the silver fox's widened eyes.

"He does look good, doesn't he? I mean, I've already painted two portraits of him, but I had to destroy them again, because somehow I never manage to capture what I see in him, which is odd, because normally I'm good at that, but there's something about Curtis, something mysterious, that evades the canvas every time, though I'm sure I'll be able to do it one day, and what I mean is you don't have to feel bad about looking at him, many people do that, especially Doms, but so far, he hasn't chosen one, which I can totally understand, because finding the right man, the right Dom, is very difficult, because sometimes the chemistry is there, but then you like different things, which always sucks, and if you told Curtis what you liked in bed, perhaps you could ask him out and you could get to know each other and then Curtis could decide if he wanted to keep you, and wouldn't that be nice?" Collin smiled happily. Andrew rushed around the counter to pat Curtis's back. The man was chocking on his éclair, which Andrew could relate to, because he himself was having difficulty getting enough air into his lungs. When his hand touched Curtis, Andrew could feel his body's warmth seeping through the shirt. It was so good, he let his hand linger a bit longer than strictly necessary, but Curtis didn't seem to mind. He gave Andrew a grateful nod, accompanied by a small smile.

"Did I say something wrong, Curtis?" Collin sounded anxious, and Andrew realized the young man really didn't seem to know what he had just done. Next to him, Curtis straightened with his hand on Andrew's arm for support. He looked at Collin with a smile. "No, you didn't do anything wrong. Andrew and I were just surprised, that's all."

The sheer relief flooding Collin's face washed away the last tiny bits of animosity Andrew had felt toward him for exposing him so brutally.

Since the cat was already out of the bag, he decided to go with the flow. "And you were right. I was staring at Curtis, because I think he's a very attractive man and I was wondering how best to ask him out."

Andrew felt Curtis's eyes drilling a hole into him. "Is that so?"

He turned to look at the stunning man. "Yes."

Curtis closed his eyes and for a moment, Andrew feared the worst, but when he opened them again, they were bright, and a smile was illuminating Curtis's features. "I'm free on Friday. And it would be my pleasure to go out with you, stranger."

The blood was pulsing so loudly in his ears over this victory, that Andrew almost didn't get the hint. When he saw Curtis's questioning glance, he hurried to introduce himself. "My name is Andrew. Andrew Granger. I'm the owner of Sweet Break." He extended his hand. Curtis took it, and Andrew was glad to feel that Curtis's hands trembled as badly as his own.

"I'm Curtis Morris. I have an art gallery here in Miami."

"How fascinating. I'd like to hear more about it on Friday." Andrew winked. "There's this great restaurant close by, OLA. They have excellent food."

Curtis grinned. "We actually just came from there. It's a wonderful choice. How about I come here on Friday, say around 7:00 p.m.?"

The positive reaction from Curtis had Andrew in full flirting mode. He was surfing on a wave of endorphins. "Shouldn't I pick you up?"

Curtis shrugged. "You could do that, though my house is near the Keys. It would definitely be easier if I drove here."

"If you put it like that…. Then at least let me offer you a private parking lot at the back of my bakery. We can walk to OLA, if that's okay for you."

"A private parking lot is always appreciated." Curtis pulled out his phone. "May I have your contact information? Just in case something happens and I can't make it."

While Andrew typed his phone number into Curtis's smartphone, he thought about how Curtis's accent got thicker the longer they talked. Andrew's people-reading skills were a bit rusty due to him having been busy with his move, but he was sure Curtis was as nervous as he was.

"Then let's hope nothing happens, because it would be a shame if we missed out on getting to know each other." He handed the cell back to Curtis.

"Yes, let's hope that."

"Cool! Leeland and Dean and the others will be so excited to hear this news. I can't wait to tell them!" Collin's enthusiasm pried Andrew from the nice bubble in which he was staring at Curtis, entirely content with the way things had gone. Curtis rolled his eyes.

"No, Collin! You can't tell them yet. Let's wait till Andrew and I have the date. I don't want them putting their noses in and pestering me the rest of the week. You have to keep this a secret."

Collin's face fell. "But won't they be miffed if we don't tell them?"

Curtis laughed. "Oh, they will be, but not for long. They will get over it as soon as they start grilling me about every little detail." He turned to Andrew, his face absolutely serious. "As you can see, the stakes are quite high. Our date has to satisfy the sensational needs of my friends."

Andrew bowed, making a sweeping gesture with his right hand. "I'll do my very best!" he said in his best imitation of Freddie Frinton. That earned him a laugh from both men, though he wasn't sure if it was because of his performance or because they got the reference. He straightened up and went back behind the counter, where he took the box with the macarons and handed it to Collin. The young man gave him his credit card in return, and after the payment was completed, Curtis and Collin turned to leave the bakery. At the door, Curtis looked back at him. "The éclair was delicious, by the way. Even though most of it ended up in my windpipe. See you on Friday." Curtis gave him another dazzling smile before he followed Collin out of the shop. Andrew kept staring at the door for a long time. He had a date. With a walking wet dream of a man who also happened to be in the lifestyle, if Andrew had understood Collin correctly. He pinched himself. This was almost too good to be true.

CHAPTER 5

ANDREW WAS standing in front of his wardrobe, trying to decide what to wear for his date with Curtis, when his phone rang. A quick glance told him it was Tim, so he accepted the call.

"Hi, Andrew, I just wanted to check if our plans for tomorrow are still good?"

Tim's voice boomed through the speaker, sounding as smooth and at the same time as commanding as the first time they had met.

"Hi, Tim, nice to hear from you. And yes, our plans still stand. It's even more important for me to find a club now, because tonight, I'm going on a date!"

Andrew knew he sounded like an overexcited puppy, but he couldn't help it. After what seemed like eons in the desert of love, he finally had the proverbial oasis in his sights.

"Man, that's great! Who is he? How did you meet? Is he in the lifestyle?"

Tim sounded almost as excited as Andrew felt. With a huge smile on his lips, he selected a blue button-down shirt that accentuated his light tan. "You won't believe it, but he simply stepped into my bakery a few days ago, and he seems to be in the lifestyle. Hopefully I'm going to find out more today. And he's so hot!"

He sighed and Tim's laughter echoed in his ears. "Somebody's eager…. Good luck tonight! I'm looking forward to hearing all about your date tomorrow. Have fun and don't fuck up!"

With this well-meant advice ringing in his ear, Andrew ended the call. He eyed himself critically in the mirror, deciding that his outfit was as perfect as it was going to get. OLA had no dress code, though a certain sophisticated yet still laid-back style was the norm there, and he found he had achieved that with the shirt, dark blue jeans, and loafers in a light whiskey color. Full of nervous anticipation, he grabbed his wallet and keys to wait for Curtis in front of his shop so he could guide him to his private parking lot in the back.

While Andrew was standing on the sidewalk, watching the traffic go by, he wondered what kind of car Curtis was driving. He'd said he was a gallery owner, though it had to be a small one, since neither Collin nor Curtis had looked like they were made of money. Something sensible, he imagined, like a Toyota Sienna, one of the older models, with enough room to transport pictures or sculptures. Or perhaps something smaller, better suited for navigating in the city, like a Honda Jazz or a Volkswagen Golf. While he was picturing Curtis in all kinds of cars, Andrew checked his watch. It was five minutes to seven. Curtis had seemed like a man who would be punctual, but one could never tell. Perhaps this was something he would want to work on with a Dom? There were all kinds of delicious punishments Andrew could implement for being late. Like putting Curtis in a cock cage for an hour for every minute he was late. Or edging him until he was a sobbing, begging mess under Andrew's hand. Or—Realizing he was most definitely getting ahead of himself, Andrew concentrated on the street again, just in time to see a shiny BMW i8 coupe in a stunning metallic blue setting the blinker and coming to a stop in front of him. Thinking the driver perhaps wanted to ask for directions, he stepped closer, only to realize it was Curtis sitting behind the steering wheel, looking delicious in a lavender-colored button-down with the two top buttons open and his salt-and-pepper hair artfully tousled. With a slightly forced smile, he gestured for Curtis to drive into the small alley between his shop and the neighboring house.

Taking the lead, Andrew showed Curtis where to park his impressive ride next to Andrew's far more modest SUV. The glaring difference between the two cars woke uncomfortable memories of his father's voice in the back of his mind, ranting about how "those above" weren't the same as "them" and didn't know the least about the "struggles of the lower classes." Andrew thought he had outgrown his father's views a long time ago, but it seemed some of them still lingered. Curtis hadn't seemed or behaved like somebody who could afford a car like that, which was why Andrew had found the courage to ask him out in the first place. Now he wondered if he would have done the same if he had known about the car. A soft clicking told Andrew that the time for contemplating his societal hang-ups was up.

He smiled at Curtis, cursing inwardly for having missed the chance to open the door for his date, and held out his hand in greeting. "Hello, Curtis. It's so nice to see you."

Curtis shook his hand with a smile that seemed a bit strained and made Andrew wonder what secret upper-class dating rule he had just violated. "Hello, Andrew. It's nice to see you too. I'm sorry I'm late, but there was an accident close to my gallery and they had to redirect traffic, which was an absolute nightmare!"

Inwardly, Andrew breathed a sigh of relief. Apparently Curtis was upset about his own delay, not something Andrew had done. "No problem. It's exactly seven, so you're not late, but super punctual." Andrew didn't know what else to say, so he blurted out what was at the forefront of his mind. "I didn't picture you as somebody driving a car like that."

The moment the last word left his mouth, Andrew flinched. That had been about as tactful and suave as a baseball bat to the head. Thankfully Curtis didn't seem to mind, or he was just too polite to show his displeasure, because he looked at the BMW with a fond smile on his lips.

"To be honest, until five weeks ago, I couldn't picture myself driving a car like that. I always preferred British models, since they remind me of home, but I'm mostly driving in the city and rarely great distances. A hybrid car was a sensible choice for me, and when my car dealer showed me this model, I just couldn't resist, even though it's a bit showy for my taste, but the riding pleasure is beyond anything I've experienced so far, even though it still hurts a bit to admit that. National pride and everything, you know? And I'm talking too much, aren't I?"

The worried tone pried Andrew from the lustful haze the movement of Curtis's perfect lips had put him into. Still a bit worried about how easily Curtis talked about purchasing a car that looked as if its price was somewhere in the six digits, he smiled at Curtis and prayed to any god who might be listening that it looked more convincing than it felt.

"Not at all. It's a beautiful car, and these days, choosing the right model has become even more important, especially regarding the environment."

Curtis looked relieved, which Andrew counted as a clear win. He offered Curtis his arm. "Why don't we walk over to OLA and start our evening? I'm sure we have a lot to talk about." He raised one eyebrow suggestively. Curtis laughed out loud and took the offered arm.

"I'd say you already know all there is to find out, thanks to Collin. Who says hi, by the way, and wants to know if you have a delivery service. He kind of got addicted to your macarons and was not pleased when he had to share them with Martin and some other people." He grinned mischievously. "One of them being me."

"Tell him I do deliver, though only when the order is more than fifty dollars. Otherwise, it wouldn't be profitable."

"Don't worry, fifty dollars is no problem at all. We were thinking of pooling our order, which will be a lot higher than your minimum. The boys all love your macarons."

Andrew felt as if he'd grown ten feet under the praise. Being looked at like that by a man he badly wanted to impress was what being bathed in liquid testosterone had to feel like. "I'd be delighted to provide you and your friends with all the macarons you can eat."

"Then you better start baking right now."

Laughing, Andrew led Curtis along the sidewalk toward OLA.

CURTIS WASN'T sure what to think. When Andrew had asked him on this date, he'd been thrilled, because the handsome man with the deep black hair that showed the first gray strands, the hazel eyes, and smooth bronze skin covering a fit yet not overly muscular body was exactly his type. That Andrew hadn't even flinched when Collin mentioned having a master and hinting at Curtis being a sub had woken Curtis's hope to have finally met a decent Dom outside of Whisper. He had taken great care to make himself presentable for this date, excited about this chance to meet somebody new.

On his drive to Sweet Break, Curtis had thought about possible topics he could discuss with Andrew and how to best breach the BDSM elephant. He knew most subs would leave that problem to the Dom, but Curtis wasn't at his current position in life because he let others take the reins when he was perfectly capable of steering himself. All these thoughts evaporated, though, when he saw the strained expression on Andrew's face the moment the man realized it was Curtis in the ridiculously expensive BMW. He still wasn't entirely sure if the car had been a good purchase. Jonathan had found and customized the car for him, and Curtis had to admit it was a great ride. Plus, ever since he'd bought it, he hadn't had to visit a gas station. The solar power system at his house was more than enough to keep the sleek sports car running and the lack of loud engine noises while driving was a balm to his nerves. He had tried to downplay the whole thing in front of Andrew, who had finally gotten a grip on himself, but now that they were at OLA, he looked strained again. Curtis had met enough Doms to know the signs. Andrew was intimidated by him, by the fact that he had the money to buy an expensive car, by the fact that the staff at OLA greeted him first, because he was a regular there, by the fact that their waiter looked at him for their choice of wine, even though the table was in Andrew's name. Curtis knew how the dating game was played, how the interactions between Doms and subs worked, and he also knew how to play along. The only question was if he wanted to do this tonight and if he did, if Andrew was worth the trouble. Curtis had to give it to him. The man was trying hard, so he decided to give him a chance. Their wine had just arrived, accompanied by an amuse-gueule from the kitchen, a delicious crème of spinach soup served in an espresso cup. After his first taste, Curtis put the cup down, smiling openly at Andrew. He couldn't deny the electric buzz he felt when close to him, something he had been missing for some time. *Ever since Jasper*. And he wasn't sure if there had been any buzz at all back then or if it had just been wishful thinking on his part.

"So, what else are you up to when you're not creating those sweet masterpieces you sell in your bakery?"

Andrew visibly relaxed, probably glad to have an opportunity to take over the reins of their conversation. "Oh, I'm up to quite a lot of things." He winked, the gesture making him look playfully flirtatious and almost irresistible to Curtis. "At the moment I'm still trying to make my apartment inhabitable. Most of the boxes are unpacked now, and my DVD collection is already in alphabetical order. First things first." He grinned broadly, making the joke obvious. Curtis was relieved. He liked men with a sense of humor.

"Don't tell me you're one of those guys who has an extra drawer for their socks and who always aligns their cutlery like it was participating in a military parade?"

Andrew put his right hand above his heart in a gesture of mock indignation. "Don't tell me there's people who don't?"

Now Curtis laughed out loud. "As much as it pains me to tell you this, but yes, there's lots of people who don't. Me being one of them."

"Okay, that's it. How could I have ever asked you out? Why don't men like you come with a warning? Looks gorgeous but can't keep his home neat and tidy."

"Perhaps you should make a questionnaire? Next time you want to ask somebody out, you hand them the sheet and give them ten minutes to answer it. That way, there won't be any nasty surprises."

Andrew pretended to think about it, his eyes gleaming merrily. "Good idea. Well, I guess it's too late for the written sheet, but how about a little oral exam?"

Curtis lifted a brow. "Was that supposed to be an innuendo? Because if yes, it was rather terrible. And I'm very good at oral exams."

"Who's being suggestive now? And no, I didn't mean it as an innuendo, but I can see how somebody with a dirty mind could interpret it that way. Also, I'm curious how good you are—at oral exams, that is."

The waiter bringing their salads and main course put a temporary stop to their friendly bantering, for which Curtis was grateful. It gave him the chance to gather himself again because he was close to becoming a puddle of goo under the assault of pure charm Andrew was raining on him. He couldn't remember when he had last flirted so easily. As soon as the waiter left again, Curtis couldn't help but poke the beast some more.

"So, what are your questions?"

Andrew put a piece of salad in his mouth, showing off his well-defined jaw muscles while he pretended to think hard. He swallowed. "Well, the first was already answered by Collin. Are you in the lifestyle? I dare say it's the most crucial one, and also the hardest."

Curtis nodded. Finding the right partner was hard enough. Finding one who also shared your kink or was willing to try it was almost impossible. It just wasn't something that usually came up during a polite conversation. *Oh, I really like the way your eyes light up when you smile, and by the way, I would love nothing more than to kneel at your feet, worshipping your cock after you flogged the shit out of me.* No, that didn't go over well, not even after a few dates.

"Since this particular hurdle is cleared, what would be your next question?"

A predatory gleam entered Andrew's eyes and Curtis felt a tingle going down his spine, knowing he was the reason for it. "I'd be asking about your preferences. I would describe myself as a rather conservative dominant who puts great value in safe, sane, and consensual. I'm not into hardcore play, but I don't just do sensual play either. I also like rules and I'm strict about them."

Curtis gulped. This sounded almost too perfect to be true. Like Andrew had taken a look into his head and was now telling him what he wanted to hear. "I like the act of submission itself. I'm not into hardcore play either, but I appreciate a strict Dom who knows what he wants and, more importantly, what he doesn't want. I don't like playing games, like acting bratty on purpose to earn a punishment, and I don't like being set up for failure. I know my submission is a gift, and a Dom who can't appreciate and respect that—and me as a person—is not for me."

Why he'd said that last sentence, Curtis didn't know. It was a bit more aggressive than he would usually be. He had a suspicion it was to test Andrew after he so obviously failed to hide his discomfort about the car and the way Curtis was treated by the staff of OLA. There was no reason to lead Andrew on with a pretend version of himself when they'd inevitably reveal their true selves sooner rather than later. And if the attractive man was just another mismatch, Curtis wanted to know before he gave in to his charms.

Andrew seemed to realize how serious Curtis was, because the playful smile vanished from his lips, exchanged for an expression of absolute sincerity. "I won't try and pretend I'm perfect. We both know nobody is. But I promise you, should you honor me with your trust, I'll do my very best not to betray it."

Curtis nodded his acknowledgment of this statement before he took another mouthful of his tuna steak. Andrew fiddled with his cutlery for a moment, and then he looked up with an apologetic smile. "So, uhm, where do you go to have—*fun*?" He put a certain emphasis on the word "fun" to make clear what he meant. Curtis found it adorable.

"I have my *fun* at Club Whisper. I became a member when I first moved here, and I can't say I regret the choice. Where do you go? You haven't been here long, but have you found a club already?"

Curtis had seen how Andrew had flinched at the mention of Club Whisper and he wondered if there was a story there or if it was something else. He was pretty sure Andrew couldn't afford the fees for Whisper, but if he was with a member—such as Curtis—he could go there to play. And even though Curtis would prefer if they always went to Whisper, he was perfectly willing to try out any club Andrew had chosen for himself should they ever get to that stage. At the moment, though, Andrew didn't look like a man with fun on his mind. More like a man who had bitten into something sour.

"Uhm, to be honest, I haven't chosen a club yet. I went to Club Submission last week, but, well, that's not exactly my scene. I did meet another Dom there, though, and we're going to check out Club Eros tomorrow. You could come with me, if you wanted…." The last sounded hopeful, and Curtis was tempted to say yes, just to see Andrew in an environment that hopefully made him more comfortable around Curtis, but tomorrow was their boys' night, and he didn't want to miss the movie Emilio would show them. The boy had remarkable taste, unlike Peyton, who loved everything Vin Diesel and Dwayne Johnson. Though Curtis had to admit *Baywatch* did have a certain appeal. No gay man with blood in his body could say no to that many tasteful muscles, even if the humor was kind of childish.

"I'm sorry, Andrew. I'd love to come with you, since I haven't been to Eros before, but tomorrow I'm meeting with my friends. It's our movie night and I can't miss that. But we could go another night if you think the club is good. Or we could go somewhere else."

Andrew looked a bit disappointed, but he managed a small smile. "Sure. That would be great," he announced with false cheer.

For some reason, Andrew clammed up after that, and Curtis found it increasingly difficult to keep even the small talk flowing. "I really like the herbal crust in combination with the lemon sauce on my fish. The chef is so good at combining flavors and giving the customers new experiences, don't you think?"

"Mmhmm," was all Andrew had to offer.

"Is your meal not to your taste? It looks delicious." Curtis was trying hard to get some words out of his sour date.

"It's fine. Bit over-the-top, if you ask me." Andrew sounded so dismissive, Curtis decided to change the topic.

"What was Colorado like? I have to admit, I've never been there. I heard winter can be hard."

"Yeah, we do get a lot of snow." That was it. Nothing more, no funny stories about Andrew learning to ski or how he got snowed in or anything like that. It was like talking to a wall.

Curtis honestly didn't know what he had done wrong, and by the time Andrew asked for the check, he was angry enough to insist on them splitting the bill. Andrew tried to argue with him over it, but Curtis was done being polite. As discreetly as possible, so as not to disturb the other guests, he hissed: "Just forget it. You were the one who asked me on this date. You were the one who said I'm hot and you wanted to get to know me. You were the one who suggested OLA even though you don't seem to like it here too much. You were the one who wanted to talk about the lifestyle on our first date, and you were the one who got his panties in a knot when I mentioned Whisper. I don't know what problem you have with the club, and considering the last forty minutes, I don't care. I just want to get out of here and forget all about this date from hell."

With that, he yanked his wallet out of his pocket, slapped a hundred-dollar bill on the table, and then left, still fuming. How could he have been so stupid as to get his hopes up about a date with a complete stranger? Just because Andrew looked good didn't mean he was a decent man, as evidenced by this evening. He didn't even run after Curtis, which made him even angrier, because he couldn't decide if he was relieved about it or insulted. It didn't matter. Curtis rushed back to the parking lot behind Sweet Break, opened his car, got in, and drove away as if the hounds of hell were at his heels. So much for finding romance outside of Whisper.

CHAPTER 6

ANDREW STOOD frozen while he watched Curtis leave the restaurant in a hurry. Angry, the man looked even better and his first instinct was to follow him and apologize. But then he hesitated, that nasty little voice at the back of his head telling him it was better like this, better to not get acquainted with somebody who was so clearly out of his league, better to let this man go, who had stirred his heart like nobody in a long time, better to not give something a try that was doomed from the start. Because in the long run, what did he have to offer to a man like Curtis? Even more importantly, what kind of Dom was so crassly inferior to his sub in real life? He didn't even have a bulky body to at least cement his physical superiority. And if he felt that way after just one date, how could he ever hope to be a good Dominant for Curtis? Andrew knew, should they play, he would constantly wonder if he did certain things to Curtis as a sub, or to Curtis, the member of a different social class who he suddenly found under his thumb.

Andrew had made a habit of never lying to himself, and he knew he could never be sure. He also knew this concern played only a minor part, the bigger one reserved for the fact that he felt insecure and like a teenager in Curtis's company. He might have been able to get over the fancy car, impeccable manners, and the fact that the staff at OLA treated Curtis like royalty. But the moment he casually mentioned only going to Whisper, as if that was the only club worth considering, and then shot down Andrew's invitation to accompany him to Eros because of some stupid movie night he could have any day of the week, Andrew had taken it personally and retreated into himself, his tried and tested approach when a situation got too uncomfortable for him to handle. He wasn't proud of it, fully aware that adults didn't pout like rebellious teenagers when something didn't go their way, but he hadn't been able to help himself. And when Curtis had made polite small talk as if nothing were amiss, it had only cemented the fact that the man was way out of Andrew's league. With a sigh, Andrew gathered his wallet and slowly went for the door, intent on giving Curtis enough time to leave so that they wouldn't run into each other at Sweet Break. He also tried to ignore the painful squeeze in his chest at letting a man he probably would have loved getting to know better go.

"Hey man, I'd ask how you're doing and how your date went, but just looking at you, I can see it wasn't that great, huh?" Tim's booming voice held a hint of pity that made Andrew flinch. He had seriously considered cancelling his night out with Tim just to avoid the rehashing of last night's disaster.

"It was a catastrophe. An absolute fuckup." Andrew didn't even try to keep the dejection from his voice. It was too late anyway. Tim frowned at him.

"Was he a jerk? Did he act out?"

Andrew shook his head. It took a moment for Tim to connect the dots, but then he raised a brow. "It was you. You blew it, didn't you?" If there had been the faintest trace of mocking in Tim's voice, Andrew would have punched him in the face and written their budding friendship off. As it was, Tim looked almost as defeated as Andrew, so he forgave him. "Man, I'm sorry. I know exactly how that feels. You try to be all nice and charming and before you know it, you've put your foot in your mouth and it's all over before it even began."

Judging from Tim's sad tone, this had happened to him more than once.

"Would it be okay if we didn't go to Eros tonight? I'm in the mood for a few beers and something stronger to swill them down."

Tim nodded. "Yeah, no problem. The way you look, they probably wouldn't let us in anyway, and if they did, no sub would be willing to talk to us. Let's have some beer, and then you can tell me all about how you managed to drive your date away."

Andrew bared his teeth. "Too soon, Tim, too soon."

Tim just laughed and hailed a cab. A night of drinking and driving didn't go well together.

When they arrived at the same biker bar they had been in the previous weekend, it was packed already. They had to drink their first beer at the bar, mostly just staring into the amber liquid or at the other patrons, because it was too loud to have a decent conversation. When they finally got a booth at the back, the drop in noise was considerable.

Without several people shouting out their orders in an attempt to get the bartender's attention, a civilized conversation was possible again. They both downed the shots they had taken from the bar before Andrew found the courage to start talking.

"To explain what went wrong yesterday, I have to start with my childhood." Andrew looked at Tim to see what impression his words made. He couldn't suppress a chuckle when he saw his friend putting on invisible glasses and taking notes on an equally invisible pad. "I was happy as a child, no problems there. The point is, we never had a lot of money. My parents both worked hard and we never lacked food or clothing, but they couldn't afford to send me and my sister to college. I learned to be a baker, and I love my job, don't get me wrong, but all through my childhood, I heard my father venting about 'those rich idiots in charge,' or the 'overprivileged scum that was born with a golden spoon in their ass.' You know, the kind of talk you expect from somebody who had to struggle all their life and feels bitter about it. Justifiably so." Andrew didn't want to paint his parents in a bad way; he loved them dearly, and he hoped Tim could understand that. His friend simply nodded.

"I get it. It's like all Indians are either doctors or computer wizzes. Or all Mexicans are drug dealers and all African Americans are in a gang and every white boy from the South is secretly a member of the Ku Klux Klan."

Andrew sighed in relief. "Yes, like that. A lot of prejudices and false assumptions. Anyway, I grew up with the class war always present in my mind. I tried very hard to shake it, but that always requires a conscious effort on my part. And it's not like I'm meeting rich and privileged people every day. And then Curtis comes to Sweet Break in a BMW that probably cost twice what I make in a year. I have to admit, that was a low blow for my ego, but he was so sweet and nice, and did I mention how hot he is?"

Tim grinned and raised his glass. Andrew followed his example, taking a generous sip of the slightly bitter beer. "So he had a great car and that intimidated you. I can understand that up to a certain point. What happened next?"

Andrew decided to let the "up to a certain point" slip for now. "We went to this restaurant in my neighborhood, OLA. He looked gorgeous, he made perfect small talk, and everything was fine. I thought I could impress him with the food there, but as it turned out, he's a regular at the place. I mean, when I asked him to go out with me, he did mention that he had just come from OLA, but I thought that was even better, because he seemed to like the restaurant. Long story short, the staff treated him like a prince. They knew all his preferences, and he basically selected our wine and food."

Hearing it out loud, Andrew couldn't decide if he sounded like a whiny brat or if his complaints were valid. Tim raised a brow. "You're aware that you sound like a white, heterosexual man from the fifties who's offended because some woman has more money than him, aren't you?"

Whiny brat it was. Andrew took another sip from his beer. At this rate, he was going to need another shot. "I know. But please, keep the context in mind. I already knew he's a sub, and I wanted to make a good impression, not only as a potential boyfriend but also as a potential Dom for him. Instead, he showed me how utterly inept I am at taking care of him."

Tim hummed at these words. "I can see the dilemma. Being a Dom is usually tied to a certain image, which contains us providing for the sub and taking the lead in everything. You do know that's just a cliché, don't you?"

"Intellectually, yes. But in reality, it felt humiliating. Here was the man I was already fantasizing about having on his knees in front of me, my cock in his mouth, handling our orders and pretasting the wine. Which should have been my job, since the reservation was in my name. I felt—uprooted. Not in my element."

Tim thought about this for a moment. "Since you were already having naughty fantasies about him, didn't it make you even hotter imagining having such a capable man at your feet? Or is that not your thing?"

Andrew sighed. "Not really. First of all, it would feel wrong for me to subjugate Curtis because of his social standing. To me, submission is all about free will and explicit consent. If I played with him, I'd never know if I didn't do certain things just because of my own hang-ups."

Tim steepled his fingers. "What I get from what you're saying is that a), you're an incredibly responsible Dom, which almost certainly rules out you abusing Curtis or his trust in you about something as petty as your different standing, and b), that you've been giving this a lot of thought, which means he's gotten under your skin."

"That he has. Though I'm pretty sure he won't want to see me ever again. He was furious when he ended the date."

"What did you say to him?"

Andrew squirmed. He needed more beer for this, so he signaled the waitress for another round. She came quickly to put two more glasses in front of them. Once she was gone, Andrew started talking again.

"We talked about BDSM. About what we like, and then I asked him where the good clubs are in Miami. He told me he only ever goes to Whisper."

"Ouch." Tim shook his head. "I can see how that threw you off."

"It wasn't the worst, though. I told him the two of us wanted to check out Eros today and asked him to come along. He told me he had a video night with his friends."

"Was that an excuse?"

"I don't think so. He suggested we could go out some other night, but at this point, I was already too pissed and hurt to take him up on his offer. I kind of didn't speak to him while we ate, and when we were done, he paid and left."

Tim's eyes had widened. "How can you 'kind of not speak to somebody'?"

"Well, he made small talk, and I—I basically answered with yes and no. I left him hanging."

Andrew lowered his head. If he thought about it, he'd been a colossal ass. Tim just shook his head. "So there was a guy who was willing to go out with you on sight alone, who, according to your own words, is hot, kind, and generally good to be around, and you blew it because he happens to have more money than you do?"

"It sounds awful when you phrase it like this!"

"Man, it *is* awful! I've had more than my fair share of disastrous dates, given that I'm too loud and unpolished for polite company, but you certainly take the crown. The fact alone that he agreed to the date should tell you a lot. The rest, you should have tried to figure out over the course of several follow-up dates, during which you would have gotten to know him. I hate to tell you this, man, but I don't see a big chance of you convincing him to give it another try."

"Who says I want another try?"

Tim just raised his eyebrow, and Andrew deflated as quickly as he had gotten his hackles up. "Fine. I would like to see him again, but as you so eloquently put it, he probably has had enough of me. Now let's get drunk. I need to forget this epic failure."

Tim stopped him with a shake of his head. "Oh no, my friend. We can't make a solid plan when we're drunk. And that's what you need to get back into Curtis's good graces. A plan."

Tim smiled so broadly, Andrew feared for a moment his face would split in half. "What do you suggest?"

"First of all, we need to find out more about him. He's a gallery owner, you said. Get your cell out. We have some research to do."

Energized by Tim's determination, Andrew did as he was told.

CHAPTER 7

ON HIS way over to Emilio's, Curtis picked up Peyton. He still wasn't sure if he should tell his friends about the date from hell, but Collin would probably implode if he didn't say anything, and that would just be cruel. Besides, he could do with some cuddling from his friends.

"You seem awfully quiet today." Curtis could feel Peyton's gaze drilling holes into his side. His friends were also terribly observant—well, at least some of them.

"I had a rough day yesterday."

"Something for the class?"

Curtis nodded. Definitely something for the class. Peyton reached over to pat Curtis's thigh. The gesture lacked all sexual innuendo and was full of friendly support. Exactly what Curtis needed. He parked in front of the building where Emilio now lived in Leeland's apartment and they got out. A quick look around showed the Volvo Leeland used to drive around, the brand-new Mercedes van Richard had gotten for Dean so he and Emily were safely encased in as much metal as possible when driving, and the white Harley with the pink and turquoise stripes that was Seth's ride.

"Seems like we're the last ones," Peyton murmured. They made their way up the stairs, and after a short ring, Emilio opened the door.

"Curtis, Peyton! Good to see you. Please, come in." Emilio stepped aside to let them in. The apartment was filled with the warm smell of curry. Peyton made a show of sniffing, which had Emilio laughing.

"There's a new Indian restaurant two blocks away, and they make the best naan bread I've ever had. And before you ask, it's heavy on the garlic."

Peyton grinned. "Then it has to be good."

They shed their shoes and light jackets before they joined the others in the spacious living room. The TV was already set up; the food sat in warming boxes on the coffee table. After the usual round of hugs, they all filled their plates, and for the next ten minutes, the only sounds were the light clatter of cutlery and some almost orgasmic moans. Curtis loved the fact that all his friends enjoyed food as much as he did. He hated eating with people who counted every single calorie. Even Emilio, whose master, Garrett, kept him on a strict diet to further improve his body—which, in Curtis's opinion was already perfect—had a free pass for their evenings together. According to Emilio, Master Garrett had grumbled and complained, but finally he had realized it was just plain cruel to make Emilio watch while his friends stuffed their faces with everything tasty under the sun. Carrot sticks with low-fat yogurt just couldn't compare to a plateful of spaghetti carbonara followed by some rich dessert.

After their initial hunger was sated and they all had congratulated Emilio on finding such a good restaurant, it was time for talking. Their evenings followed a routine that was never strictly implemented, but helped them to keep track of one another's lives, since they couldn't always talk openly at Whisper and Peyton and Seth weren't members there. It was always a merry-go-round, this evening started by Dean. He wore a silly smile that made his eyes glow.

"I can finally tell you all! The surrogate is pregnant, and it's the first week of the second trimester. We wanted to wait until we started telling people in case something went wrong again." For a moment, Dean's face fell. He doubtlessly remembered the two times the surrogate miscarried within the first eight weeks. That wasn't uncommon with in vitro fertilization, but for Dean, who had been looking forward to a sibling for Emily, it had been devastating. Now those dark times were behind him, and he accepted the heartfelt well-wishes of his friends.

"I'm going to be an uncle again! I need to tell Martin that we have to go shopping, and, Peyton now you get to design another nursery, just don't forget to leave one wall free so I have room for the mural, because shifting the furniture in Emily's room was exhausting, and I think I could use dragons or perhaps all the best characters from fairy tales, though fairy tales can be pretty cruel and bloody, and I found a book about how Snow White was originally told, and I didn't know one could die from having to dance in heated iron shoes, though I think dancing itself is hard when your feet are burning, and yes, she was evil, but killing her like that seems a bit over-the-top, and I don't think I want to draw somebody who's dying because their feet are on fire, but then again, children often see things differently. I mean Emily had no problem when Dean killed the evil racoon in our first story, though I'm not sure if she really knows what death means, and that is something I envy her."

Collin had to finally get some air, which gave Peyton the chance to chime in. "Dear Collin, if I'd known you back when I designed Emily's room, I would of course have left at least one wall to your artistic genius. As it is, I'm definitely taking your ideas into account and a fairy-tale theme can also be done gender neutral." He looked at Dean, who just shrugged.

"This is up to you, Peyton. You know Richard and I have no strict policy on that subject."

"You just find the single-color schemes boring, don't you?" Leeland grinned and poked Dean in the ribs.

"Hey, that's perfectly okay! I just think it's more fun having different colors and not just shades of blue or pink." Dean shuddered. Emily was a little over three now, and there had been a brief period around her third birthday when her favorite color had been pink. In all shades, preferably with glitter. After a concerted effort from Collin, Peyton, and Curtis, her taste in colors had broadened again, though Curtis would never forget the sea of pink balloons and streamers for Emily's birthday. He still couldn't look at his light pink button-down without hearing the delighted squeals of a bunch of three-year-olds, let alone bring himself to wear it. Perhaps he would give it to charity.

"You're absolutely right, Dean. My congratulations, and I could do a quilt for the little one as soon as Peyton and Collin have decided on a theme." Seth smiled warmly at Dean. The latest addition to their little group was a study in contrasts, a fascinating mixture of bad biker boy and trendy twink. Seth's stature leaned more toward muscular leather stud, while his grooming choices branded him as a stereotypical gay. Though the eyeliner and lip-gloss did look good on him, and he somehow managed to combine the two looks and own them.

After they had all congratulated Dean thoroughly, Peyton told a funny story about one of his clients. Leeland had nothing to contribute, but since he was busy with his studying, nobody expected him to. Emilio shyly announced that Master Garrett had deemed him ready for his first fitness convention, where he would show off for Garrett's chain of fitness clubs.

"That's great, Emilio! You worked so hard on your body and you're so disciplined, you've earned this!" Dean smiled at the youngest member of their group. Emilio blushed and looked down on his now empty plate.

"Thank you, Dean. I'm pretty nervous. I don't want to disappoint my master."

"You won't." Leeland's voice held a hint of steel. "And if he gives you any trouble, you tell me, Emilio. Okay?" Leeland winked at Emilio, and for somebody who didn't know Leeland well, it seemed like a playful gesture. Curtis knew Leeland and Dean *very* well, and if the wink had managed to distract Curtis from the strange undertone in Leeland's voice, Dean's visible tensing would have put him right back on track. Something was going on, but neither Leeland nor Emilio seemed to want to share it, and from the way Emilio reacted more to the wink than the words, Curtis wasn't sure if they had talked about it yet and if Emilio was aware that Leeland seemed to have latched on to something. Curtis furrowed his brows. They usually were very open with one another, and he wondered what was going on. Before he could ponder that thought any further, Emilio smiled at Leeland.

"I will, Leeland. Thank you so much for being there for me." Curtis looked at Dean, who just raised one eyebrow. So this was something Leeland was chewing on, and he wasn't ready yet to voice his problem. Curtis knew the best course of action in this case was to let Leeland work it out for himself. They would find out sooner or later.

Now it was Collin's turn, and the radiant smile on his face told Curtis it had to be something good.

"Martin and I have set a date!"

"What?" It came from Dean and Leeland in unison. Peyton made a face, while a smug grin appeared on Emilio's lips. Seth looked suspiciously unperturbed. He must have known.

"That's great, Collin! My congratulations!" Curtis hugged Collin, who was sitting right next to him. He was truly happy for his young friend, though it only made the date from yesterday look even worse. Curtis felt a twinge in his heart, not of jealousy, but of sadness, because it seemed as if he would watch all his friends finding their men and going steady while he stayed alone. He knew he was being a bit overly dramatic, but after the date with Andrew, he definitely had a right to be.

"Man, couldn't you have waited another four weeks?" Peyton didn't look too happy. "Now I owe this little stud over there a hundred dollars and can't collect his workforce to clean my apartment."

Emilio grinned broadly before he stuck his tongue out. "I told you Master Martin was getting impatient. But you never listen to me. Serves you right, Peyton."

"Wait, you agreed to clean that dump Peyton calls his apartment?" Leeland sounded incredulous. "And you'll only get a hundred dollars from him? He tried to pull one over on you, Emilio."

"Shut up!" Peyton interrupted him. "You make it sound as if I'm like one of these hoarders. Just because you can't eat off my kitchen floor—" Leeland made a gagging sound. "—doesn't mean my apartment is some kind of war zone."

"It's not a war zone, Peyton. It's a breeding station. You have a healthy dust bunny population, every single corner of your home is listed on the spider housing market as a prime location, your kitchen and bathroom are officially silverfish territory, and last time we were there, I think they were thinking about mounting an attack on the living room as well." Leeland shook his head.

"Hey, that's not fair. Those dust bunnies do no harm, the spiderwebs are kind of quaint, and having silverfish in your home means there's no nasty toxic things in your walls or paint or floor."

Curtis couldn't suppress his grin. It was an old argument between Peyton and Leeland, though Peyton's apartment wasn't that bad. He did clean it once a month. It wasn't his fault that Leeland was after every bit of dust like the devil was after poor souls. The two stopped their bickering when Dean turned to Collin.

"So when's the big day, Collin?"

Collin looked to Seth, who grinned broadly. "In October. We didn't want it to be too hot, but it shouldn't be cold either, and Seth has already composed the perfect cake for me, and he's shown me the most beautiful flowers, and I'm going to wear a suit, and we'll have the ceremony at home in our garden, with a big party afterward, and the only decision I had to make was picking my best man, and I really love you all, you know that, but for my best man there's only one choice, so Curtis, I hope you say yes, because Seth has already picked out a suit for you as well so that we all look good when we're standing in front of the officiant."

Collin smiled broadly at him, and Curtis couldn't help the welling of tears in his eyes. It was good to be loved so much, good to be among friends.

"It would be my honor, Collin."

With a squeal, Collin threw himself in Curtis's arms, and the others hooted and cheered. When the noise finally died down, Leeland turned to Seth. "I guess we know what your big news is. I can't believe you kept that from us."

The wedding planner shrugged. "Secrecy is my middle name. You know the difficulties I had to overcome to get this wedding. There's no way I'd have compromised my success by telling you meddlers."

Leeland threw his hands in the air. "So much for helping you with Collin's likes and dislikes! I'm through with this. Where are the sweets?"

They all laughed. Helping Seth plan the perfect wedding for Collin without Collin realizing it had been their mission for the past few months. The work had paid off, it seemed, if Collin's relaxed stance was any indication. Even the cake conundrum had been solved when Martin decided they would simply have two layered cakes instead of one after the bakery had informed Seth that having the waterfall of fruit *and* the semi-liquid chocolate coating wouldn't work.

"Now all we have to do is teach Dog to carry the rings and we're golden." Seth looked very pleased with himself, as he should be. As much as Curtis loved Collin and liked Martin as a friend, he was the first to admit that they weren't the easiest clients to have. While Collin's inability to make a decision could be considered mildly annoying, though still kind of sweet, Martin's demanding manner that stemmed from knowing exactly what he wanted and having the money to back those wants up, was anything but.

"Great, we have a baby, a first competition, a wedding, and two cases of blissful boredom." Peyton counted on his fingers. All eyes went to Curtis, and for a moment he considered not telling them. Theirs had all been good news or no news, which was good news, no matter what PR people thought. He would seriously dampen the mood if he aired his less than satisfying personal life in front of them.

"You're hesitating. That means it's bad news and you don't want to ruin our evening. Forget it, Curtis. You all were here for me when the surrogate miscarried. That's how our group works. You should know better than to hide things from us."

Curtis gave Dean a grateful smile.

"Yes, you'll feel better once you've told us everything." Peyton managed to keep his curiosity to a minimum, for which Curtis was grateful. He knew Peyton didn't mean to pry; he just wanted to help— and satisfy his need for juicy stories. To his credit, though, Curtis had to admit that he never gossiped. For Peyton, it was enough that *he* knew.

"I probably will. Thank you, guys. This means a lot to me." Curtis drew a deep breath. "I had a date yesterday, and it went terribly wrong."

The boys made sympathetic sounds.

"Who was he?" Dean asked.

"The man who made the macarons," Collin volunteered before Curtis could answer.

"The macarons you shared with me?"

Collin nodded. He took Curtis's hand and squeezed it. "That man kept staring at Curtis as if he wanted to eat him and when I asked him why he was doing it, he said he found Curtis hot and that he wanted to ask him out but didn't know how. He was also glad when I mentioned that Curtis doesn't have a Dom at the moment, so I figured he has to be one."

Curtis raised his brow. Leave it to Collin to be perceptive when you least expected it. The man usually lived in a happy bubble, mostly unaware of what was going on around him. But when he picked something up, it was always accurate, and it made Curtis wonder if Collin's constant absentmindedness was his brain's way of coping with the fact that he could absorb everything.

"That doesn't sound too bad so far. He asked you out and you decided not to tell us." Leeland grinned at him. "I wonder why."

Curtis sighed. "You know why. Because I didn't want to be driven up the wall by all your good-natured meddling." He held up his hands. "As it turns out, I could have told you, because that date couldn't have been worse even if all of you really tried."

"Hey." Peyton pouted. "We're helpfulness personified. We could have come to the place you had your date and helped you out when things went south."

Curtis buried his face in his hands. "You know what the worst part is? I actually think that would have been a good idea."

"Don't be so hard on yourself." Dean leaned forward from his seat left of Curtis to pat his thigh. "You had a traumatic experience with an asshole. Happens to all of us."

Which wasn't entirely true, because Dean had conveniently stayed with his first boyfriend ever and then married him. He knew next to nothing about the agonies of dating, but Curtis still appreciated the sentiment.

"He was a good-looking asshole, though." Curtis remembered Andrew's thick hair, the light stubble on his chin, the way he moved with easy grace. Oh yes, he could have seen himself with that man.

"So what did he do? Was he mean to you?" Seth looked at him over the rim of his glass.

"No, not really. He acted a bit strange when I came with my car, but that could have been nerves. I mean, it's just a car. A nice one, granted, but just a car. When we arrived at OLA, he was definitely nervous, but that's fine. It was a first date, after all. Anyway, we started talking and he pretty quickly inquired about my views on the lifestyle."

Leeland and Dean winced collectively. "It was kind of forward, but then again, he is a Dom, he knew, through Collin, that I'm a sub, and of course he would have wanted to talk about our sexual preferences. I mean, we're adults. Did I wish for a more romantic approach? Yes, definitely. But I wasn't appalled either. It was fine. And he was nice about it, charming. Anyway, he then told me he's still looking for a club to play and he wanted to know where I go to. When I told him it was Whisper, he seemed shocked. Then he asked me out for today and after I declined, he more or less stopped talking to me. I made polite small talk for forty minutes, and then I left, because I was pretty pissed."

"How awful!" Collin took Curtis in his arms. "That was just mean. Why would he do that? He was the one who said he found you hot and he asked you out. If he didn't want to go anymore, he could have just told you!"

"Yeah. That was really shitty of him." Dean looked furious. "I wonder what his problem is."

"He was intimidated." Emilio's voice was soft, as if he wasn't sure if he wanted to be heard. All eyes went to him.

"Intimidated?" Dean raised a brow.

"Yes. Try to see it from his point. He's new in town, you said. He's a Dom, and he's looking for a club to play, so he probably doesn't have a lot of contacts in the scene yet. He meets you by chance and can't believe his good luck when you agree to go out with him. Then you come by in a car that costs more than Leeland or I make in three years. You said he owns a bakery. No matter how successful he is, I'm sure he doesn't have that kind of money. He takes you to OLA, which is not a Michelin restaurant, but upscale. It's the kind of restaurant I would go to if I had something to celebrate. I guess he wanted to impress you, and then he finds out you're a regular there. I bet the staff treated you accordingly, because that's what they do in places like this. So you have a Dom who has the burning wish to impress you and is thwarted at every turn. To top it off, you tell him you're a member at Whisper. He probably thought he doesn't have a chance at all."

Emilio panted as if he had just run a marathon. He rarely spoke so much, and he seemed flustered.

"But I agreed to go out with him! Why would he think he doesn't have a chance? I get that most of the Doms at Whisper have some hang-ups about me because of the way I act and who I am, and because they like their subs more dependent, but this was a normal situation. I didn't go all upper-class on him!" Curtis knew he sounded bitter and he didn't care. If his behavior was too posh for the Doms at Whisper and his money scared all the other Doms away, he would die alone.

Leeland leaned forward and handed him a cupcake, their dessert for tonight. "I'm sure you didn't. You're the most modest man I know, and you only unpack your scary social skills when you want to sell a painting or you don't like somebody. The problem is, your date didn't know you. He could only go with what he saw, and I guess when he asked you out, he pegged you as, well, normal. You never dress up when you're out with Collin, and Collin always wears his ratty jeans, so why would he suspect you to be different than what his first impression of you was? My guess is, he wouldn't have asked you out if he'd known."

"Just great. Now I feel bad about having money in addition to having been dumped before there was anything to be dumped for. Thank you, Leeland."

"That's not how I meant it and you know it. He's still an asshole for being mean to you. I was just trying to tell you that his behavior had nothing to do with you as a person and everything with him being an insecure jerk."

Curtis smiled weakly. "I have to admit, when you put it like this, it sounds a lot better. The problem is, where does that leave me? I may not be a 24/7 sub, but I like my sex kinky, and Doms seem to be deterred by either my money or my manners, two things I can't really change."

Curtis hesitated a moment. "Well, I could give away my money, but to be honest, I like having it. And I was trained in social skills from the day I was born. That's not something you just shake off."

"Plus, it's a part of you. One we like a lot." Dean handed him another cupcake. "I know it sounds like mockery, but you can't give up. Just because Jasper was an asshole of the highest order and this Dom yesterday proved to be in the same league doesn't mean all Doms are bad. You're going to find your perfect match, and we're going to help you. You're not alone in this, Curtis. We love you."

Curtis already felt better. Andrew had been a mistake, but thankfully a small one. After all, that was what first dates were for. To find out if there was more than just chemistry.

"And I love you. All of you." He grinned. "Now, Emilio, what film did you choose for us tonight?"

Peyton groaned. "Please tell me it's not one of those artistically valuable pieces again."

Emilio pointedly turned his back on Peyton. "To be honest, I don't know this one myself, but I fell in love with the poster art, and I think we're going to enjoy it— Most of us," he added with a backward glance at Peyton. "It's called *El laberinto del Fauno*, or *Pan's Labyrinth*. It's from 2006, and Guillermo del Toro directed it. The reviews say it's a great fantasy film and when I saw the trailer, I just had to choose it for tonight."

Emilio hesitated for a moment, which gave Curtis the chance to smile broadly at Peyton. "I liked the movie when it was released and would very much enjoy seeing it again."

Peyton groaned. "I knew it! Artistically valuable! Emilio, how could you do this to me?" He rolled his eyes dramatically.

Emilio simply shrugged and turned his gaze to Seth. He had by now learned to ignore Peyton when he embraced his inner drama queen. "The only problem is it's in Spanish with English subtitles." He looked at Seth. "I know the others all know enough Spanish to follow a film. If you're uncomfortable with it, we can turn the subtitles on."

Seth leaned back in his spot, a lazy smile on his lips. "It's fine, Emilio. My Spanish is far from perfect, but I know enough to get by, and I view it as a challenge to see how much I can understand. If things get dicey, we can always have the subtitles, but I think they always kind of distract from a film."

With a relieved sigh, Emilio pushed some buttons on the remote control and the large flat-screen came to life. They all settled on the couch, Curtis flanked by Collin and Dean, who both cuddled him close. Seth dimmed the lights, and the movie began. Curtis smiled in the embrace of his friends. Life was good, even if he didn't have a special someone at the moment.

CHAPTER 8

CURTIS SPENT his Sunday in the garden, working with Sophia, the landscaper who also did Dean's and Collin's gardens. She was teaching him how to take care of the beehives she had put up at the back of his garden, where it bordered on a patch of wilderness. At first, Curtis had been skeptical about getting bees, but after his first taste of the honey Dean's and Collin's bees had produced, he'd asked Sophia to set him up as well. By now he found it comforting to work with the insects, and the constant low buzzing that came from the hives soothed his nerves like nothing else. When Monday rolled around, he felt ready to face whatever the week could throw at him. Or so he thought.

Patty, his PA, greeted him with a blinding smile as soon as he set foot in the gallery. Her being in such a good mood on a Monday morning was far from her usually cranky personality and therefore highly suspicious.

"Patty, what has you so excited? Did your mother-in-law finally decide to move to the North Pole?"

For a moment Patty's face fell. Her wife's mother was a constant thorn in her side. The woman was convinced Patty had used some voodoo magic to turn her poor, innocent daughter into a lesbian who wasted her best years on "some coal-black slum creature" who was just after Lydia's money. Curtis had met Lydia and knew the woman never did anything she didn't want to and was as far from innocent as the devil from heaven. She was also a cutthroat lawyer whose services Curtis required whenever there was trouble with some of his more entitled clients. She also kept a close eye on all transactions regarding Collin.

"There's a special place in hell reserved just for her, and I'm tempted to do something really bad just to get there and watch her squirm. For eternity."

Patty's eyes had gotten that dangerous sparkle Curtis had learned to fear. "Well, you're married to a lawyer. I guess you're going to have front row seats."

"Hey, don't go dissing my girl. She's sweet as can be."

"Yes, when she's not devouring unsuspecting wrongdoers alive."

Patty smiled proudly. "She's great, isn't she?"

"As long as she's on my side, yes."

Patty threw her long black curls over her shoulder, even though they came bouncing back immediately, and laughed. After drying some tears from her heavily made-up eyes, she focused on him again. "All jokes aside, you got a delivery waiting for you in your office. Came in around nine via express. Just what were you up to this weekend, you naughty boy?"

Before Curtis could give her an answer, she bypassed him on her impossibly high stilettos, creating a familiar background sound that never failed to put Curtis in work mode. Driven by curiosity about her remark, he stepped into his office, where a huge vase with surely more than a dozen white roses stood on his desk. In front of the vase sat a bright yellow box with a familiar logo on it—Sweet Break. Curtis felt sweat gathering on his forehead. His heart hammered away like crazy, and hope flared in his chest. Yes, Andrew had behaved like a bastard, but he was a hot bastard with whom Curtis definitely had chemistry. Still, Curtis tried to stamp down that hope. It was probably just a coincidence. Somebody had wanted to send him flowers and added some sweets from Sweet Break. Yes, that was entirely possible. He approached his desk slowly, not sure what he was hoping for. Between the vase and the box sat an envelope. It wasn't a fancy one made from thick, expensive paper but one that could be bought cheaply in any supermarket, and his name on it wasn't done in elaborate ink letters but scribbled with a ballpoint pen. Somehow, that made it even more endearing in Curtis's eyes. That hint of imperfection. His parents and most of the other people he knew from growing up wouldn't be caught dead using something *cheap* and *mundane*. He took the envelope and opened it. There was a letter inside, together with two tickets for an exhibition at the PAMM, the Perez Art Museum Miami. Curtis read the letter first.

> *Dear Curtis,*
>
> *I'm so sorry for the way I behaved on Friday. I know I made the worst possible impression and the only thing I can say in my defense is that you caught me on the hop, as the Britons say. (Yes, this reference is deliberate to increase my chances of you forgiving me, and yes, I did think about how to word this letter for a long time.) As*

you may have guessed, I'm not from a rich background, unlike you, which is my problem in a nutshell. I admit I felt intimidated by you, but as a friend of mine pointed out, that is my problem, not yours, and shouldn't keep me from trying to have a relationship with somebody I felt an instant connection to. I'm not going to promise I'll be a changed man from now on—we both are old enough to know these things don't happen overnight—but I do wish to explore our chemistry and see where it leads us to.

If you think you can give me a second chance, we could go to the opening of the new exhibition of Haroon Mirza on Wednesday. If you can't forgive—which I would understand—you can perhaps take Collin with you or give the tickets away.

Andrew

PS: The macarons are for you. If Collin wants more, he has to buy some. :-)

Curtis stared at the letter for quite some time. It was a lot more than he had expected and even though he was afraid things would go south again, he could hardly say no to a man who had pleaded his case so eloquently. Before he could think about it anymore and maybe lose his confidence, Curtis took out his cell to dial Andrew's number, determined to see where things would lead.

Andrew answered after the second ring, almost as if he had been waiting for this call—or as if he had his cell nearby, just like everybody else. Curtis was a romantic at heart, but he was also old enough to know things were rarely as easy or nice as they seemed at first glance, just like Andrew had pointed out in his letter.

"Curtis?" Andrew sounded hesitant, as if he couldn't believe Curtis was really calling.

"Yes, it's me." A moment of awkward silence stretched over the line. Just when Curtis got ready to break it, half willing to tell Andrew he was forgiven, but that Curtis didn't want to take another chance with somebody who couldn't even manage a simple phone call, Andrew started to speak.

"I…. Are you calling to tell me to back off or to listen to my apology?"

That was so sweetly blunt it had Curtis chuckling. "If I wanted you to back off, I wouldn't have bothered calling. You would have gotten a pointed text."

"Oh. Well, then I guess I better tell you what an idiot I am, and how sorry I am for blowing our first date. I was so happy when you agreed to go out with me and then incredibly nervous. You see, I haven't been here long and outside of work, the only other acquaintance I've made beside you is Tim, another Dom who I met at Club Submission. I'm obviously looking for something permanent, and when I realized you were a sub—I couldn't believe my luck. I admit, I wanted to go all Dom on you, sweep you away with my charming personality and firm but respectful demeanor." Andrew chuckled, and Curtis realized he was trying to make a joke. A rather good one too. He laughed.

"If it helps, I did like your firm but respectful demeanor. About the charming personality I don't know, because so far I've only seen glimpses. Those are promising, though."

"I guess I earned that. Anyway, seeing my plans so completely thwarted was like a bucket of cold water. Things weren't as I expected them to be, and I'm man enough to admit that I don't deal well with surprises."

Curtis grinned. "I saw that. And I like the flowers, the macarons, and the letter. Thank you for that and you're forgiven. Though, in the interest of full disclosure, I have to tell you I already have tickets for that opening. As a gallery owner, I get them automatically. I wouldn't mind going there with a certain good-looking Dom at my arm."

For a moment Andrew didn't say a word. Then he started to laugh. "I should have known. Am I right in assuming you want me as arm candy?"

"I want you as my date. In a place where most people know me and will talk to me about business. For me, openings are work. Having you with me would make the work less tedious and afterward, we can go to a restaurant of your choosing." Curtis knew it was risky. He had just spelled out for Andrew that going to the opening with him would probably be even more intimidating than ending up in a restaurant where Curtis was a regular. This time, Andrew was warned and now was his chance to back out. Curtis held his breath.

"I understand. I better dress up, then."

Curtis inhaled deeply. "You don't have to. The world of art is about carefully constructed individualism. You should be fine in jeans and a shirt. Maybe, if you feel extravagant, you could add a silk shawl or come barefoot. It's all in the details."

Andrew laughed. "I'm not coming barefoot. I have a nice pair of jeans and a few good shirts. You won't be embarrassed by me, I promise."

Even though the last sentence was said lightly, Curtis could hear the tension underneath. "Don't worry. Once I start telling you the more outrageous stories about some of the participants, you'll realize how absolutely upstanding and nonembarrassing you are. I want to go there with you because of who you are, because you had the guts to ask a complete stranger out, because you apologized even though you could have just filed our date away under disastrous mistakes. So no, I could never be embarrassed by you, Andrew. I'm not that shallow."

A sigh of relief came through the line. "I didn't think you were. But you were open with me about what to expect, so I thought a warning would be fair. I'm not bad with people, but I'm also not used to upper-class crowds. I'm going to be on my best behavior, and afterward, I'm going to take you to a diner."

Curtis giggled. "Alternative program?"

"Yeah, something like that. Showing you my world, so to speak."

"I can't wait." Curtis knew he sounded breathless. He was excited at the chance of getting a second try with Andrew and wary at the same time. It made for an interesting mix of emotions that had his heart racing.

"I'm looking forward to it. Shall I pick you up or do we meet at the museum?"

"If it's all right with you, we could meet at my gallery. It's only a few blocks from the museum. Let's see, the opening starts at four. How about you come here at three? I can show you around a bit, and then we can walk to the museum."

"That's fine with me, Curtis. I already have your address, so I'll just come by."

Curtis gripped his phone a little tighter. "Perfect. See you on Wednesday."

"Yes. See you on Wednesday. And, Curtis? Thank you." Andrew sounded so genuine, Curtis felt a shudder running down his spine. Perhaps there was a chance for them, after all.

"You're welcome. I'm looking forward to the opening. Bye, Andrew."

"Bye, Curtis."

THE LINE went dead and all Andrew could do was stare at his phone. Curtis had forgiven him. Curtis was willing to give him a second chance. Curtis wanted him at the opening, with all his posh acquaintances. That was a sobering thought. Andrew had no illusions—he would stick out of that crowd like a sore thumb. He only hoped Curtis would be true to his word and not mind. Though the man hadn't struck him as somebody who said one thing and meant something else entirely.

"Hey, boss, stop staring at your cell like some lovestruck teenager and give me a hand. We need to refill all the macarons and the éclairs before the eleven o'clock rush!" Debbie, Andrew's part-time help at Sweet Break, pried him from his whirling thoughts that were gearing up for a minor panic attack. He put his cell in his back pocket and looked down at her meager five foot two. Debbie was nearing her midfifties, had a full, plump figure with generous breasts, a mass of thick hair that was currently dyed different shades of blue and framed her head like a halo. Her light brown skin always had a healthy glow that made her look a good ten years younger, and her dark brown eyes drilled into him with an intensity only a mother of six could achieve so effortlessly. Andrew flashed her a quick smile before he followed her into the pantry, where the macarons and éclairs were waiting.

He had a date. A second chance with Curtis. Should he bring some more macarons? Curtis had liked the éclair, so perhaps he should box some of those to bring. Andrew knew he would need all the help he could get, and he wasn't beneath using underhanded methods to win Curtis's favor. If it could be done with the liberal distribution of sweets, all the better for him.

"Andrew! What's wrong with you?" Something poked his belly with just enough force to be painful without causing real damage. He looked down at the griddle full of éclairs Debbie was using like a battering ram.

"I… uhm. I get it." He made a grab for the griddle, relieved when Debbie let go. Of course he wasn't off the hook so easily. Having her hands free meant she could fold her arms across her chest, pinning him with a glare that was usually reserved for her teenage sons.

"What's going on? Last week you were hyped up like my youngest when he's gotten his hands in the candy jar, and now you're zoning out when we should be preparing for the next rush."

Andrew bit his tongue to not point out that at the moment, she was the one keeping them from getting their work done. Even though she'd been working for him for only a short time, he had already learned not to try to distract her when she thought she was onto something. That only prolonged the torture. He licked his lips, trying to find a way out without revealing too much.

"I, uh, have something going on."

Debbie's eyes narrowed. She stared at him so long that he started to squirm. Finally, a smile blossomed on her lips. "You've met somebody! Finally."

The griddle almost fell from Andrew's hands. "What? I mean, how?"

Debbie turned around to get a plateful of orange macarons. "You forget I have six sons, five of which are already at an age where they have dates. I know the signs. Who is he?"

Despite the rainbow sticker on his shop door, Andrew had never told her he was gay. He was out and proud, but he never advertised. Leave it to Debbie to figure it out, though he assumed there were enough clues for her to work with. Plus, the woman was sharp like that. Andrew decided to wave the white flag.

"I'll tell you everything about him, but can we refill at the same time?"

Debbie just rolled her eyes, took a second plate stacked with chocolate macarons, and brushed past him toward the front of the shop. Andrew only had to lift the griddle slightly to let her pass. While they were filling the empty displays, Andrew tried to explain about Curtis.

"He came into the shop last week and I asked him out. He looks so hot with his salt-and-pepper hair and his big, kind eyes. He dresses up nicely, and his accent is to die for. He's British, you know?"

Debbie placed the last macarons before she looked up at him. Her gaze was soft now. "I see. You like him a lot, don't you?"

Andrew thought about this. "We've only had one date so far, and that didn't go too well. But yes, I feel drawn to him, and it's definitely not just physical. There's something about him I would love to explore."

"And he's willing to give you a second chance?"

Andrew raised a brow. "What makes you think I was the one who fucked up?"

Debbie just snorted.

"Fine, it was me. I just want to point out it could have been him as well."

"Of course, dear."

"Now you're just humoring me. Anyway, he's willing to try it again. Which reminds me, do you think you can take over the afternoon shift on Wednesday? We're usually sold out around four."

Debbie didn't hesitate. She usually only did the morning shifts to be home when her children got back from school, but she was surprisingly flexible, probably because her oldest boys were already eighteen, sixteen, and fifteen. "No problem. It will give Geoff a chance to get off my shit list. And when he's babysitting his brothers, he can't get into any trouble."

Geoff was her second oldest and currently going through a rebellious phase. Andrew nodded.

"Thank you, Debbie. I'm leaving around half past one."

"That's fine, boss. Don't worry, at least not about the shop. Just don't blow that date as well."

Andrew threw his hands in the air. "Thanks for the vote of confidence! Oh, how I can feel the love!"

"Just a tip, sarcasm won't get you far with your date. Charm and eloquence are what you want to show."

Andrew prepared for a sharp answer, because he loved the constant bickering with Debbie, but the chime of the shop door put an end to this particular match. He grabbed the empty griddle and plates to return them to the kitchen before he joined Debbie in the fight against the eleven o'clock rush. Glad his business was going so well after three short months, Andrew didn't complain.

CHAPTER 9

ANDREW WAS sitting in his car outside Curtis's gallery, taking a last look at his face in the rearview mirror. He was dressed in black jeans, his black biker boots, which he had polished until they gleamed, and a deep red button-down with the sleeves rolled up. Since he knew there was no way he could compete with the kind of styles the other guests at the opening would probably be wearing, he had opted for something he felt comfortable in. That the shirt and the jeans were just tight enough to nicely highlight his ass and shoulders without being too obvious about it was a bonus. With Tim's encouraging words in mind—*Don't forget, just be yourself, and trust Curtis to come to his own conclusions*—and a box of macarons in hand, he exited the car.

The gallery was at the ground floor of a modern building that also housed an international law firm and an accounting firm. Through the huge glass doors, he could see part of the showroom and some interesting sculptures. There was no flashy sign anywhere, just a discreet brass plate to the right side of the door, announcing he was entering the *Curtis Morris Gallery*. For a brief moment, Andrew wondered how people knew the gallery's opening hours when there was no sign, but they probably checked on the internet, like he had done, or simply knew. Perhaps he could ask Curtis about it later. Andrew stepped through the doors into the cool air of the gallery. Before he had a chance to take a look around, a tall, African-American woman who was made even taller by her stilettos, descended on him like an eagle on a lamb.

"You must be Andrew! Curtis has told me you're picking him up. I'm Patty, his PA. He's getting ready for the opening, so why don't you come with me? I can make you a cup of coffee or an espresso, if you'd like. Oh, and you brought him something? How sweet of you." Her perfectly manicured hands dug into his biceps like claws while she dragged him through the first showroom, as he now realized, toward a short hall with two doors on each side. They entered the first room to the left, which turned out to be some kind of common room, with a small, blinding white kitchenette, a huge coffee maker, two white leather sofas, and a small coffee table made of blue glass. "Please, sit down. Espresso?" Patty took the box with the macarons from him and placed it on the coffee table before she turned her attention to the coffee maker. Grateful for this short reprieve, Andrew sank into one of the sofas. It was sinfully comfortable. "Uhm, yes. An espresso would be great."

"On the way."

Spitting and hissing, the coffee maker came to life, gurgling out a cup of espresso with a more than satisfying layer of crema on top, as Andrew could see when Patty brought him the cup. He smiled at her, still not sure how to handle the situation. Patty made herself a café latte in an elegant glass cup and came to sit down on the other sofa. For some time, neither of them spoke. Andrew was almost sure Patty was testing him in some way, but as a Dom, he knew about power play, and the silence game never had an effect on him, much to his mother's and sister's dismay. After Patty had stirred her latte long enough to not only destroy the artful pattern on the foam, but also to swirl the layers of coffee and milk until it was all one light brown mush, she raised one perfectly plucked eyebrow.

"I can see you have the backbone. That's good. What about the heart?"

As it seemed, Andrew had passed part of the test. Now he wondered how to proceed. He didn't know this woman, though it wasn't terribly hard to deduce that she felt protective of Curtis, which was good but also unnerving. Being honest to her would certainly earn him some brownie points, though he wasn't sure how much of his private life he should bare to her—if any. He didn't even *know* if there was a private life with Curtis for him.

"Unlike you, he has one, Patty." Curtis's voice sounded amused, not angry, so this had to be normal behavior for Patty. The woman pouted.

"I do have a heart, Curtis. You should know; you're one of the few who live in it."

This time Curtis laughed out loud. "I do know, Patty. I was just trying to rescue my date. Hello, Andrew."

Curtis approached the sofa and Andrew hurried to get up. The man looked gorgeous. His salt-and-pepper hair was once again artfully tousled, his eyes twinkled in amusement, the light blue button-down with the white pinstripes he wore harmonized perfectly with his anthracite slacks and black loafers. Andrew couldn't believe his luck.

"Hello, Curtis. You look beautiful."

Curtis actually blushed. Andrew's self-confidence rose, and with a cocky grin, he took the box of macarons and held it out to his date. "Here, for you. I thought you might have eaten the others already."

"Thank you, Andrew. That's so thoughtful of you." Curtis took the box with a happy smile that made Andrew feel as if he were ten feet tall. He opened his mouth to give a reply but was cut short by Patty's delighted squeal.

"You're the bringer of macarons? Wonderful!" She clapped. "Curtis only gave me two, can you imagine? He's so bad at sharing." The dark look she threw in Curtis's direction was probably meant to be menacing, but Curtis only laughed.

"They were a gift to me, you vulture. Besides, they have, like, a ton of calories, so I was actually doing you a favor."

Patty stuck her tongue out at them. Andrew decided this was a good chance to sling an arm around Curtis's waist. They hadn't reached the kissing state yet, though the tingling that went through his body just touching Curtis promised something special. Curtis didn't seem to mind. He snuggled into Andrew's side as if he belonged there. His head was just high enough to rest comfortably against Andrew's shoulder, and Andrew decided he loved having Curtis so close. Patty's gagging noises drew him out of his happy haze.

"There's nothing worse than young love. Gah." She made a shooing gesture with her hands. "Come on, leave. Before I barf all over the white leather."

Curtis just shook his head. "Sometimes I don't know why I'm putting up with you. It can't be your charming personality, for sure." He looked up to Andrew. "I'll give you the tour, and then we can head to the PAMM."

Andrew nodded. "I'd love to see your workplace."

Curtis stepped out of Andrew's embrace, much to his regret, but made it all better when he entwined their fingers. With a goofy smile on his lips, Andrew followed his date out into the showroom.

ALMOST TWO hours later, Andrew and Curtis were standing in one of the garden sections of the PAMM, sipping champagne from fragile-looking flutes. The tour of the gallery had been interesting, even though Andrew wasn't that into art. Just hearing Curtis getting all excited over certain pieces or even single colors in a painting was worth looking at abstract pictures of flower fields and cities. There was a fire in Curtis Andrew hoped transferred to other areas as well. Now the speeches for the opening were done and it was time to mingle. Andrew looked around. Curtis had been greeted by a great portion of the guests, many of whom were dressed as elegantly and posh as Andrew had feared. Curtis had been right, though. There were also some guests, artists, he assumed, whose style was relaxed, highlighting the carefully staged individualism Curtis had mentioned before.

An elderly couple approached them, both with huge smiles on their faces. "Mr. Morris, it's such a pleasure to meet you here. What a great exhibition, don't you think? We've already talked to the artist, such a delightful man."

The man's voice was just loud enough for other people standing nearby to hear him, and given how quite a lot of heads swiveled their way, Andrew knew it was calculated. Curtis smiled graciously, taking the woman's hand and kissing the back of it before he shook the man's. "Mr. and Mrs. Abrego, it's such a pleasure to meet you. Yes, I think the exhibition is vey well done. May I introduce my date, Mr. Andrew Granger, to you?"

Andrew put a smile on his face as well and extended his hand. He didn't kiss the woman like Curtis had done, but he bowed his head slightly to show his respect. "It's nice meeting you, Mr. and Mrs. Abrego."

The woman let out a delighted titter that didn't manage to move the skin on her face even a bit. It remained a stiff mask of indifference, and Andrew wondered if this inability to show any real emotion made her marriage happier. Realizing that he was getting sarcastic, Andrew focused back on the couple. The man was talking animatedly about a sculpture he had just purchased from Curtis. Mrs. Abrego put her hand on Andrew's forearm, feeling him up a bit without being subtle. Andrew decided to let it slide in favor of listening to Curtis talking business. Andrew had to admit Curtis was very good at it. When they said their goodbyes to the Abregos, the couple agreed to make an appointment with Patty to see Curtis's new pieces. After the Abregos came the Wallaces, the Fuenteses, the Rosenbergs, and many others. Half of them were in their late fifties or sixties, and some were younger, clearly wanting to impress customers and peers with their taste in art. And they all came to Curtis. The longer Andrew listened to the discussions, the more he realized only a few of these people knew anything at all about art. They treated it as an investment, both financially and socially, and Curtis, genius that he was, catered to their needs in his perfect, gentlemanly way. At some point, the artist came to talk to Curtis as well, thanking him for coming to the exhibition. This talk was a bit different, Curtis changing his behavior from polite firmness to a softer approach.

After the artist had been whisked away by his agent, they had a moment's peace. Curtis smiled at him apologetically. "I'm sorry, this must be boring for you. I promise, just one more hour and we can make our escape."

Andrew picked two virgin mojitos from a tray one of the many waiters moving around held out and passed one to Curtis. They had stopped with the alcohol after the first glass of champagne, Andrew because he didn't like being inebriated and Curtis probably because he needed his wits about him.

"No, it's fine. Believe me, nobody is more surprised than me, but I actually enjoy listening to you talk to all these people."

They clinked glasses and each took a sip. Curtis winked at him. "Don't say that too loud or I'm going to drag you to every single event I have to attend. I have to admit, it's a lot nicer with a hot guy by my side."

Andrew laughed and mock bowed. "It would be my pleasure." He reached for Curtis's hand. "I'm really enjoying myself, Curtis. Though I have to admit, those sound installations are not my cup of tea."

Curtis entwined their fingers, squeezing lightly. "I can understand. Some forms of art are more elusive than others. It's the same with sweets, I guess."

Andrew raised a brow. "What do you mean?"

"Well, I love your macarons; they're great. And I do love all kinds of other sweets, like éclairs or cookies, but then there's things like meringues or petit fours with orange liqueur, and I just don't get those."

"Ah, now I understand. And you're right. It's funny how different people's tastes run. Though I'm glad you like my macarons. Gives me an advantage." He winked and enjoyed the blush creeping up Curtis's neck. The man was adorable, and Andrew couldn't wait to see where else Curtis could blush.

"Curtis! There you are! I've been looking for you everywhere!" Andrew knew that voice and was just in time to turn around to see Collin flitting past him to hug Curtis, who let go of his hand so that Collin's assault wouldn't knock the glasses over.

"Collin! I thought you wouldn't come?"

The young man leaned back a bit in Curtis's arms. He seemed completely oblivious to the ruckus he had created. People all around them were whispering and staring, but nobody dared to come closer. A shift in the air to his right alerted Andrew to another presence, and when he looked, he knew why everybody kept their distance. The man next to him was built like The Rock, had the menacing air of a mafioso, and a dark scowl to go with it. He watched Collin like a hawk.

"I thought so, too, but then Martin suddenly had the afternoon off, and he suggested we could come here, even though I know he's not that interested in other artists, but he insisted and I really wanted to come, because, you know, I love sound and what you can do with it, and so we drove here, and this garden is amazing, have you seen, there's lots of birds and insects here, and I ate one of those small breads with a funny spread, though it was too salty, and now I'm thirsty, but I can't wait to have a look around."

With a smile, Curtis gestured to his mojito. "If you want, you can drink this. But I'm sure there's going to be a waiter around soon. Hello, Martin. It's good to see you. May I introduce Andrew Granger to you? He was reckless enough to come here with me on a date. Andrew, this is Martin Carmichael, Collin's fiancé."

Andrew offered the huge man his hand. Curtis's playful tone told him the men knew each other well, so he was anxious to make a good impression. "Nice to meet you, Martin."

Martin smiled. "Likewise. Has your brain already tried to leak out through your ears from all the art talk, or is it all still new enough to be interesting?"

Andrew couldn't suppress a grin. Martin was charmingly blunt, which reminded him of Tim and made him feel at ease. It also helped that Martin and Collin were probably the most underdressed people at the opening. Collin's jeans had several holes in them, his sneakers had most probably been white once, and his T-shirt was old enough to be thin around the shoulders. Martin wore black jeans and black boots, similar to the ones Andrew sported, and a black button-down that did nothing to hide his powerful build.

"No, not yet. This is my first rodeo, so to speak, and only my second date with Curtis, so everything is still new. Hopefully you can ask me the same question in a year."

It was a bit daring, but it did the trick. Martin chuckled. "I like a man with ambition, so I'll keep my fingers crossed for you."

"You have forgiven him?" Collin looked at Curtis, his blue eyes devoid of any malice.

"Yes. Andrew explained everything to me and we decided to give it another try."

"Oooh, that's so great! I'm happy for you, Curtis, but I have to ask, when did Andrew apologize, and how did he do it, because Peyton and Seth and Leeland need to know because of the bet, though I'm probably not supposed to tell you that, but you would have found out anyway when you told us about this date, and so it's just a bit early, and since you like Andrew again, perhaps we can get more macarons, and éclairs, and our next meeting is at my place, so I can order it all, and perhaps we just skip the main course, that way we can eat more sweets."

Martin chuckled and reached for Collin, tugged him against his broad chest. Collin looked very small and vulnerable, very submissive yet, at the same time, completely safe. It was obvious that these two had found not only their common ground, but also their rhythm.

"Collin, baby, you can't just eat sweets and nothing else. We've talked about this. Now why don't you and Curtis look at the exhibition while Andrew and I tag along in the background?"

"Oh, yes, let's do that." Without hesitation, Collin broke free of Martin's hold to link his arm with Curtis. The two men led the way, while Martin and Andrew followed. Again it was funny to see how the people in front of them parted like the Red Sea for Moses.

"You have an interesting effect on people," Andrew muttered.

Martin grinned. "I know. I'm in the security business, so it comes with the job. And now that I have Collin, it's even more useful. Those vultures would eat him alive."

Before Andrew could comment on that, Haroon Mirza, the artist, approached Curtis again with his agent in tow. He greeted Collin with a warm smile and offered to give him a tour, all under the watchful and more-than-sour expression of the agent.

"What's gotten her panties in a knot? She looks like she wants to kill somebody."

Andrew leaned a little closer to Martin, to make sure they couldn't be overheard. Martin did the same when he answered. "Well, given the chance, she probably would sink her claws into Curtis and rip his heart out. None of the agents in the scene like that he's taking care of Collin's business."

"Why not? He's a gallery owner."

Martin nodded. "Yes, exactly. A gallery owner, not an agent. But I don't trust anybody else with Collin, and now the other agents are afraid Curtis might expand into agent work."

"Is that a possibility?" Andrew didn't know much about owning a gallery, but he was sure Curtis couldn't complain about a lack of work.

Martin just snorted. "No, surely not. Curtis is probably the most capable businessman I know, apart from another friend of mine, but I know for sure he neither has the time nor drive to start another venture. Just the galleries are keeping him busy like hell, and Collin is in high demand. Managing him is like a second full-time job, and yet he pulls it off with apparent ease. They're all just jealous."

Andrew didn't respond to that. He was still chewing on the plural of gallery. It seemed his date was a lot higher up the food chain than he'd originally thought. His brief internet research had been focused on getting the address of his gallery in Miami and on finding some general information to help him get the man back. He had to give Curtis credit, though, for not even remotely seeming like a too-rich-to-care snob.

The tour took about half an hour, and by the end of it, Andrew was ready to leave the world of art behind for the day. Curtis said his goodbyes to Haroon Mirza, seemingly oblivious to the daggers his agent was throwing at him. With lots of nods and smiles in every direction, they made their way out of the museum.

"Where have you parked?" Martin turned to Andrew, as if he had already read their dynamic, which Andrew still hoped to establish.

"We walked here from Curtis's gallery."

"Ah, a good idea. Do you have plans for the evening? Collin and I will be at Whisper."

Andrew swallowed. Of course friends of Curtis would be at the most exclusive club in the city. Before he could come up with an answer that was elusive without being impolite, Curtis saved him. "We don't know yet, Martin. Andrew has promised to feed me, and after that, we'll see. We both have to work tomorrow, so don't get your hopes up."

Laughing, Martin patted Andrew's shoulder. "No problem. I have to work tomorrow as well. But Leeland has the early night shift today and Collin wanted to see him."

Curtis nodded gracefully. "I understand. We'll see if we're in the mood."

"Even if you're not in the mood"—Martin waggled his eyebrows—"you can still show Andrew around. No pressure, though."

"Thank you." Andrew shook Martin's hand and nodded at Collin, who embraced Curtis before he snuggled back under Martin's arm. The scary-looking Dom herded Collin toward a black Escalade whose lights greeted them when Martin took out the key from his pocket and pressed one of the buttons. Andrew took Curtis's hand to lead him back to the gallery. They walked in silence for a few moments. "Martin seems nice."

Curtis snorted. "You don't have to be polite about it. It's his job to be scary."

"Yes, he said something about being in the security business. I can see that working well for him."

The dry humor in Andrew's voice had Curtis chuckling. "It certainly does. He runs his own firm, together with his twin sister." He turned serious. "Thank you for this, Andrew. I know this isn't exactly your scene."

Andrew squeezed Curtis's hand, enjoyed the shiver that ran through both of them. "Well, I had a lot to make up for, and it wasn't as bad as I'd thought. To be honest, meeting Martin and Collin stressed me more than all those entitled rich people who wanted to show off their financial prowess to you."

"You did well, Andrew. In case you're worried, Collin isn't able to hold a grudge if his life depended on it, and Martin invited you to Whisper, which he wouldn't have done if he didn't like you."

Andrew's eyes grew big. "Him asking us over was his way of showing his approval?"

A smile bloomed on Curtis's face. "Yes. You passed with flying colors. But we really don't have to go tonight. You promised to feed me, remember?"

"Oh yes, I do. And I'm a man of my word. We need the car, though. The diner I want to take you to is close to Little Havana."

"I can't wait."

CHAPTER 10

THE DINER Andrew took him to was nice. They didn't just serve the typical American diner foods like burgers and apple pie, but also had a selection of Hispanic food like arroz con pollo and Cuban sandwiches. At Andrew's recommendation, Curtis ordered the mango-avocado salad and the Havana burger, which turned out to be a delicious blend of American and Cuban ingredients. Andrew had another fusion cooking meal with rice, cheese, and a steak. After they had eaten their first bites, Andrew looked at Curtis with a half smile on his lips. "So this was a typical workday for you?"

Curtis took some time to chew some of his salad before he answered. This seemed like a loaded question to him, and he wasn't entirely sure where things were going and if he liked the direction. "Yes, more or less. Having somebody at my side was new, though."

Andrew nodded. He, too, seemed insecure. "I liked it. Really." It sounded a bit as if he wanted to assure himself as much as Curtis. Curtis sighed. Things were going nowhere fast and he decided to stop trying to read Andrew and just be upfront.

"Andrew, you can tell me if you didn't like it. Just because we have chemistry doesn't mean we have to work out. I think it was big of you to apologize to me and come to the opening, but if you don't feel comfortable with my work, it's no use pretending otherwise. My work is a big part of my life, and I can't always separate it from my private affairs."

For a moment Andrew seemed taken aback, but then a smile bloomed on his face. "I see, you're a power bottom, aren't you? I wasn't trying to back out of this. I'm merely in the process of understanding it all. Martin mentioned that you've got a lot of work with your galleries, as in plural, and on top you have Collin to manage, which I first didn't see as a big task, but I'm beginning to think he's a lot more successful than his appearance lets on?"

"Is this your way of asking me to put my cards on the table?" Curtis tried to sound casual, though he was wound tight as a bowstring inside. Andrew didn't sound freaked out, just curious, and Curtis found he wanted to explore what could be between them.

"Well, yes. I was already blindsided once, and I almost lost my chance to get to know you. I think we can both agree that there is something between us. Something I want to delve deeper into, but I want to do it with my eyes open. As for the cards on the table, you already know I own a bakery here in Miami. I come from a small town in Colorado, which I left because I started suffocating there. I have a sister, who lives close to my mother. My parents divorced ten years ago but are still on speaking terms. They know I'm gay and I think they have a suspicion as to how I like my sex, but they have never said anything about it. I make decent money, though surely not nearly as much as you do. Not enough to be able to afford a membership at Whisper, which is the main reason I don't want to go there. No need to dangle that particular carrot in front of me when I know I can never have it. That's about it."

Andrew's smile was open, but it was the hint of vulnerability in his eyes that convinced Curtis that he really wanted to give him a chance. "Fair enough. Fist of all, if we work out, the fees won't be a problem. It's in the club rules that you can bring a steady partner to play as long as he has been vetted by Richard and Martin. As a Dom you have to pass a little test that is more extensive if you express the wish to play with other subs as well. If you only play with me—which I would prefer should we come to an agreement—the test is a formality to make sure the privacy of the other clients is protected." Curtis hated to refer to their potential relationship with such clinical terms, but even though there was a chance of them being together, he didn't want to get too enthusiastic yet. That way, rejection, if it came, wouldn't sting so badly… or so he hoped. "As for my businesses, I do own several galleries in Europe, the US, and Asia. My name is a brand in the world of art, and I make seven-figure sums every year. My parents are British nobility, and if I stopped working today, I could still live in the lap of luxury for the rest of my life on my trust fund alone. In addition to these very happy circumstances, Martin has also asked me to manage Collin's career. He is one of the stars in the art scene, and his pieces sell for six- to seven-figure sums. Martin is also one of the owners of Whisper, in case you were wondering. I have no siblings, and my last relationship is almost eight years in the past and ended with me being dumped for a younger model."

Curtis knew the last sentence sounded bitter, but he couldn't help it. He had realized long ago that Jasper had just been an asshole who'd managed to deceive him for five years, but he'd still been the longest relationship Curtis had ever had. For a few moments, Andrew didn't say anything. He seemed to be in shock.

"Wow. That's… more than I anticipated. And a lot to address." Andrew's tone changed. All of a sudden, Curtis could see the Dom shine through. "First, whoever dumped you was an idiot. Second, if we reach an agreement as you called it, I would never play with other subs. I don't like to share, and I'm conservative when it comes to my relationships. Conservative as in exclusive, I mean." Andrew winked. "As for the vast difference between our incomes, I'm not going to lie to you, it will take me some getting used to. I'm not a fan of stereotypes, but I have to admit I seem to be caught up in quite a few regarding Dom/sub relationships."

Curtis lifted a brow. "I didn't think you were a 24/7 guy." That would be a deal breaker for Curtis.

Andrew shook his head. "No, I'm not. I prefer keeping the Dom/sub dynamic in the bedroom and the club. That doesn't mean I don't have certain images of what a Dom and a sub should be like internalized. We'll have to work on those together."

Hearing these words, Curtis dared to hope a little more fiercely. Andrew was definitely interested in more, and he was smart enough to see his own hang-ups as well as brave enough to address them. Curtis put his cutlery down to reach for Andrew's hand over the table. He entwined their fingers with an encouraging smile on his lips. "It would be my pleasure. Thank you, Andrew, for being so open with me. For giving me—us—a chance. I like to think I'm a good sub, but a lot of it is just routine, and I would love to go about exploring my submissive nature anew with you as my Dom."

Andrew squeezed Curtis's fingers. "You honor me, Curtis. I promise, I will do my best to be worthy of your submission. And hopefully of your love as well." He smiled crookedly. "I know it's early to talk about the L-word. I just wanted to make my intentions crystal clear."

"You did. And they do match mine. I'm getting too old to play games."

Andrew laughed. "You're not the only one. Though playing games never appealed to me. I like things that are real."

They stared at each other over the table, all the time holding hands like lovestruck teenagers. Curtis found he could get lost in Andrew's dark gaze that seemed to devour him alive. The waitress politely clearing her throat yanked them out of their blissful haze.

"I'm sorry to interrupt, guys, but are you done?"

They both looked at their empty plates. Curtis couldn't remember having eaten anything. He blushed. "Of course. Sorry. We got—lost here."

She winked. "No problem. Being in love is great."

"We would like the check, please." Andrew's cheeks sported a healthy pink color, but he didn't let go of Curtis's hand. When the waitress was gone with their plates, he lifted their hands and pressed a kiss to Curtis's knuckles. "The night is young. How about you give me that tour of Whisper?"

Curtis lifted a brow. "Are you sure? I mean, I would love to, but you've already had a busy day."

"I am sure. And why put it off when I seem to be on a roll today?"

The waitress came back with the check, and after paying it, Andrew took Curtis's hand again. They both rose. In front of the diner, Andrew suddenly stopped. He turned around to face Curtis, a hungry look in his eyes.

"Before we go to Whisper, I need to do this." He bent down to press his lips on Curtis's. Automatically, Curtis tilted his head to give Andrew better access. He felt Andrew's breath ghosting over his face, warm and with a faint aroma of mango. Their lips met tentatively at first, both of them testing the waters. When he felt the same electricity surge through his body that he experienced whenever Andrew touched him, Curtis parted his lips in invitation. It seemed as if Andrew had just waited for that. His tongue entered Curtis's mouth, started exploring right away, while Andrew's arms tightened around Curtis's waist, pulled him so close he had trouble breathing. Though that could have been the kiss as well. It was determined and dominating, but with a sweet undertone that had Curtis wishing for more. When Andrew finally broke the kiss, they were both panting.

"Damn, I should have done this sooner." Andrew sounded satisfied, and he looked like a sated lion basking in the sun.

"Yes, you should have."

Laughing, they sauntered toward Andrew's car. Once they were inside, they started kissing again, like two parched men in the desert. In

Curtis's case, it was definitely true. When their lips were red and swollen, Andrew sat up straight in the driver's seat. "Let's get going. Can you give me directions?"

"Of course." Curtis leaned back in his seat. What a perfect day.

THE DRIVE to Whisper took them about twenty minutes. Twenty minutes during which Andrew had every chance to freak out. Only he didn't. Being with Curtis almost half the day, seeing him in his element, had somehow lessened Andrew's fears of being inadequate. On the contrary, he was proud Curtis had subtly leaned on him by way of his body language. Andrew was nervous, though. Whisper was a great club with an impeccable reputation. When they drove through the gate into the fenced-off parking lot, Andrew got a first taste as to why the club was so popular among the upper crust. Curtis had shown his membership card at the gate and now, in front of the huge double doors leading into the building, his card was swiped by a scary-looking security man who could easily pass as a hardcore Dom in Club Submission. Once inside, they had to get through two more security checks. The interior was tasteful and classy, with red carpets and huge photographs of BDSM scenes on the walls. At what Andrew thought had to be the reception area, they handed all their electronic devices to a sub in leather shorts and a black fishnet T-shirt. Andrew was given a day pass, and he was asked if he wanted a leather bracelet to announce his status as a visitor. Since he was here with Curtis and not looking to play with anybody, he declined. The sub wished them a nice evening and another broad-shouldered security man opened the oak door for them that led into the club. There was a short corridor leading into an open space with a raised stage. Andrew felt himself drawn there, but Curtis dragged him through a door to the right first.

"We need to get changed," he explained with a smile.

Andrew looked around in what seemed to be a locker room. Or what a locker room would want to become when it ever made enough money. The benches were decked in white leather; the massive lockers were made of wood with black iron doors. The floor was a grayish marble that went perfectly with the light gray walls and blinding white ceiling. If Andrew hadn't known he was technically in a dungeon, his guess would have been law firm or beauty clinic.

"This is the room for guests. The subs and Doms who are here regularly have their own changing areas. I thought you might want to leave your shirt here."

"You're still using me as arm candy, boy?" Andrew winked at Curtis and was more than happy to see a faint blush creeping up the man's neck.

"Could be—Sir." Curtis had hesitated for a moment, and Andrew realized it was time for them to talk about their expectations for the evening.

"You don't have to call me sir if you're not comfortable with it. You know that, don't you?"

Curtis gave him the sweetest smile. "I know. I wanted to hear how it sounds. How it feels on my tongue."

"And?"

"It felt good. Right. I mean, there's no way we're doing an evening on high protocol here, since you're a guest and we haven't even talked limits or anything, but I'm comfortable with you calling me boy and me addressing you as sir. If it's okay for you as well."

Andrew leaned forward to kiss those full, inviting lips. When he came up for air again, he grinned broadly. "It's more than okay for me." Andrew started unbuttoning his shirt but stopped at the second button. "Why don't you do this for me?" He looked expectantly at Curtis, wondering if he'd gone too far. The blush on Curtis's cheeks deepened, and Andrew knew he had done the right thing.

"Of course, Sir."

Curtis stepped closer to reach the buttons. Slowly he began undoing them, his hands trembling slightly. Andrew stood perfectly still, afraid to break the spell coming to life around them, wrapping them in a wonderful bubble of intimacy. His cock reacted to Curtis's body heat and close proximity. The poor thing had gotten quite the workout already, since kissing Curtis had turned Andrew on like few things had ever managed. Now his shaft made another valiant attempt at getting his attention, but Andrew kept his focus on Curtis's elegant, perfectly manicured hands and the way his breath hitched at every button sliding free. When he was finally done, Curtis slowly lifted his hands, looking at Andrew with a clear question in his eyes. "May I, Sir?"

Andrew smiled. He had tried to imagine what Curtis's submission might look like, but the quiet dignity paired with a smoldering passion outdid any fantasy. "Yes, boy, you may."

Curtis's breath was coming more quickly now, his arousal fueling Andrew's. The first touch of those soft yet skilled hands on his skin had Andrew gasping. He couldn't help himself—he grabbed Curtis's wrists and held him still to bask in the heat seeping through his palms into Andrew's body where they were connected. They looked at each other, drowning in the lust that was simmering between them.

"One thing's for sure. We have killer chemistry," Andrew rasped.

"Yes. I haven't felt this desperately turned on since my teenage days. You make me want so much." Curtis moaned, a deep, beautiful sound that had Andrew almost spilling in his pants. How could one man be so sexy? In a bold move, Andrew took Curtis's left hand and directed it to his bulging erection, showing him what kind of effect he had on him. Curtis whimpered. He caressed Andrew's hard-on through the jeans, and Andrew knew there was no way he was walking out of this locker room without both of them getting some relief. Since they hadn't discussed anything yet, he went for the safest option, opening his fly with feverish movements and taking out his shaft before he did the same with Curtis. Curtis's hands dug into his shoulders when he pressed their leaking shafts together, causing a delectable friction. Curtis whimpered incoherently close to his ear, and Andrew let go of their cocks just long enough to spit into his hand for a little lubricant. Then he closed his fist around their shafts again, started working them with firm, determined strokes. He was so close, there was no way he could prolong this, so he went directly for the kill.

"This isn't going to last long, darling. Kiss me."

Curtis complied, his hips bucking wildly into Andrew's fist. After Curtis's hot tongue had entered his mouth, it took only two more strokes for Andrew to come. He felt the familiar pulsing in his balls, and then the orgasm washed over him with so much force, he almost lost his footing. The best thing was that Curtis followed him right over the edge, their cocks twitching in a wild rhythm in his fist. The scent of cum was thick in the air, and their gasping breaths filled the room like the sweetest music.

"Wow. I needed that. Thank you, Sir." Curtis leaned his sweaty forehead on Andrew's chest, still trying to fill his lungs with oxygen.

"It was my pleasure, boy. Is there somewhere we can clean up?"

Curtis nodded, his head still buried in Andrew's chest. "Over there." He pointed in the opposite direction of the door.

Andrew saw the sign for toilets over an unobtrusive door flanked by two locker rows. "Let's go, then."

He managed to get Curtis upright without smearing his clothes with cum. It felt a bit strange, walking around with his dick hanging out of his jeans, but they were in a BDSM club, after all. It should be fine. The toilets had that same classy elegance as the locker room, with two bidets, four different kinds of lube on a small shelf, and a stack of wet wipes. Andrew raised his brow and Curtis just shrugged. "Those annual fees have to be good for something," he muttered with a wink. After they were cleaned up, they went back to the locker Curtis had chosen for him. They were both a bit tense, but not in an uncomfortable way. To Andrew, it felt more like the sexual tension between them had gotten more intense with their first shared orgasm. There was one thing, though, he wanted to be clear about.

"I hope you don't mind that there was no blowing or licking off cum. This is something I want to hold off until we know each other better."

Curtis smiled. "I understand. And I'm glad. I think this is very thoughtful of you. Thank you, Sir."

Relieved, Andrew put his shirt in the locker before he turned to Curtis. "What about your clothes?" He lifted an eyebrow in a slightly challenging manner.

"I have a set of clothes in the sub's changing rooms. Since you're technically my Dom for tonight, you're allowed to come with me. Single Doms are not allowed there so that the subs have a quiet place to change or catch some breath."

Andrew nodded his approval. He was a big believer in making the subs as comfortable as possible. Because when it came down to it, there would be no playing without them. "If you think they don't like seeing a stranger there, I can wait outside."

Curtis raised his hand to touch his cheek. "That's very considerate of you. But it's fine. You're with me, so they won't mind."

Andrew entwined their fingers and let Curtis lead him back into the short corridor and through another door to a much larger room where the subs had their realm. This room made the one where he had changed look like a public toilet in a big city. For one, there were no simple lockers here but individual, antique wardrobes with small, polished silver plates to announce the owner/user of the piece. They were in different styles, ranging from what looked to Andrew like nineteenth-century furniture to the almost futuristic pieces of the seventies. Before Andrew could really register the deep blue marble tiles or the crème-colored leather benches, his eyes fell on the wall to his right. There were no wardrobes there and for good reason. The entire wall was covered in the most intriguing picture he had ever seen. The man depicted was obviously a sub, the collar around his neck and the cuffs on his wrists making it abundantly clear. He also looked like an angel. His blond hair fell to his shoulders, framed his gorgeous face like a halo; the eyes were of the brightest blue, and his half-open mouth spoke of absolute ecstasy. His wings were fully open, the tips a deep black that almost shimmered and turned to a blinding white close to his body. The space between was intermingling shades of gray so perfectly blended, Andrew thought he saw the wings moving. The man was naked, his torso covered in red welts, his thighs a deep red. Andrew swallowed. Whoever had done this painting, they had captured the essence of submission perfectly, the vulnerable strength, the combination of opposites. It was what he as a Dom was striving for with every encounter he had—the perfect balance between pain and bliss.

Curtis's hand on his forearm broke the spell the picture had woven around him. "And this is the reason why Collin needs an agent." The words were said with a small chuckle, but Andrew could feel that Curtis was moved by the picture as well.

"Collin painted that?"

"Yes. He's a very talented young man. Now please follow me, Sir."

Andrew allowed Curtis to lead him to the far end of the room, where he stopped in front of a wardrobe with two doors in a deep mahogany color. The plate read "Curtis Morris" in loopy letters. Andrew watched Curtis opening the doors without using a key.

"Don't you have locks on these?"

Curtis shook his head. "No. Nobody here steals. This may sound contradictory to you, especially considering the times we live in, but at Whisper the sense of being in a safe space comes from the absence of security measures—at least in here. Outside, things are of course different."

Andrew thought about this for some time while Curtis changed into black leather trousers and a black leather vest that accentuated his well-defined but not overly muscular arms while it diverted attention from his small—miniscule in Andrew's opinion—paunch. Curtis was by no means untrained; he just wore his age well. And it made sense to not have visible security measures in a place meant to create a relaxing atmosphere. Given the rigid controls upon entering, Andrew doubted there was no surveillance in place. It just wasn't visible.

"Are your ready, Sir?" Curtis looked at him with an expectant expression. Andrew took one last look around. They were almost alone, but on a Wednesday night, that wasn't surprising. The three subs who were currently changing acknowledged Curtis with a friendly nod but ignored Andrew like well-trained boys. They left the changing room, and this time, Curtis led him into the main area of Club Whisper. Andrew had to correct his estimate about Wednesday evenings immediately. Apparently the lack of subs in the changing room only meant they were all too busy in the club area. The place was not packed but fuller than any other club Andrew had ever seen on a weekday. He could also easily see why. If he could afford the fees, he would be here for downtime every day of the week. The huge room gave the atmosphere of a very posh living room where instead of watching TV, people amused themselves with demonstrations of various BDSM techniques.

One was taking place at the moment, and Andrew walked more slowly to take a good look. The Dom wore black leather pants with white laces at the sides and nothing else. He didn't have to, because his perfectly sculpted body was a joy to watch. The muscles in his arms and torso gleamed under the spotlights illuminating the stage, where he had a naked sub chained to a St. Andrew's cross. The sub was completely naked and built as well. Not as stacked as his Dom, though the dimples at the sides of his ass, the long, sleek muscles in his back, and the perfectly defined lines of his legs still made him a feast for the eyes. Especially with the angry red stripes decorating his back and ass in a neat pattern of parallel lines. The Dom changed his position behind the boy, lifted his arm with a vicious-looking cane in his fist, and let it come down on the sub's thighs with more force than Andrew would ever feel comfortable administering. The boy screamed, his back went rigid, his hands balled to fists, but he didn't safeword. Instead, he sobbed out a broken "One, Master," followed by "Please, give me more, Master." And the Dom complied. The only reason Andrew could watch this scene that normally would have been too brutal for his liking was the fact that the Dom kept on checking on the sub in the mirror that hung behind the cross, and the air of absolute control that surrounded the two. Without knowing the pair, Andrew could sense they were used to this kind of play, used to each other. Still, just thinking about doing the same to Curtis had him break out in a cold sweat. He was glad there were so many different possibilities to enjoy the game of dominance and submission.

Andrew was so busy thinking about the caning on the stage, he barely noticed when they reached the bar. It was Collin's enthusiastic "Oh, you made it, Curtis, how wonderful!" that yanked him out of his stupor. He watched Curtis embrace the young artist when a heavy hand landed on his shoulder.

"Andrew, nice to see you again. I didn't think you'd come tonight."

Andrew turned around to greet Martin, who looked even more intimidating than at the opening. He wore black leather pants that seemed painted on his muscular thighs and a leather harness with a silver D-ring resting on his breastbone. All those muscles made Andrew wish for a moment he had kept his shirt on. It was easy to feel intimidated by somebody as packed as Martin.

"Hello, Martin. Nice to see you as well. Our decision to come here was quite spontaneous, but I can't say I regret it."

Martin laughed. "I hope not! Richard and I put a lot of effort into the club. Speaking of the devil!" He looked at somebody approaching from Andrew's left, and when he followed Martin's gaze, Andrew had to concentrate to keep his mouth closed. The man coming toward them was as tall as Martin and also as packed. His black skin glistened under the soft illumination from above, and his gaze seemed to burn holes into Andrew. He wore clothes similar to Martin's, minus the harness, but it was the air of absolute authority surrounding him that caught Andrew's full attention. A leash was wrapped around his left hand, leading to a beautiful blond man who followed Richard at the perfect distance, his gaze respectfully cast down. He completed his master in a way Andrew had rarely seen in a Dom/sub couple, and he suddenly found himself wishing from the bottom of his heart to get the same with Curtis. Even though Andrew knew it was bad manners to stare at someone else's sub, he couldn't take his eyes off the blond. There was no mistaking it. He was the man from the picture in the subs' changing room.

"Uhm, Andrew, this is Richard Miller, the other owner of Club Whisper. Richard, this is Andrew Granger, my guest tonight." Curtis's voice wavered between amusement and a tiny bit of worry, which prompted Andrew to stop his staring. He looked at Richard, who extended his hand with a stony expression. Andrew took it, inwardly shaking his head at himself.

"I'm sorry, Richard. I didn't mean to stare at your sub. It's just, he's the man from the picture in the subs' changing room, isn't he?"

Musical laughter resounded from behind Richard, and his strict features softened considerably. "You can't blame him for being a little shocked, Master. Thank God I left the wings at home."

Martin and Curtis started laughing and were joined by Richard after a short moment. He made a small step to the side so his sub could come forward. The man extended his hand on his own, and Andrew was still too confused to think about proper protocol and shook it.

"Hi, my name is Dean. Are you the macaron man?"

"Hi, I'm Andrew, and yes, I'm the macaron man. Unless Curtis is having a secret affair before ours really started."

Dean's smile broadened. "I like him," he said to Curtis, who was standing close to Andrew now. Richard cleared his throat.

"Boy." There wasn't any heat behind the word, but Dean lowered his hand to his side.

"Sorry, Master. Hi, Curtis, hi, Collin."

Collin escaped from Martin's arms to hug Dean, which made a very nice picture. Both subs wore leather shorts that could have doubled as belts and nothing else.

Richard threw his hands in the air. "There goes high protocol again. I blame your boy, Martin."

The amused twinkle in the huge man's eyes belied his sharp tone. Dean seemed to know his master very well, because he went on tiptoe to kiss his chin. "You can go all high protocol on me during our scene, Master. I promise I'll be naughty."

Richard moaned and kissed Dean in earnest. "You're a bad, bad boy. Just the way I like it."

When the kiss ended, Richard turned to the others. "Let's order some drinks and sit down. Andrew looks as if he could use a break."

Andrew followed Curtis back to the bar, where a slim, androgynous-looking man was waiting for them. He had his long, shimmering black hair in a messy bun at his nape and wore a very short red vest that accentuated his flawless body. Curtis, Dean, and Collin hugged the man over the bar counter, while Martin and Richard nodded at him. Curtis dragged Andrew forward. "Andrew, this is Leeland Drake, another friend of mine. Leeland, this is Andrew."

Andrew shook the slim hand while Collin did the talking for him. Apparently all of Curtis's friends knew everything about their disastrous first date. Andrew didn't know if he should be offended or not. "He apologized, and Curtis is giving him another chance, isn't that great? Also you lose the bet, but I think you hoped you would do so, which I think is totally cute of you and now you can't punch his nose in, especially not here, though we're all used to it somehow, but not in the way you do it."

That sounded ominous enough for Andrew to take his hand back as quickly as possible while pretending he didn't see the small smirk at the corner of those thin lips.

"Hi, Andrew. Nice to meet you." The silent threat in those words was obvious. Curtis came to his rescue.

"It's fine, Leeland. As Collin said, he apologized and we're giving it another try. Please don't ruin it for me by scaring him off."

"I would never do that, Curtis." Leeland sounded offended. "I'm just looking out for you." He stared at Andrew. "If you hurt him again, you'll never know what hit you."

Andrew nodded. "Fair enough." He didn't feel offended. On the contrary, he was glad Curtis had such a strong support system. Those were important in everybody's lives and especially in a sub's. "Can I order now?"

"Ha, you got guts, I like that." Richard's hand came crashing down on Andrew's shoulder. "I'll take the virgin caipirinha. And a water for Dean."

"Of course, Master Richard." Leeland sounded perfectly smooth and didn't appear ruffled.

"Leeland here is not only an excellent bartender, but also our go-between for sub-Dom relationships. If you become a regular here and you fuck up, he's the one you have to face first. And believe me, afterward, Martin and I seem like the *good* guys."

Andrew felt his eyes going wide. He'd never heard of a sub middleman before. "If I hadn't loved your club before, this would have sealed the deal. I take sub safety very seriously, and I've never heard of a club where a sub is responsible for sub safety."

"It's something we came up with a couple of years ago. The system works perfectly." Richard sounded very smug and rightfully so in Andrew's opinion. "Of course Leeland is the main reason for it. He's approachable for the subs and firm with the Doms. Nobody dares to mess with him."

"Leeland is a UFC champion. When he threatens to kick your kidneys out through your ears, he has the means to actually do so." Dean grinned at Andrew, his glass of water in hand. "He's nice, though."

"I heard that, Dean."

Andrew listened to the playful bickering between the subs while he waited for Leeland to finish their order. Even though they wouldn't be playing tonight, both Andrew and Curtis stuck to sodas. Andrew felt he needed to keep his wits about him in the company he was keeping. When they all had ordered, they went to a booth a little in the back that provided a perfect view of the entire main area, where the demonstration had obviously come to an end. The good-looking Dom/sub couple was nowhere to be seen. Dean went to kneel at Richard's feet, and Collin followed suit, although he was by far less graceful than Dean. Martin put a hand on the nape of his sub to pull him closer to his body, a gesture that was strangely tender for such an intimidating mountain of a man. Andrew sat down and looked at Curtis, who seemed a bit torn as to what he should do. They weren't here to play—they weren't even official yet—but Andrew had to admit he would have liked it if Curtis had kneeled for him. Still, until they had a contract—and even then—it was his decision.

"Whatever you feel comfortable with, boy." He gave Curtis an encouraging smile. His boy—because Andrew had every intention to make Curtis his—sighed in relief and then knelt down next to him even more gracefully than Dean, at least in Andrew's opinion. It felt good, having him there, and without thinking about it, Andrew weaved his fingers in Curtis's hair and started petting him just to feel the silky texture of those salt-and-pepper strands as well as the happy shudders that went through Curtis's body. Andrew had always been a very tactile person, and he loved nothing more than a constant connection with his sub.

"So, Andrew, you're new in town?" Richard's tone sounded nonchalant, as if he were just making polite conversation. A barely audible "Very smooth" from Dean's direction made it perfectly clear, though, that this was more an interrogation. Andrew didn't mind. If he was to spend more time here, a prospect that seemed more alluring by the minute, Richard and Martin would want to know what kind of Dom they let in.

"Yes, I moved here almost five months ago. I'm from Colorado, and I wanted some sun for a change. I have a bakery close to the botanical garden, which I opened about twelve weeks ago. I'm forty, and I've been a Dom for about ten years. Two weeks ago I started looking for a club and decided it was a good idea to try Club Submission first."

"Ouch. That must have been a shock, unless you're hardcore, which would surprise me." Martin took a sip from his sparkling water.

"It was a shock. Though I did meet another Dom there who also just moved to Miami. We decided to try Club Eros next, but then I blew up my first date with Curtis and we went drinking instead."

"And now you're in Club Whisper." Richard grinned.

"Yes, now I'm in Club Whisper, and I have to admit it's everything I could want from a club—except for the fees." Andrew hadn't meant to add the latest comment, not wanting to spoil the mood, but it had somehow slipped from his mouth and now it was too late to take it back. A quick glance at Curtis and back to Richard and Martin told him they weren't offended. Richard shrugged.

"We know the fees are high, and we have good reason to keep it that way, though I want to assure you it's not to keep people with less money out. When we planned Whisper, Martin and I had to make a decision as to how we wanted the club to be. Since we both like our luxuries, it was only logical to go the route of exclusivity. In order to open the club for people with less financial prowess, we have the rule that partners of members are free."

Andrew nodded. He could see where Martin and Richard were coming from, and when he thought about it, it wasn't much different from Club Submission. Theoretically, everybody was welcome, but in reality, the clubs catered to a special clientele that automatically excluded another kind of customer. That, in the case of Whisper, he was the other kind of customer sucked, because the club was more than fine, but if things with Curtis worked out, he might be seeing more of it in the future.

"I understand, Richard. There is no customer-oriented business that doesn't exclude somebody. Even my bakery is off-limits for some groups, like people with diabetes or allergies. And so far you haven't given me the impression of seeing me as lesser because I don't earn as much money as you do, which, to be frank, is an unexpected but nice surprise."

Richard laughed and toasted him with his cocktail. "I really like how straightforward you are. I hope we'll be seeing more of you in the future."

Andrew raised his glass as well. While he drank, he felt Curtis relaxing against his leg. Knowing he had done everything right this time, Andrew kept making small talk with Richard and Martin while constantly stroking Curtis's head, which he seemed to enjoy immensely. When their drinks were empty, Richard took Dean to one of the private playrooms. Collin went off to talk to Leeland while Martin excused himself. He still had some paperwork to do. Andrew and Curtis stayed in the booth a little longer, simply content with their positions. At around eleven, they gathered their stuff and left the club. Curtis asked the sub at the reception area to call a cab for him. Andrew tried to protest, but Curtis simply shook his head.

"No, Andrew, it's fine. I'm in the opposite direction from you, and we both have to get up early tomorrow. There's no need for us being more tired than we absolutely have to be. Now let's get outside and kiss some more before my cab arrives."

Andrew lifted a brow, ready to remind Curtis who the Dom was, but the prospect of more kissing let him do a salute instead. "Yes, Sir."

Curtis laughed happily about his antics, a sound Andrew thought he would never get tired of hearing. The ten minutes until the cab arrived were spent in lustful bliss neither of them wanted to break. It was the impatient honking of the cab driver that finally pried them off each other.

"Good night, boy." Andrew stared directly in Curtis's beautiful eyes.

"Good night, Sir. Thank you for tonight."

Curtis's voice was soft, full of awe, and his kiss-swollen lips stirred feelings of possessiveness in Andrew's chest. "I have to thank you. See you soon, boy."

One last kiss and Curtis entered the cab. Andrew watched until the taillights disappeared through the gate before he went to his own car.

This date had definitely been a success.

CHAPTER 11

ANDREW WAS busy cleaning up his kitchen when his phone rang. It was Tim, and Andrew decided he had earned a little break.

"Hey, Tim, how are you doing?"

"Hey, Andrew. Dying of curiosity, man. How did it go yesterday? You don't sound defeated, so I assume it wasn't bad?"

Andrew felt his face splitting into a huge grin. "It wasn't only not bad, it was great. Don't get me wrong, at the opening there were a lot of your typical stuck-up rich snobs, but that only made me see that Curtis is definitely not one of them. Afterward we had dinner, and then we went to Whisper. It's even better than we thought it would be."

"Oooh, I'm getting jealous just listening. Tell me everything about it!"

With a light chuckle, Andrew complied. "Well, for one, their changing room for guests is posher than the entire Club Submission, even though compared to the subs' changing room it looks like a dump. Everything there is the best of the best, and the atmosphere is very different from any club I've ever been to. They even have a spokesman for the subs, can you imagine? And he doesn't take shit from anybody, believe me. He's friends with Curtis, and when he realized I was the one who made him sad, he didn't hesitate to threaten me."

"You sound awfully happy about that."

Andrew dried the gleaming steel counter with a towel while he contemplated his answer. "Well, I told you I'm big on safe, sane, and consensual, especially the consensual. Everything that helps making subs feel secure is good in my book, even if it means some unpleasantries for me."

"Gah, you sound like a model Dom. How boring." Tim's tone was teasing. Andrew knew him well enough by now to realize he was the same, even though he tried to hide it behind his gruff demeanor.

"Ha, at least I'm man enough to admit it. Unlike some other Dom I know."

Tim's laughter exploded over the phone, causing Andrew to hold it away from his ear. "Touché. So you would recommend Club Whisper?"

"Definitely. If you can afford the fee."

Tim snorted. "Maybe I should give it a try. Will you let Curtis pay your fee? Since he seems to have his entire social circle there?"

The question was loaded, and Andrew sensed Tim wasn't only asking about the fee. He sighed. This was where things were still complicated. "Apparently, when I'm with him, I don't pay a fee at all. Partners are free. And no, I'm not sure if I like it. Granted, Whisper is scarily close to being the perfect club for me, despite it being filled mostly with super rich people, but I still feel that as the Dom, I should be the one paying for it. It's stupid, I know. Lots of preconceived ideas and toxic ideals of masculinity. But intellectually understanding a concept and acting accordingly in reality are two very different pairs of shoes. I've decided to take things slowly. Tonight, I go over to Curtis to discuss a contract. The chemistry between us is undeniable, and I also like his personality. I can easily envision myself in a domestic situation with him, which hasn't happened with anyone since I outgrew my romantic teenage phase. I just have to wait and see how things work out between us."

There was a moment's pause at the other end of the line. "Wow. He must be really special for you to even contemplate this. After that first date, I had the impression you hated everybody with money."

Andrew sighed. "I don't. I just never had contact with any people significantly richer than me. At least not with people as loaded as Curtis. Apparently, his yearly income is in the millions, which is intimidating. And a bit frightening. I'm not really sure I fit in, you know?"

"Well, you said you met some of his friends. Were they different?"

Andrew thought about it. "They certainly weren't what I would call 'normal,' but then again, normal is a pretty stupid term anyway. Collin is nice. He takes some getting used to, but he's a doll. And Leeland, that's the one who threatened me, he works at Whisper, so I don't think he's rich. Martin and Richard, though…. They're the owners of Whisper. They didn't come off as particularly snobbish, not in the least, but there's something about them that screams money. I don't know, perhaps they're just very secure in their manliness."

Andrew furrowed his brows when Tim erupted in laughter. "I'm so glad I could entertain you with the string of unpleasant truths that's my life at the moment."

The laughter sounded almost hysterical for a while. When Tim had calmed down enough to speak, the amusement was still evident in his voice. "I'm sorry. I know it must be terrible to fall in lust with a gorgeous, cultivated man—your words, not mine. It's just, hearing you talk about Richard Miller and knowing your hang-ups is hilarious. He's a billionaire, Andrew. A very influential billionaire. And since you didn't realize this while talking to him, I think it's safe to say your prejudices are exactly that."

Tim's words gave Andrew pause. He had known Richard had to be rich since he owned—co-owned—Whisper. Thinking the man had even more money than Curtis didn't quite fit with the Dom who had been more than patient with Collin and whose eyes lit up in pure love whenever he looked at Dean. The ideas Andrew had about rich people and what he had experienced with the men at Whisper were impossible to reconcile. He also knew what that meant—he had some readjusting and learning to do.

"You're right. It's high time I got over my silly ideas and started judging people for who they really are, not what social status they have. Damn, common sense can be a bitch sometimes."

Tim chuckled through the line. "Damn if I don't know, man. I wish you luck tonight, and keep me in the loop. I guess you're not up for trying Club Eros out?"

Andrew hesitated. It was true, now that things were looking promising with Curtis, his determination to find a club had diminished a bit, but it wasn't wise to put all his eggs in that particular basket, even if he desperately wanted to. Besides, Tim was his friend.

"I am. I can't let you go alone, can I?"

"Yeah, I need a keeper or there will be nothing but crying subs in my wake."

"Idiot. Let's see, it's Thursday, so how about we meet Saturday? At eight?"

"Sounds good to me. Thanks, man."

Andrew grinned. "That's what friends are for. Plus, I don't have the money to make bail for you."

"Where's the trust, Andrew? Of course I have an account set up for situations like this."

"You're incorrigible. See you later."

"Bye, Andrew."

After ending the call, Andrew finished cleaning his kitchen, braved the afternoon rush until he was sold out yet again, sent Mark, his other part-timer, home, and then went upstairs to prepare for his evening with Curtis. After a short internal debate, Andrew opted for casual, which was kind of inevitable, since he didn't own any other clothes. Simple jeans, a dark green T-shirt that accentuated his slim waist and toned arms, and a pair of brown loafers would hopefully impress Curtis into a nice make-out session and perhaps a little more. After the negotiations were done, of course. Speaking of which, Andrew went to the small breakfast table by the kitchen window to grab the contract he had printed from the internet. It was a standard form that could be easily adjusted to individual needs. There were dozens like it to be found online. The reason Andrew had chosen this one and sent it to Curtis as well was because of the extensive list of BDSM practices mentioned there. He wanted to make sure he and Curtis covered all their bases before entering into a contract, even if it was only a preliminary one since everything was still so new. Contract in hand, Andrew grabbed his keys and left the apartment.

FORTY MINUTES later he stood in front of Curtis's door, waiting for him to answer the ring. The two-story house wasn't as grand as Andrew had envisioned on his drive through the definitely upscale neighborhood, but charming with the outer walls painted a soft pink hue and the iron-wrought balcony and wooden shutters in a blinding white. The generous front yard teemed with flowers of all colors and hinted at an at least equally big backyard. Andrew had no problems admitting to himself that he would love living in a place like this.

The door opened, and Andrew was overwhelmed by Curtis's unique smell and stunning good looks. He wore light gray linen slacks and a baby blue Henley shirt that made his eyes shine.

"Hello, Andrew. You're right on time. Our dinner was delivered only ten minutes ago."

"Lucky me and hello to you, too, Curtis." Andrew decided to be bold. He leaned forward to press a kiss on Curtis's lips and was delighted when Curtis opened right up. They kissed until they were both breathless.

"Wow, we didn't even make it through the door. It's been some time since I made out in public." Curtis grinned happily.

"I don't know about public, but yeah, it's kind of nice to be overcome by hormones." Andrew took Curtis's hand. "May I come in?"

An adorable blush crept into Curtis's cheeks. "I'm sorry. I'm a terrible host, aren't I?"

"No, darling, you're not. You're just swept off your feet by my charming personality." Andrew hoped the teasing was evident in his tone. When Curtis's eyes began to sparkle, he knew he had won.

"That must be it. Anyway, why don't you come inside? Maybe I can sweep *you* off your feet with my impeccable taste in furnishing."

"Consider me swayed. No matter what your taste, it's sure better than mine. I'm more of a practical guy."

Curtis gave a delicate shudder and led him into the house. The corridor was broad and well lit, opening into a huge living room/kitchen area that looked out onto the gigantic backyard through a floor-to-ceiling window front. An L-shaped couch in a warm orange hue faced a flat-screen TV on the blinding white wall. Two armchairs and a low wooden coffee table completed the living room. The polished hardwood floor reached into the British-country-style kitchen with a generous cooking island in the middle. Andrew usually preferred stainless steel in a kitchen due to his job, but the brass pans hanging from a hook rack above the cooking island actually worked perfectly with the more modern style of the living room.

"You have a beautiful home, Curtis. Consider me swept off my feet."

Curtis smiled. "Perfect. Keep that in mind and let's agree to never have me cooking for you. That way, your adoration for me will never wane."

"You're not a cook?"

Curtis shuddered. "I never learned because I grew up having a cook at home and in the boarding schools I went to. My mother considered cooking as something dirty, and after my first attempt at producing a meal on my own, I had to agree with her, which doesn't happen often. It took me two days to get the kitchen clean again. Since then, I've entered a stable relationship with several restaurants that do deliver and haven't looked back once."

"So your kitchen is just for show?"

"More or less. It's a place where I can transfer the delivered food from the boxes onto plates. In my book that counts as cooking."

Andrew slung his arm around Curtis's waist and kissed him soundly on his cheek. "It does, darling. And if the two of us work out, which I very much hope, your kitchen is going to see a lot of action. More baking-wise, since I'm not into cooking that much, but at least those pricey appliances will earn their keep."

"You're trying to bribe me with the prospect of sweets." Curtis waggled his eyebrows. "I approve."

"I'm so glad. Now how about we plate the food you ordered so expertly and then we sit down and talk."

Curtis nodded, suddenly nervous. "Yes, let's talk."

They put the salad in two bowls, the spaghetti vongole on plates, and grabbed two glasses and a bottle of red grape juice to go with their meal. Andrew would have loved nothing more than to have real wine, but negotiating a contract—just like doing a scene—had to be done while all parties were sober. He was glad Curtis took this all seriously enough to stay away from alcohol without Andrew having to mention it. Then again, Curtis wasn't some untried, young, new-to-the-scene boy. He was an experienced sub and mature man. Of course he would take their negotiations seriously. They settled down at the dining table in a little nook next to the kitchen. After he had taken several forks of the delicious pasta, Curtis looked up.

"That was a very thorough contract you sent me." He sounded a bit hesitant.

"I know. I like using that one because as far as I know, it covers all bases considering BDSM practices. Makes it easier to rule things out. I like to get a feel for my partner, and sometimes the things people cross off the list tell me more about them than the things they choose."

"Sneaky." Curtis smiled. "And true."

"Now tell me, what's your list of hard limits?"

Curtis sighed. "Quite a lot, which is why I'm a bit hesitant to start."

"I understand. Let's do it like this. You tell me one of yours, I'll tell you one of mine. Is that fine? Whenever we're not in agreement, we discuss it."

"Sounds like a plan to me."

"Well, I am the Dom here. Having plans is in the job description." Andrew waggled his index finger. "Now start."

"Bossy." Curtis contemplated his plate for a moment. "I'm not into pup or pony play or anything like it."

Andrew nodded. "Me neither. Okay. No blood play, no knives, no whipping where blood is drawn."

"No piss play."

"No mummification. No breath control."

When Curtis lifted a brow, Andrew shrugged. "I love dominating my sub, but I have a problem when the potential for serious damage gets too high."

Curtis smiled. "I'm glad. And I think I can already see a pattern here. We're both not into the more hardcore stuff. To me, submission is more of a state I want to achieve on my own, not something the Dom pushes me into through pain. Ideally for me, the pain comes when I'm already firmly in my subspace."

Andrew couldn't believe his luck. It was as if Curtis had looked directly into his head and then spoken his very thoughts. "Seems like we don't only have chemistry. We're on the same page. How do you feel about restraints?"

Curtis thought about this for a moment. "I do like some shibari. But only when the mood is right and when there is absolute trust. I'm not totally against being tied to a St. Andrew's Cross or a spanking bench, but I always prefer being free."

"Because then it's your decision, the entire time."

Curtis inclined his head. "Yes."

"I like my boy to submit to me because it's his choice. I don't want him to give in because I hurt him just right. To me, the pain is the reward I give for submission. And I don't need a lot of toys. I find a simple spanking is often more satisfying than an elaborate whipping."

"I agree. My ex—don't worry, it's been a long time and I don't miss him one bit—he liked complicated setups. The more furniture and toys, the better. It was never ideal for me, but I went along because I was in love and he wasn't bad at coaxing a reaction out of me. My heart was never in it, though, and I think that was one of the reasons he turned to somebody else. The other reason, of course, was that he's a bloody idiot with the spine of a mollusk, but it took me a while to realize that. I'm telling you this because I want you to understand why I might be coming on a bit strong about the negotiations. If I learned one thing from Jasper, it's that one-sided compromise never leads to anything good."

"I appreciate your openness, Curtis. And I thank you for it. I can definitely see where you're coming from. And just for the record, that man was a total idiot. It's the Dom's job to make sure the sub is happy and content. And since we're being open, I'm telling you I never had a serious relationship, BDSM or otherwise. I did have some affairs and partners I regularly played with, but I always worked hard, first to finance my training, then to make my business a success. There was no room for romance or anything lasting. Those times are gone, though, and I want to make it clear to you that I'm pursuing a relationship with you. Long-term."

Again that adorable blush entered Curtis's cheeks. Andrew couldn't control himself anymore. He reached out and took Curtis's hand. "What we have between us could work out great in my opinion, disastrous first date notwithstanding."

"I think so too. We do seem pretty compatible in every aspect. Now tell me, where's the catch? What despicable little secret are you hiding, because that's just my luck."

The merry twinkle in Curtis's eyes told Andrew he was teasing. For dramatic effect, he closed his eyes for a moment and sighed deeply. "I'm afraid you got me. I wanted to keep this from you until you had fallen too hard to care anymore, but if you must know... I like to fart in bed. Multiple times, under the covers. When I've built up a good stink, I lift the covers to get the full blast."

"Eww. Deal breaker. You're out, no rose for you, Mr. Neanderthal!" Curtis was laughing so hard, he had tears in his eyes. Emboldened by this reaction, Andrew lifted a brow.

"And what's your disgusting little secret, Mr. British Gentleman? What do I have to put up with for the joy of having you in my life?"

"Corny much? You do like to exaggerate, don't you?"

"You still haven't answered my question, boy." Andrew infused a little dominance in his tone. The effect on Curtis was baffling. The mischievous twinkling in his eyes intensified while his body started to shudder. Andrew silently thanked the heavens for having sent this incredible man into his bakery. He did love a boy with a healthy sense of humor who could at the same time appreciate a sexually charged situation.

"Well, I'm British. I like my five o'clock tea with pressed cucumber sandwiches."

"If I didn't know better, I'd say you stole that one from *The Importance of Being Earnest*."

"And if?" Curtis asked teasingly. "Oscar Wilde is one of the greatest figureheads of British literature. And I didn't steal, I kind of quoted."

"How can you 'kind of quote'? Anyway, I want to know about a real vice. Something you don't dare admit in polite company."

Curtis threw his hands in the air. "Fine. You win. I like to sit on the couch warming my crotch with my hand Al Bundy-style while I watch *The Gilmore Girls*. Happy?"

Andrew couldn't help it. He started laughing so hard, his sides hurt. "That's hilarious! I never thought it possible to have Al Bundy and *The Gilmore Girls* in one sentence!"

"Two series that definitely aren't compatible...."

They looked at each other. Heat flared in Andrew's belly. He licked his lips and watched Curtis's gaze following the movement with hitching breath.

"What do you think? Are you up for a small scene? Or do you want to wait? Get to know me better? Both are fine for me."

Andrew held his breath while Curtis thought about his proposal. "I think I'm good. I mean, technically, we already had sex—or at least a mind-blowing hand job—and on our second date no less. It's moving fast, but then again, we're no spring chickens anymore. We're consenting adults who have needs."

"You don't have to sell me on it, boy." Andrew lifted a brow.

Curtis sighed. "I'm not trying to. I think I'm trying to rationalize the need I feel for you. It's been a while since I last felt so reckless."

"Then let's be reckless together, boy."

Curtis nodded. "How do you wish to be addressed?"

"'Sir' or 'Master.' I like both." Andrew hesitated a moment. "I'm not planning anything harsh, but I still need your safewords, boy."

Curtis seemed surprised by his request.

"You didn't think I would suggest playing without safewords, did you, boy?"

"No, of course not. It's just—I only realized now that I don't want to use green, yellow, and red for playing with you, and I'm wondering what words I should choose."

"You never had individualized safewords?"

"No. Jasper—my ex—always said the traffic light system was easiest for him to remember during a scene, and I never cared enough to put my foot down." Curtis sounded almost relieved. "Now I'm glad, because this is a first I can give you. My own safewords."

Andrew knew something so simple shouldn't make the butterflies in his belly do a little dance, but here he was, giddy with joy about Curtis's words.

"I'm honored, boy. And I'll gladly help you find other firsts for both of us."

They looked at each other with such deep understanding it almost hurt, though in the best way. "Do you need time to think about it?"

Curtis shook his head. "I think I already have them. How about 'Degenerate Art' for stop, 'Dali' for slow down, and 'macarons' for go?"

"Combining both our interests. Clever boy. I can definitely remember those." Andrew rose from his seat, extending his hand toward Curtis. With a happy smile, his boy took it and led the way upstairs to a generous bedroom with a plush lavender carpet on polished hardwood floors, and a king-size bed with a wooden frame and a headboard with a stylized tree in black metal that was ideal for holding on to during sex or a scene. Or both. Andrew had a lively imagination. Next to the bed, on the wall across from the door, hung a picture that was most probably from Collin, and Andrew knew he would take a closer look— later. Now he had his boy to focus on. Curtis was standing in front of the bed, seemingly unsure how to proceed. Andrew smiled. He would take care of his boy. He took Curtis's hands in his and kissed the palms reverently, showed his boy how much he appreciated the gift he was about to give him.

"I want to undress you, boy. Is that okay?"

"Yes, Master." It came out breathless, which had Andrew's cock straining against the confines of his jeans. He reached for the three buttons on Curtis's T-shirt and opened them. Then he took the hem and slid the T-shirt over Curtis's head, revealed that fine upper body with a smudge of silver-black hair trailing down from the navel to the waistband of the slacks, and just enough additional flesh around the waist that Andrew would be able to properly grab him during sex. Not yet, though, and probably not even later tonight. They were still trying to get to know each other. There was no rush. This wasn't a one-night stand or a casual scene with some stranger. This was so much more, and Andrew was determined to be patient, even though his libido was killing him.

He went for Curtis's slacks next, exposed his long, fine legs and satin briefs in dark red. Andrew gulped when he saw Curtis's cock tenting the smooth fabric. "You're gorgeous, boy."

Curtis whimpered. "Thank you, Master."

Since Curtis wasn't wearing shoes or socks, it was soon just his briefs hiding the most private parts of his body. Andrew took some time to watch his fill, to enjoy the faint flush on Curtis's shoulders and neck. When his own cock screamed at him to finally do something, anything to break the tension, Andrew hooked his thumbs under the waistband of the briefs and tugged them down. Curtis stepped out of them easily and just like that, he was naked. Andrew stepped backward, took off his own T-shirt, and then resumed ogling his boy.

Curtis stood in a natural pose, his arms dangling loosely by his sides, his feet slightly apart, cock standing up proudly. It was obvious that he wasn't ashamed of his body or his arousal. This easy, unforced display of self-confidence had Andrew drooling. He had always preferred partners with a backbone, a strong opinion, and he had thought it was because with such partners, the chances to mess up during a scene or unintentionally abusing them were smaller. Looking at Curtis in all his graceful glory made him realize he hadn't been honest with himself. What he liked most about this situation was that a self-reliant man like Curtis was submitting to him. The thought made Andrew hesitate for a moment. Was this right? Was it okay to use a part of Curtis's personality to feed his own kink? This was definitely something he would have to contemplate in more depth later on. Now he would concentrate on making it good for them both, so that even if he took unfair advantage of Curtis, he would have nothing to complain about.

Andrew stepped forward, circled Curtis, touched his soft, smooth skin, brushed his fingertips over the enticing curve of his ass, enjoyed the goose bumps following in their wake, teased Curtis's spine with featherlight touches until his boy whimpered and a quick look assured Andrew that Curtis's cock was already leaking precum. He pressed a few soft, wet kisses on his nape, between his shoulder blades, and on Curtis's hard nipples when he stepped around him. Then he went to the bed, sat down at the edge, and looked Curtis in the eye. His boy's gaze was soft, already a bit dazed. This was good.

"Would you kneel for me, boy?"

The low, whimpering sound that escaped Curtis's throat almost had Andrew coming. And when Curtis went down on his knees in one graceful, elegant movement, Andrew had to actually pinch the tip of his cock through the jeans to anchor himself. Curtis was beautiful on his knees, his gaze now respectfully lowered, his spine still straight, his hands behind his back, and his knees slightly parted to give Andrew a better view.

"So beautiful, boy. So beautiful and perfect for me." Andrew was whispering because talking too loud would have felt like a sacrilege at that moment. He spread his own legs.

"Come here, boy. Come to me."

Andrew held his breath. The bed was just far enough from where Curtis was kneeling that it would make sense for him to get up to come to Andrew. But Curtis didn't rise to his feet. He brought his arms forward, went on all fours, and started crawling toward Andrew. It was perfect. For many subs, being forced to stay on all fours was part of their humiliation kink, part of what got them going. And that was fine, because many Doms liked their subs on their knees. Andrew did, too, though for different reasons. Of course the humiliation was part of it, but the biggest turn-on for Andrew was that Curtis had chosen to come to him like that. There had been no order, no punishment in case Curtis disobeyed. All there was between them at this point was insane chemistry and the beginnings of a wordless understanding that he had been dreaming of since he first discovered BDSM. Because having to ask for something and simply getting it were two very different things indeed.

CHAPTER 12

CURTIS'S ENTIRE body tingled in anticipation. Deciding to get on all fours to get to Andrew had been a bold move on his part, but given how Andrew's breath hitched, it had also been the right decision. Unlike many other Doms Curtis knew, including Martin and Jonathan, Andrew's behavior didn't change much when he slipped into his Dom-mode. It felt more like some aspects of his personality became more heightened while others dimmed a little. Curtis found he liked that a lot. It felt natural.

It also felt natural to crawl to his master. The feeling of deep satisfaction he got from just hearing Andrew's pleased reaction did more to send him into his sub-headspace than any amount of pain. Once he was between Andrew's spread thighs, Curtis went back to his kneeling position, hands behind his back. His eyes were now focused on the impressive bulge under Andrew's jeans, since he was too close to be able to look at the floor.

"Good boy. Such a good boy for me. Thank you, darling."

Andrew petted his hair and Curtis almost started purring. This was it, mutual respect that infused even a simple gesture like kneeling with so much meaning and sexual tension that Curtis could feel his cock twitching, ready to shoot.

"Now, would you use those pretty lips to free my cock and show me how much you appreciate it?"

Curtis shuddered. Again, there was no order. Just a simple request. One he could decide to decline. Only he didn't want to refuse Andrew anything he asked for, equal parts because it was Andrew doing the asking and because he knew his master would never demand something Curtis couldn't give. It was another way of showing mutual trust—giving and receiving perfectly balanced.

"Yes, Master."

Curtis started to lean forward, to get the zipper of Andrew's jeans, but Andrew stopped him by petting his cheek.

"That's not all, boy. Can you do it without using your hands? And can you hold it in for me? I want to see you aching with need, desperate to come, but not doing so because it's my will."

Curtis gulped. Things were getting hotter by the minute, and Andrew's words alone were enough to make his balls draw up.

"What if I fail, Master?"

Andrew's fingers glided under Curtis's chin, lifted it so their eyes could meet. The smile playing around Andrew's lips was enough to melt Curtis completely.

"There is no failing, boy. Just you trying is enough for me. And if you come I get the double pleasure of seeing you in the throes of passion and of coming up with a suitable punishment. Win-win."

Curtis grinned. "At least for one of us."

"It's my pleasure, Master."

Curtis leaned forward again, this time with his hands firmly clasped behind his back. With his teeth, he grabbed the zipper of Andrew's jeans and dragged it down. It caught halfway because of the odd angle, but Andrew didn't hesitate to help Curtis out. He lifted his hips to create a straight line and the zipper went down easily. Curtis took a moment to inhale the rich musk of Andrew's crotch. His own cock twitched just at the thought of having that delicious-smelling piece of meat in his mouth. When his senses could detect nothing but Andrew anymore, he carefully grabbed the waistband of his cotton briefs and tugged on the elastic to get it over Andrew's massive erection. He didn't have a lot of room, since the jeans were still up, but it was enough to free Andrew's cock and balls. In this setup, Curtis wouldn't have the pleasure of licking the skin behind the sac, but on the other hand, the confines of the jeans presented the cock and balls almost obscenely. Curtis could certainly work with that. He started with tiny licks along the hard shaft and the smooth skin of the balls, testing Andrew's reactions. If the groaning was anything to go by, his master was in heaven.

Curtis intensified his efforts, started circling the tip of Andrew's dick with his tongue, sucking at the slit to get the first trickle of precum into his mouth, before he devoured the cock like it was a Popsicle. Andrew gripped his hair, held him without demanding anything, gave him security just being there, a not-so-subtle reminder of Andrew's trust, passion, and self-control. The romantic part of Curtis wanted to melt while the mischievous part wanted to shatter that self-control.

Curtis let the tip of Andrew's cock slide out of his mouth again before he went farther down to pay some attention to the sensitive skin of the sac. Andrew's hips jerked when he sucked one orb into his mouth, massaged it with his tongue.

"Curtis, boy! So good."

Curtis grinned inwardly and did the same to the other ball. Then he licked his way back up to the tip. For a few happy moments, he played with the bulbous head, nibbled at the fleshy fringe, and dug the tip of his tongue into the leaking slit. He had always enjoyed giving head and Andrew was such a responsive and vocal recipient, it took all of Curtis self-control to not come when his master's moans grew in intensity. He finally swallowed the shaft, let it bump against his palate before he relaxed his throat to take it in. Andrew was perfect, appreciated the act with loud praise and never forgot to draw back so Curtis could get some air. All too soon—or after an eternity, Curtis wasn't sure—Andrew started to babble.

"Boy, I'm coming!" He stilled for a moment, and Curtis immediately recognized the gesture for what it was. Andrew was holding himself back, giving Curtis a chance to draw back if he didn't want to swallow. The act was so sweet, it made Curtis's heart beat even faster. To show Andrew how much he wanted to have him come in his mouth, he sucked the pulsing shaft deep into his throat and swallowed around it, massaging the orgasm out of his master. Andrew came with a scream, his hips bucking wildly, and only his hands on both sides of Curtis's head prevented Curtis from falling back on his ass.

The hot semen ran down his throat, and Curtis regretted not being able to really taste it. There was a slight salty muskiness in his mouth, but that was mostly from Andrew's sweat. Andrew still clung to him after the last spurts had stopped and his shaft had started to soften. He was panting.

"Boy, that was perfect. Just perfect. I've never…. You're too good to be true. I can't be that lucky."

The words stirred something deep inside Curtis. He realized how much he had missed being appreciated like this. A single tear slid down his cheek. Andrew must have seen it, because he gently freed his cock from Curtis's mouth and lifted him onto his lap.

"Curtis, darling, is everything all right? Was I too demanding? Too rough?"

The concern in Andrew's voice coaxed more tears from Curtis.

"Everything is fine, Master. It's just, I missed this. And I didn't realize how much until now. Thank you for that."

Andrew looked at him for a long moment, as if he was trying to inspect the inside of Curtis's head. Then he slowly nodded.

"I believe you. And since you were such a good boy, you get a reward."

Andrew's hand slid between Curtis's legs, to his still very hard cock. "Spread your legs for me, boy. I'm going to make it good."

Curtis obeyed, enjoyed the rough grip of Andrew's hand, the raspy texture of his palm. Andrew's voice was hot in his ear, the words turning Curtis on almost more than the physical administrations.

"I wanted to edge you, wanted to make you suffer for the rest of the evening. I even considered asking you to hold it in until tomorrow or even till the weekend. The thought alone of that gorgeous cock of yours being all hard for me, unable to find relief… it's so erotic, I could come again right away."

That was enough. With a shudder and a cry, Curtis came, released his cum into Andrew's hand in violent spurts. It took him some time to come down from his erotic high, especially since Andrew was petting and cuddling him all the time. When Curtis could finally think clearly again, he squirmed to get out of Andrew's lap.

"Where are you going, boy?"

"To the nightstand, getting tissues. Your hand is smeared with my cum, Master."

"Not anymore, boy." Andrew grinned broadly and showed him his slightly glistening palm. Curtis realized that Andrew had licked his sperm off his hands. Not knowing if he should cry because he missed the sight due to his postorgasmic high, or if he should simply go back on his knees for this perfect member of the male species, he settled for kissing Andrew, chasing his own taste on his master's lips. Andrew engaged happily and very soon, they were lying on the bed, making out like teenagers. It felt good. So incredibly good to just enjoy another man's body, knowing that there were rules in place but that those rules could also be ignored by mutual agreement. It was bliss.

THEY MUST have fallen asleep, because when Curtis woke, it was already dark outside. He yawned and stretched, the entire time aware of Andrew's comforting weight at his back.

"You're awake, boy." A hint of amusement tinged Andrew's tone.

"Yes, yes, I am. Sorry, I didn't mean to doze off."

Andrew pressed a kiss on Curtis's shoulder. "It's fine. I was napping as well. Are you rested enough to talk about a contract, or do you need some more cuddling?"

Curtis chuckled. That was a no-brainer. "More cuddling. I like cuddling."

"That I've noticed." Andrew closed his arms around Curtis's body, buried his nose in his nape, and ground his erection none too subtly against Curtis's lower back.

"You want to go again, Master?"

"I'd love to. I want to ram my cock into your tight hole, boy, make you whimper and squirm and twitch with need for me. I want to see you fall apart in my arms."

Curtis mewled. His own cock was starting to swell at those words, definitely on board with the idea.

"But I also want to do this in the right order. Which means talking about the contract, signing it, and then we can agree on a date in the very near future where we go all the way. I want our first time having penetrative sex to be special. I want everything with you to be special. Hence the need for patience."

Curtis sighed. "You take the fun out of it when you're being all logical about it."

"That's my job as your Dom. To keep things in perspective and to look out for your best interests. In real life, that might be a bit hard for me because of the difference in our incomes, and because I've gotten the impression that you're entirely capable of taking care of yourself, but in our relationship and especially when it comes to the BDSM aspects of it, I have every intention of being your rock."

"Thank you, Master. And you do know I don't care about our social or financial differences, don't you?"

"Yes, Curtis, I do know. I'm just asking you to be patient with me, because I'm still getting used to it."

"Oh, I can be very patient. Very." Curtis waggled his hips, intentionally rubbing over Andrew's very hard shaft.

"Is that meant to be a challenge, boy? Because I'm up for that."

Curtis snorted. "I can feel it."

Andrew laughed. "Careful, boy. Or I'm going to hump your delicious ass until I come without letting you have any fun at all!"

"I'm good, Master. I promise, I'm a good boy."

Andrew's lips came close to Curtis's ear. "I appreciate it, darling. Today. Some other day, I want to find out just how naughty you can be. I'm looking forward to it."

"The things you do to me!"

Andrew sat up. "I know. I'm that good." He grinned broadly and swatted Curtis's thigh playfully. It was nowhere near enough to really hurt, but Curtis was so ramped up he felt his cock taking an interest. His moan was cut short by a deep kiss from Andrew, which he only broke when they were both out of breath.

"Clothes, boy. Then we talk and maybe have a little snack. And then we set a date."

Curtis grumbled a bit before he got out of bed to put his underwear and slacks back on. Andrew did the same, though he didn't put his T-shirt back on. Curtis only hesitated for a moment before he threw his own shirt in the hamper. Two could play the naked game.

The knowing look on Andrew's face and his delighted grin made Curtis feel all fuzzy inside. It was good to have a Dom again. A Dom who intended to stay, who wasn't just there for a night of kink without the kind of deeper connection Curtis so desperately craved. They went back to the dining room, where the contracts still were on the table.

"Would you like some tea before we begin?"

Andrew smiled. "Black tea?"

"Not this late." Curtis shuddered. "I'm way too old to consume stimulating beverages before going to sleep."

Now Andrew laughed outright. "You're not that old, Curtis. In fact, I'm pretty sure you're not much older than me and I'm forty-four."

"I'm forty-eight, which isn't ancient, but I'm also no spring chicken anymore. But to tell you the truth, I couldn't have caffeine after six o'clock since I turned twenty. Somehow, my body just doesn't like it."

"I can see that being the case. Me, I've lived off coffee during my training and in the first years when I started building my business. Though I have noticed that I'm not coping as well as I used to."

"Herbal tea it is. Do you have any preferences?"

Andrew shrugged. "Not really. I rarely drink tea, and if I do, it's either iced tea with so much sugar you wouldn't know the ingredients anyway, or whatever bag I have available."

Curtis stared at him in horror. "You're a heathen! I knew there was something wrong with you. I knew it. Let me tell you, the farting under the covers, I could have learned to tolerate, but this—I'm not sure there's a future for us." He winked.

Andrew winked right back before he schooled his features into a pleading expression. "I know I'm clueless, but I'm also willing to learn at your feet, boy. Do you think you can find it in your heart to give me a chance?"

Curtis pretended to ponder the question. "I don't know. There's so much to learn…."

"Please, Curtis. Pretty please?"

Now Andrew looked at him like a puppy that had been kicked, while waggling his eyebrows like crazy. Curtis couldn't keep his laughter in. It had been so long since he'd had such relaxed fun with somebody who wasn't a sub. If he thought about it, he'd never had such fun with Jasper, whom he had thought to be in love with.

"You get your chance, Master. But you have to promise to study hard. We Brits take our tea seriously. Very seriously."

Andrew took him in his arms and kissed him while laughing at the same time, which made for an interesting experience. "Thank you, boy. I'll do my very best."

There was that Freddie Frinton quote again. Sometime soon, Curtis would have to find out if Andrew truly liked old films or if he just thought the line was funny. Not tonight, though. Tonight, he would give his Dom a first lesson in tea.

"Rule number one: No bagged tea. Not ever. Whole leaves and a tea strainer are the way to go."

Andrew nodded and followed him eagerly into the kitchen.

CHAPTER 13

ANDREW WATCHED while Curtis prepared their tea. He moved with effortless grace through his kitchen, pulling an old-fashioned teakettle out of a cupboard and filling it with water from a water filter. Then he went to an open cupboard next to the fridge, where an array of colorful metal bins was waiting. None of them looked the same: some seemed to be very old, others fairly new, some had Chinese and Japanese landscape pictures on them, others simply showed one color with the word "TEA" emblazoned on the bin, and Andrew spotted one or two with art prints on them. Curtis's hand hovered over a deep red bin with black kanji signs on it.

"How about something refreshing? Peppermint and lemongrass."

Andrew shrugged. "Sounds good to me."

Curtis took a small measuring spoon out of a drawer, hooked two tea strainers into the mugs he had chosen, filled them each with four spoons of tea, and poured the hot water over it. While the tea steeped, Curtis took out a small plate and arranged some chocolate chip cookies on it.

"I'm sure they're not as good as what you bake, but I have to admit, I've already eaten all your macarons."

Andrew stepped toward Curtis to press a light kiss on his cheek. "That's so sweet, boy. You should have told me. I can always bring more."

A mischievous twinkle appeared in Curtis's eyes, made him look like the proverbial cat who got the canary. "That's a dangerous promise, Master. I might take you up on it."

Andrew kissed Curtis again before he looked at him with a serious expression. "I will always keep my promises to you, boy. Always."

Curtis opened his mouth to answer when the timer he had set for the tea started to beep. He broke free from Andrew's arm to take the strainers out.

"Do you want sugar or honey with your tea?"

"No, thank you. At this time of night, I don't want anything sweet. That tends to keep me up longer than is good for me."

"We really seem to be a match made in heaven." Curtis beamed.

"If my preference for unsweetened tea at night is all it takes to make you mine, I won't complain." Andrew winked.

They took their mugs and the plate with the cookies into the living room, snatching the contracts on the way. Curtis got a ballpoint pen from a secretaire that stood on the left wall of the living room. He sat down next to Andrew instead of opposite to him, which told Andrew how relaxed Curtis already was in his presence. It was a good sign. He put his arm on Curtis's lower back, petting him gently.

"Since both contracts are the same, we can put one of them aside and work on the other. We've already established that our sexual preferences are quite similar, but let's go over the list real quick."

Curtis nodded. They read through the list, crossing out everything neither of them wanted to try. The things both of them enjoyed were also pretty consistent, with only mummification on Curtis's list of soft limits while this was a hard limit for Andrew, and CBT on Andrew's soft limits. It wasn't that he didn't find the idea of cock and ball torture appealing. He was simply intimidated by the possibility of seriously hurting his partner, especially when said partner was Curtis. Andrew glanced at their list.

"We agree on plugs, dildos, floggers, paddles, and the riding crop. Caning or whipping with single or bull tails are off the table. No public scenes, no heavy bondage, but some shibari. Blindfolding and chastity devices are welcome as well, as are wax play and sounding, though we're going to wait with that for a bit until I have time to polish my skills. Sound good?"

Curtis smiled broadly. "Sounds perfect."

"We already established your safewords. Now let's talk about daily life."

Andrew saw Curtis wincing. "As you may have guessed, I don't do 24/7. With my work, it's fairly impossible, and it's also not what I want or need. Is that okay with you?"

Andrew put his hand on Curtis's forearm to soothe him. "That works for me, Curtis. To be honest, I don't think I'd have the determination to enter into a 24/7 relationship. We both have demanding jobs, and I like to spend time with you without the restrictions a Dom/sub relationship can bring. Besides, I think the contradiction between who you are in day-to-day life and what you would have to be for me in a 24/7 arrangement would be too strenuous for both of us. Don't get me wrong, I won't say no to some intense fun over the weekend, when we can both relax and really sink into our respective roles, but not when there could be a call from work at any minute for you. I'd rather explore our kinky side in the bedroom or the club."

Andrew looked for the paragraph in the contract and made some adjustments with the wording. "Next is living arrangements." He looked up. Curtis had seemed uncomfortable saying no to a 24/7 relationship, but now he was squirming in his seat as if somebody had set his pants on fire.

"Curtis, relax." Andrew reached for Curtis's tea and held the mug out to him. His boy accepted it with slightly trembling hands and took a huge gulp before putting it back on the coffee table.

"I'm sorry, Andrew. It's just… I know how hard it is to accommodate me. And I'm aware I'm not an easy sub to deal with. I think I still wait for you to get fed up and leave."

The way Curtis looked at him, his beautiful eyes all big and vulnerable, Andrew knew that now was not the time to make a joke to ease the tension. He took both of Curtis's hands in his and made sure to establish steady eye contact before he started to speak. "Curtis, the whole point in talking about a contract is to find common ground. I knew what I was getting into when I printed those contracts. You're not a young man in your twenties anymore. Neither am I. We're both mature men, with full, demanding lives. We're both here because we are attracted to each other and because we want our relationship to work. Which is why we're talking instead of assuming. Now tell me what's on your mind regarding living conditions, and don't assume I'll get mad and leave."

Curtis shook his head with a smile. "I'm sorry. I got a bit carried away by my own fears."

"It's fine, boy. Now tell me what you want."

Curtis took a deep breath. "Ideally, I'd want for you to live here with me. I know that's not practical, because you have to get up early for work. And to be honest, I don't want to move into your apartment in the city. The area is nice enough, and I have nothing against the occasional— or regular—sleepover, but this house is my sanctuary. I bought it after Jasper broke up with me, and I've spent a lot of time and energy to make it perfect for me. That said, I'm up for any flexible solution we can come up with."

Andrew nodded. He had expected as much. Since they weren't going for a 24/7 relationship, moving in together wasn't a requirement, and Curtis was right about everything he'd said.

"I like your house, Curtis. Or at least everything I've seen to far. But you're right. I can't live here during the week. I have to be at the shop quite early and the commute is not something I'd like to take on when I can easily avoid it. But I would like for us to spend as many nights together as possible. Perhaps we can agree on me coming over to your house for the weekends and you spending the nights at my apartment whenever it doesn't conflict with your work? It'll be trial and error in the beginning, but if we keep talking to each other, we should be able to find a rhythm that suits us both. What do you think?"

Curtis looked at him with so much hope in his eyes, Andrew couldn't help himself. He leaned in to kiss those gorgeous lips. The way Curtis responded by letting him in eagerly and moaning hungrily, Andrew knew the discussion about the contract was done for the time being. It was fine. They had talked about the most pressing things. Everything else was details they could always revisit at another time. Now he had to kiss his boy senseless, because that was what they both needed.

CHAPTER 14

THE NEXT morning, Curtis was late coming to work. He was never late. But after the glorious evening with Andrew, he felt justified sleeping in. They had made out for what had felt like an eternity before Andrew reluctantly announced he had to get home. He suggested the following day for a follow-up date, but Curtis had to decline.

"I'm sorry, Andrew. I'm already meeting my friends tomorrow." Curtis had drawn a deep breath when he had seen the disappointment in Andrew's eyes. The atmosphere between him and Andrew was so open, he had decided to take the risk and be brutally honest. "As harsh as it may sound, these men are my best friends. They were here before I met you, and if things don't work out between us, they're going to be the ones to gather all the pieces of my heart and glue it back together." Curtis hadn't been sure if it was wise to be so blatant, but he had done enough tiptoeing around certain topics with Jasper to know it never amounted to anything good in the long run. And he wanted to have something good with Andrew. And Andrew proved to be every bit the man Curtis could wish for.

"I have to admit, it stings, but I can definitely see where you're coming from, Curtis. I want to be your first priority and your best friend, the one you turn to when things go wrong, but I know this kind of trust takes time, and I know how important it is to have a safety net, especially as a sub. Since tomorrow doesn't work, how about I come to your place on Sunday since I'm tied up on Saturday, and we celebrate the signing of our contract?" Andrew had waggled his eyebrows playfully.

That suggestion was music to Curtis's ears. It also made his cock harden to the point of pain, and his cruel, sadistic Dom had only laughed, stroked him through the fabric of his pants, and then left him horny as hell with the order not to touch himself until Friday. Now he was late to work, his balls were still aching with a low-burning need, and he had a meeting with his friends and Sunday to look forward to. Life couldn't get much better.

The happy spring in his steps vanished when he saw Patty breezing toward him with a strange expression on her face. It looked like a cross between annoyed and amused, and Curtis wasn't sure he wanted to know what had caused it.

"Patty, good morning."

"You're late." Patty winked. "Had a good night?"

"The best. So good, indeed, that your casual ignorance regarding our boss-employee relationship can't faze me in the least."

As always, Patty simply ignored his attempts at playing work superior, for which he was grateful. He liked having somebody around him who always met him at eye level. "Hold on to that feeling, *boss*, because there's a sleazebag waiting for you in your office with a huge bouquet of roses, but he ain't your good-looking bringer of macarons."

Curtis sighed. It wasn't that he hadn't had his fair share of admirers in his time, though the number had dwindled a bit in the past few years, but that didn't mean he took kindly to people who overstepped their boundaries simply because they wanted to. "Do you have a name for me?"

Patty shook her head. "He said he's an old acquaintance. I didn't want to cause a disturbance first thing in the morning without you even being present, which is why I sent him to your office. If you want him gone, just say the word."

Patty's brows rose in open threat. Curtis put a restraining hand on her upper arm. "It's fine, Patty. I'll see who our guest is first. You can still unleash the full force of your death glare on him later."

For a moment Patty seemed hesitant. "You sure?"

"Absolutely. I'm in too good a mood to have the police over."

"Call me if you change your mind. I'll be close by."

That Patty felt the need to hover was not a good sign. She had an excellent nose for people and had yet to misjudge somebody as far as Curtis knew. Taking a deep breath, Curtis headed to his office, the clacking of Patty's heels a strangely comforting war drum at his back. He opened the door and almost staggered backward when he saw who was waiting there for him with a bouquet of red roses in his hands.

"Patty, I don't want to be disturbed. But please keep your phone ready."

She nodded and pulled out her cell as if it were a weapon. With one last menacing glance at the visitor, Patty closed the door. Curtis was alone with the man he had hoped to never see again.

"Jasper, what an unpleasant surprise. What are you doing here?"

Jasper had risen from the guest chair when Curtis entered. Now he was offering the roses with a smile on his lips that didn't reach his eyes. Or perhaps his smiles had never reached his eyes and Curtis had just been too blind to realize. He would have loved to say the years hadn't been kind to Jasper, but Curtis made a habit of not lying to himself, and Jasper did look good. He was only slightly taller than Curtis, but with broader shoulders and a more muscular build. The gray streaks at the side of his head gave him a distinguished look, and his elegant suit with the light blue shirt would have once had the power to turn Curtis into a puddle of goo. No longer, though. Looking at Jasper, Curtis could only wonder why he'd never seen the appeal of jeans and biker boots before he met Andrew.

"Can't a man visit an old friend?" Jasper's tone hadn't changed either. He still sounded like an untroubled boy who couldn't understand what he had done wrong.

"First of all, you're not an 'old friend.' You're an ex. Second, old friends don't bring overpriced roses to a reunion, and they have the decency to announce their visits."

"Somebody's taken grumpy pills for breakfast. And I didn't announce my visit because you wouldn't have agreed to seeing me, am I right?"

Curtis stared at Jasper in disbelief. "You're right. I wouldn't have. Which should tell you everything you need to know about your welcome here. Now take your roses and get out of my office. Don't bother coming back."

A vein started pulsing under Jasper's left eye, a sure sign he was getting angry. "Stop being such a drama queen, Curtis. I mean it's more than eight years now, and you have to admit, we weren't that compatible in bed. You were always hard to please."

"*I* was hard to please?" Curtis couldn't believe his ears. "You were the one who always needed to ramp things up. And if you had gone about our breakup like a decent human being, I might be inclined to listen to you now. But you just got yourself a barely legal twink without bothering to tell me we were over. I had to find out through friends, Jasper! That's not okay, and I have every right to be pissed at you. Now, for the last time, take your flowers and leave before Patty calls the police. This is private property, and you're not welcome here."

Jasper's face contorted into a menacing growl for a moment before he schooled his features to a pleasant smile, though his eyes were still shooting daggers. "I'm sorry, Curtis. I apologize for coming here unannounced. You see, I have good reason. I'm in a bit of a pinch, financially speaking, and I was hoping we could discuss how you could help me out."

Curtis felt as if he'd been catapulted into some sort of twilight zone. Was Jasper for real? "You come to me, after you dumped me quite cruelly and never took the time to at least apologize for your abysmal behavior, and now you want me to give you money? Did you have a lobotomy back in good-old England, or are your really so dumb as to think I would give you so much as a single penny?" Curtis could feel the blood thundering through his body. The audacity! But then again, that was Jasper in the flesh.

Now his ex wrinkled his nose as if Curtis's outbreak had disgusted him. "Fine. I can see there's no talking to you at the moment. I'll come by at a more convenient time."

Jasper got up and left the room, leaving the roses on Curtis's desk. Curtis stared at the door for a long time, wondering if he'd just had a very realistic nightmare or if Jasper's blatant disregard of everything Curtis had said was for real.

"What an ass." Patty's voice broke through Curtis's thoughts. Her tone managed to put a smile back on his lips.

"Indeed. I assume you heard everything?"

She shrugged, not ashamed in the least. "I didn't trust him, and you asked me to stay close. That's hardly snooping."

"Having a lawyer for a wife works well for you, doesn't it?" Curtis kept his tone light. He was too grateful to give Patty a hard time about her nosy habits.

"It does. Not so much when I have to deal with her, because man, she's too damn good, but in comparison, everybody else is a piece of cake. Now, what do you plan on doing about the asshole?"

"Nothing—for now. I kicked him out and hopefully he gets the message. If not, I might have to talk to your wife."

The smile on Patty's face was that of a shark who had just homed in on a juicy seal. "You say the word, boss, and she's going to crush that roach."

"Thank you, Patty. Do you want the roses? I can't stand looking at them, but they're too beautiful to be thrown away."

"I'll take them." Patty's heels clicked past him. Once she had the roses removed from his sight, she gave him his schedule for the day before she returned to her own desk. Curtis looked at the long list of things he had to do, sighed, and got to work. At least this little morning drama would be of some entertainment value when he met the other boys tonight.

At half past seven, Curtis rang the bell to Dean's home. Originally their meeting would have been at Collin's place, but Richard had gotten a last-minute call from work, and Dean's other babysitters had all been tied up as well, so they had decided to meet at Dean's place. Curtis had picked up Emilio and Leeland on his way. A roaring sound told them Seth was on his way as well. Dean opened the door the same moment Seth parked his bike next to Curtis's BMW. Peyton hopped down from behind Seth, a broad smile blinding them all as soon as he took off his helmet.

"Hello to you all!" Peyton sounded a little drunk.

Dean just grinned. "Hello to you, too, Mr. Speed Junkie. How fast did Seth go to have you beaming like that?"

"Hey, I didn't break any traffic rules!" Seth sounded indignant. Dean simply stared at him. "Fine." Seth huffed. "I might have gone a bit faster than strictly necessary on the highway, but it was almost empty, and we were running late!"

Dean shook his head. "One of these days…," he muttered. "Just remember, there's lots of people who would miss you two a lot."

Seth stepped onto the stairs to the front door and hugged Dean. "I know, Dean. I know. I promise, I'm careful."

"You better be. Curtis, it's good to see you. I hope there is lots of news on the macaron front. Collin told me about meeting you and Andrew at the museum."

"You had a date and didn't tell us? I'm wounded, deeply wounded!" Peyton grabbed his shirt in the area of his heart in a dramatic fashion.

"I didn't have a date without telling you." Curtis did his best to keep a straight face. "I had two."

"Two! What have I done wrong to be kept in the dark like this?" Peyton's impersonation of a mortally wounded mama bear could have fooled Curtis if he hadn't known the man for so long.

"That's it. No more speed dates with Seth for you!" Dean put his hand on Peyton's shoulder and dragged him toward the house. "You act even crazier than usual. Must be all the adrenaline in your system. As for you"—Dean glanced sternly at Curtis—"I hope for your sake the story is good. Two dates without saying a word!"

"I'm sorry." Curtis grinned, showing how not-sorry he truly was. Dean rolled his eyes before he ushered them all in. The food was already there, in huge insulated boxes, waiting to be plated. Once they all had their favorites on the plates, they went to the dining room and started eating. As always, the first ten minutes were spent in happy silence, only broken by the occasional moan. For all of them, eating was a lot like good sex, and Curtis was more than happy to spend his time with men who knew how to enjoy life. As usual, Peyton was the first to be sated enough to start a conversation.

"Now, Curtis, I believe we all want to hear about your *two* dates."

Curtis rolled his eyes, took another sip from his sparkling lemon water, and dabbed his mouth with a napkin, a move he knew would make Peyton explode with tension. When Peyton's left eyelid started twitching, Curtis winked at him. "Well, as you all know, my first date with Andrew was kind of terrible." They all winced. It had been bad. "I had resolved myself to forgetting about him, and I was on a good way, if I do say so myself, but then he sent me flowers and tickets to an exhibition at the Museum of Art."

"Aww, that's sweet. I can see how you could forgive him." As an author, Dean tended to romanticize things, when he didn't come up with gruesome ways of killing people off.

"I called him back to tell him that I already had tickets and that the exhibition would be full of rich people trying to outdo each other. He told me he had expected as much and that he was willing to try again if I let him. I couldn't say no to such a determined apology."

"Good for you!" Seth toasted Curtis with his Coke.

"It must have gone well, given the smug grin on your face." Leeland elbowed him.

"It went very well. Andrew endured over two hours of pompous idiots ogling him while talking to me about all the money they have spent on art. Then Martin and Collin came, and he survived his first meeting with Martin in full-on protection mode as well."

"He just doesn't like how people often talk to me." Collin defended his fiancé immediately.

"Which is a good thing, Collin. Nobody said anything to the contrary." Dean was quick to interject. Collin took another bite from his pasta, a happy grin on his lips.

"What happened then?" Peyton was practically bouncing on his chair.

"Andrew took me to dinner at a diner, which was very romantic, and then we went to Whisper. Martin had invited us, and even though Andrew was a bit reluctant—this whole money thing makes him very uncomfortable—he decided to grab the bull by the horns, so to speak. We had a very nice evening there, with Dean, Collin, and Leeland. Emilio was there as well, but I doubt you noticed us. Garrett was doing a demonstration on caning." Curtis dropped their names casually. He had no problem revealing that the three had known about one of his dates. Emilio blushed a little, though Curtis wasn't sure if it was from embarrassment or arousal.

"You traitors! You could have mentioned something!" Peyton slammed his bony fist into Dean's biceps, causing him to wince.

"Ouch, Peyton. I'm sorry, I was busy this week."

Peyton huffed before he looked accusingly at Collin and Leeland. "What's your excuse?"

"I didn't know you didn't know, because you always seem to know everything, which is kind of impossible, now that I think about it, but I couldn't have told you anyway because I lost my cell again, even though this one's so big, and I think Dog took it, because he knows Martin wants me to carry it with me all the time and he loves teasing Martin, because he doesn't allow him on the couch, and when Martin isn't there, Dog totally sits on it, even though Martin always finds out because of the hair, and I hope he hasn't buried this cell like the last one, and anyway, it's run out of power by now, so I just have to wait until Dog brings it back." Collin beamed at Peyton, obviously satisfied that he had defended his case so well. Peyton stared at him for a very long moment.

"Sometimes I'm not sure if you aren't doing this on purpose," he muttered, though Collin didn't hear him since he was too busy shoveling the last of his pasta into his mouth. Peyton turned his glare of death on

Leeland, who appeared completely unfazed. He was quite a good poker player. "What do you have to say for yourself?"

"I threatened his life to make sure he treats Curtis right from now on."

"Good man!" Peyton grinned. Seth clapped.

Curtis sighed. Peace was restored. "Anyway, I invited him to my home for the second date...."

"Wasn't it the third?" Emilio interrupted.

"Most certainly not! Who would want to count a disaster like their first date as a date?" Seth replied.

"You just called it a date." Leeland grinned. Seth made a face and flipped him of.

"What else am I supposed to call it? Their first meeting was at the store!"

"Can we please get back to what's really important here?" Peyton cut off whatever Leeland had wanted to say. "I don't know about you, but I'd like to find out what happened when Curtis had Andrew in his lair."

"Fine." Leeland huffed. "I was just trying to be accurate."

"You're not being accurate, Leeland. You're being a bean counter." Peyton waved him off.

"Excuse me, since when does the attempt at being accurate count as bean counting?" Leeland puffed his chest out. His eyes had taken on that gleam they always got when he was bickering with Peyton. The two loved their little verbal sparring matches, which provided an endless source of entertainment to the rest of the group.

"Since you're dealing with me, sugar. I thought you knew that by now." Peyton smiled sweetly at Leeland. His tone was soothing, which meant he had a bigger bone to pick at the moment. Curtis had no illusions as to what that bigger bone was, even before Peyton focused on him again.

"He had sent me a contract before he came. A very thorough contract. Some of the practices listed there I didn't even know." When he saw the worried looks on Dean's and Leeland's faces, Curtis hurried to clarify. "He said he didn't want to miss anything. And that he usually finds it more interesting what people put on their list of hard limits than what they actually choose. Which is right. We quickly realized that we're compatible in our needs. More than compatible. Our next date is the day after tomorrow, when we plan to celebrate the signing of the initial contract for six months by doing our first official scene."

Curtis couldn't help the happy smile on his face. The others congratulated him, and in the joyful atmosphere, he almost forgot to mention Jasper's visit. When Dean started handing out dessert, Curtis suddenly remembered the unpleasantness in the morning. For a moment he debated simply ignoring it, but Jasper's visit had been gnawing on him the entire day, and he knew he had to tell somebody to let it all out. Even though only Dean knew Jasper personally, albeit not very well, they all knew the story about the breakup as well as others, and that didn't paint Jasper in a very good light, be it as a man or as a Dom. It was astounding how long subs could remember a bad Dom. Some of the stories about Jasper's misdeeds had been blown out of proportion over the years, though Curtis did nothing to correct them. First, because Jasper wasn't at Whisper anymore, and second, because he was a faulty human who took a tiny bit of pleasure out of it. So even Leeland, Collin, and Emilio, who had come to Whisper after Jasper had left, knew him from tales, and Peyton and Seth knew that Jasper was the shitty ex who had dumped Curtis without telling him because of one drunken night where they all had confessed their past lovers or, in case of Collin and Dean, past crushes.

Curtis cleared his throat. "That was the good part of my week. The bad part—Jasper is back in town. He came by my gallery today with a bunch of red roses and wanted to talk. I threw him out."

"What? Shouldn't he be somewhere in Britain, drowning in a moor?" Dean was usually a gentle man. His angry outburst warmed Curtis from the inside, since it showed how much his friend cared about him.

"Jasper, as in 'Jasper, the gigantic asshole'?" Leeland let his knuckles crack. "Do you know where he's staying?"

"No. He didn't say, and I certainly didn't ask. I told him to leave me alone, and I hope the message has gotten through."

"What could he have wanted anyway? I mean, bringing a man you traded in for a younger model flowers is about as vulgar as you can get. Then again, I don't think this Jasper is known for his class from what you told us." Seth shook his head.

"He definitely isn't. Good thing he can't get back into Whisper. Richard and Martin have revoked his membership permanently." Dean grinned smugly.

"If he contacts you again, you tell me immediately. Stall him until I can get to you." Pure murder shone in Leeland's eyes. He despised few things more than cheating.

"Thank you, Leeland. I'll do that. Though I do hope he's gotten the message. Now that my heart feels lighter, let's forget about that lying weasel and enjoy the rest of our evening together. Dean, what film have you chosen?" Curtis used his business tone to signal the others that he didn't want to talk about the topic anymore. He wanted to bask in the happiness about having met Andrew and the love he felt coming from his friends. Dean picked up on his intentions immediately.

"I've found something great. First, we're going to watch *From Dusk Till Dawn,* one of Quentin Tarantino's classics. And then, to keep a red thread, I have *Frida,* also with Salma Hayek."

Collin squealed in delight. "Oooh, that's great! I love the paintings by Frida Kahlo. She had such a unique view of the world, though when you think about it, it probably wasn't that great for her, since she was always in pain, but her art is like this beautiful flower with hints of darkness and decay, like something you would find blooming on a graveyard at midnight, full of poison and pain and sadness and yet filled with light and hope and determination."

"I like *From Dusk Till Dawn.* A young George Clooney isn't to be sneezed on." Seth smiled and grabbed his bowl of panna cotta.

This was their cue to get dessert and move to the living room, where everything was already set up. Curtis sat down between Collin and Peyton, who gave him an encouraging nod that let Curtis forget what a pain in the ass the man could be. Dean started the first film, and Curtis simply enjoyed being with his friends.

CHAPTER 15

ANDREW DID a last mental check of his two supply bags—one for food, the other for sex—before he rang the bell on Curtis's door. After a few moments, Curtis opened with a broad, happy smile.

"Hello, Andrew. It's so nice to see you!" Curtis sounded a little breathless and eager, just like Andrew wanted him.

"Hello, Curtis. It's great to be here. I've been thinking of you all the time."

"Even when you were at Club Eros?" Curtis stepped aside to let Andrew in, his tone slightly teasing. Andrew grinned and kissed him on the mouth before he entered the house.

"Club Eros was nice, definitely more suited to my tastes than Club Submission, but none of the subs there could hold a candle to you, if that's what you wanted to know."

"That *is* all I wanted to know." Curtis winked. "No, seriously, I've heard good things about Club Eros." He wanted to take Andrew's bags, but he declined.

"It's a very decent club. Mixed, like most of the BDSM clubs in the area. The people are solid middle class, and the club management is big on security. I couldn't stop comparing it to Club Whisper, though, which kind of spoiled the evening a bit. Can you imagine, they don't have three different kinds of lube in the bathrooms?"

He grinned when Curtis opened his eyes comically wide, pressed his hands against his chest as if he were wounded, and let out an exasperated gasp. "No! What kind of club hasn't? The horror!"

They both started laughing while they went to the kitchen, where Andrew placed the basket with the food on the counter and the bag with the sex toys on the ground. These two would get mixed up soon enough if everything went the way he planned. Andrew took Curtis in his arms to kiss him more thoroughly. Tasting his boy again was such a delight, especially since Curtis reciprocated the kiss enthusiastically. There was no feeling like having been missed. After a few moments, though, Curtis tensed in his arms. Andrew drew back to look into those mesmerizing eyes.

"What's the matter, boy?"

Curtis sighed deeply, freed himself from Andrew's grasp. "I don't want to talk about it, but I know I have to, and I'm not sure how to start."

Andrew felt alarmed, tried to find a clue about what this was all about in Curtis's expression, but all he saw there was a mixture of worry and anger he couldn't quite place.

"Is this about us, boy? Do you have second thoughts? Do we need to talk about the contract again?"

Curtis shook his head. "No, I'm not having second thoughts. Though what I have to tell you is, in a way, about us." He lowered his gaze for a moment and took another deep breath before he lifted his gaze to Andrew. "On Friday, my ex visited me in the gallery. I didn't even know he was back in the States. He came uninvited, and I threw him out almost immediately. I just think you should know this. He came with flowers, roses, to be exact, and though I didn't let him stay long enough to explain his reasons to me, apart from him needing money, I'm sure it can't be anything good. And I don't want to think about him or whatever he's planning, but I also can't just let it go unspoken."

Andrew felt like a rock had just been removed from his heart. He'd feared Curtis might have decided to end their relationship before it even began. So hearing about the visit from the evil ex was not welcome news, but news he could deal with rationally as soon as he got the spike of jealousy piercing his guts under control. He reached for Curtis to draw him back into his arms.

"It's fine, Curtis. Boy. I appreciate you telling me so openly about it. I can see this isn't easy for you. Is there anything I can do to help except being my understanding, supportive self?" Andrew infused the last words with just enough humor to make his intentions clear. To his relief, Curtis smiled broadly.

"No, thank you, Sir. You being your awesome self is all I need. If he shows his face again, I already have a cutthroat lawyer on speed dial who I can unleash."

It irked Andrew a tiny bit that Curtis seemed to have the situation already under control, but then again, this was better than him having to take action against a man he didn't even know.

"Wonderful, boy. Does this mean we can leave this unpleasantness behind and start our celebration?"

Curtis's smile could have lit an entire small town. "Yes. I can't wait."

"Very well. Since this is our first official, thorough scene together, I thought we'd do something special." Andrew allowed a salacious grin to appear on his lips. The shudder he got from Curtis in return made his already half-hard cock swell instantly. "You told me you're not much of a cook, boy, which is why I brought food with me. It doesn't need hours of preparing and isn't very complicated, but it's tasty and allows me to concentrate on you while I'm preparing it. How does that sound?"

"Wonderful, Master." Curtis was already panting slightly. His cheeks had a healthy, rosy color Andrew wanted to turn into a full, blazing red until the end of the evening.

"Good. Your safewords?"

"Degenerate Art for stop, Dali for slow down, Macarons for go."

Andrew nodded. Good. The fun could begin. "I want you to strip, boy. Do it slowly, for my viewing pleasure."

The red in Curtis's cheeks deepened. He nodded and started by opening the first buttons of his light blue shirt. Curtis's fingers trembled lightly, and Andrew wasn't sure if it was arousal or nervousness. Probably a mixture of both, he decided. Which was good. It showed how into this Curtis was.

Each undone button revealed more of Curtis's pale, smooth skin. The tan practically everybody in Miami seemed to have was completely absent in Curtis. Given how light his skin tone was, Andrew could imagine that he had to be careful in the sun. Something to always remember. Curtis had now opened the last button. He looked up at Andrew while he slowly let the shirt slide from his shoulders. Andrew's own breath quickened, while more of his blood pooled in his groin. At this rate, his brain would be empty before Curtis was completely naked.

"So beautiful." He stepped forward to take the shirt from Curtis's hand and place it on the breakfast counter. "Go on."

Curtis smiled and reached for his fly, opened the button and the zipper. He hooked his fingers under the waistband to push the trousers down, when Andrew stopped him with a gesture. Curtis immediately froze.

"Turn around."

Seeing his boy obey without hesitation had Andrew leaking precum into his underwear. Curtis was so perfect, so beautiful, so elegant. How he could decide to give his submission to an unrefined man like Andrew was a mystery. One Andrew didn't want to solve.

"Take them down. Show me how flexible you are." Andrew knew he sounded like a caveman and he didn't care. Especially not when Curtis did exactly as he was told. It appeared he was in good shape because his upper body went down with the trousers in a graceful, fluid motion while his legs stayed perfectly straight. Andrew made a small choking sound when he was assaulted by ideas about how he could use this flexibility to his advantage.

Curtis stepped out of the trousers, tensed his back muscles to get upright again.

"Stop. Stay down. Now hook your fingers under the waistband of your underwear and pull it down. Take your time."

Again Curtis obeyed without hesitation. Completely mesmerized, Andrew watched as the two most perfect asscheeks he had ever seen appeared. They were even paler than the rest of Curtis's body, with a minimum of fuzzy hair and just the right amount of flesh to make Andrew drool at the thought of spanking them.

Curtis stepped out of his black underwear but made no move to get upright this time.

"Good boy. Let me look at you."

Andrew stepped forward and placed his hands on the two globes he intended to spank later. Or perhaps some light smacks to get the evening started? "I want to warm your backside, boy. Just enough to get the blood flowing."

"Whatever you wish, Master."

"Spread your legs a bit. I want to see your balls and cock."

Shuddering, Curtis did as he was told, spreading his legs farther until they were a little wider apart than his hips. Andrew took Curtis's balls in his hands, marveled at how heavy they felt, full of arousal. Curtis's cock stood proudly, and when Andrew reached through Curtis's stretched legs to grab the tip and drag the whole shaft back toward his balls, he could feel the steady stream of precum welling from the slit. Curtis moaned but kept his position.

"Such a good boy. So ready for me. I love it."

A desperate whimper was the answer. Andrew smiled, enjoyed the rush of power surging through him. Curtis was like this because of *him*. He adjusted his hand until he had Curtis's cock in a nice firm grip without it being too tight. Then he stroked his asscheeks in circular movements with the other hand for a few moments, until the skin felt hot under his touch.

"You don't have to count them, boy. Just feel."

Before Curtis could answer, Andrew delivered the first blow. It was just hard enough to leave his handprint on Curtis's left cheek, but his boy twitched a bit forward anyway, which heightened the tug on his still rock-hard shaft. Curtis whimpered.

Andrew smiled, delivered the second blow. They soon found a rhythm, Curtis's moans accentuating each contact of Andrew's hand with the rapidly reddening skin on Curtis's cheeks. The sight was so erotic, Andrew knew there was no chance he could control himself for much longer, and he didn't want to. One of the perks of being the Dom was that he didn't have to suffer through edging or orgasm denial. He delivered two more blows before he let go of Curtis's shaft and stepped away from him. Good boy that he was, Curtis kept his position, only swaying slightly back and forth. Andrew went to the bag with the sex toys he had brought and searched for the lube. When he got it, he went back to Curtis.

"I'm going to play with your hole now, boy. Make you all soft and stretched out. And when it's all puffy and creamy, waiting to be taken, I'm going to masturbate all over your delightful back, just to give you a taste of what is coming. Are you ready?"

There was another moan before Curtis managed a breathless "Yes, Master." Andrew opened the lube, scrutinized Curtis's still bent-over body for a moment before he put his free hand on Curtis's hips to guide him toward the kitchen counter. "I want you to hold yourself open for me, boy. I think this is easier for you if you can rest your upper body on the counter."

"Thank you, Master."

The simple gratitude in Curtis's tone, gratitude for something every good Dom should have realized, made Andrew grow at least five feet. This was his sub, his boy, and he was taking excellent care of him, thinking of his needs. The part of him that wanted to dominate had already taken over completely, and that beast thought along simple lines. When he had made sure Curtis was comfortable and stable, Andrew enjoyed the sight of his boy spreading his reddened cheeks for Andrew to inspect.

Curtis had some hair around his hole, and Andrew started teasing him by pulling on it. "Your hole is beautiful, boy. Tight and yet anxious, already twitching in anticipation. One day soon, I'm going to wax you down there, make you even more sensitive."

He poured some lube directly in the crack, watched it dripping toward the quivering hole. Standing between Curtis's spread thighs, Andrew could feel the muscles trembling, just like the hands that held Curtis open for him. Andrew massaged the lube into Curtis's crack with the tip of his right index finger. Every time he passed the anus, he applied a bit more pressure, watching in fascination as lube slid through the wrinkles and into the hole before it had been breached. He could have played this game forever if it hadn't been for his own raging hard-on. So he started playing with the hole, entering it with his finger down to the first knuckle, then withdrawing again. Curtis was tight, though his moans and the way his hole yielded showed his experience. It didn't take long for Andrew to penetrate him with two fingers, stretching them inside Curtis's hot channel to prepare him for the game Andrew had planned. Soon, Curtis was trying his best not to writhe on Andrew's three fingers, but to stay still like a good boy should.

"You're so brave, boy. So good." Andrew rubbed over Curtis's prostate and enjoyed the painful shudder he got in response. "Seeing you squirm like this makes me so hot, so hard for you. Knowing I'm going to torture you the entire evening almost has me coming in my pants."

Curtis whimpered. The sound was so raw, so helpless, it spoke to Andrew's inner sadist like nothing else. "Yes, you like that idea as much as I do, don't you, boy? Do you enjoy being speared by my fingers, knowing you can't come without my permission?"

"Master, please."

"What, please? Please stop? Please make me come and punish me for it? What do you want, boy?"

Curtis panted. "Please, Master. Just a moment. Can't...." He sounded so desperate, Andrew stilled the movement of his fingers immediately.

"Everything okay, boy?"

"Yes, yes. I just need a moment...." Curtis took deep breaths while his inner walls still constricted around Andrew's fingers. Andrew didn't move until Curtis wiggled his ass a tiny bit, indicating that he was ready to continue. Andrew had wanted to torture him a bit longer, but seeing Curtis so compliant, so willing, had his balls so hard he thought he would shoot from the friction of his pants alone. He opened his own fly and zipper, freed his cock, and squeezed some more lube onto his right hand before grabbing his painfully erect cock. He stepped back between Curtis's spread thighs, nestled his shaft between the still slightly red cheeks, and started moving. Curtis's moans cheered him quickly toward his orgasm, made him shoot so hard, Andrew had to grip Curtis's hips because otherwise he would have fallen over. He watched his cum pool in the dip of Curtis's lower back and start dripping down his sides. With a choked moan, Andrew dipped his fingers into the semen and massaged it into Curtis's skin to mark him in this most primal way.

After he came down from his high, Andrew checked Curtis's erection, satisfied when he found his boy hard and leaking, his balls and cock swollen and red. He took another generous amount of lube, applied it around Curtis's soft and yielding hole before pushing as much of it inside as possible. Then he cleaned his hands in the sink. Curtis was still bent over the kitchen counter, waiting for his master to give him a new order.

"Come here, boy."

Curtis swayed a bit when he put his full weight back on his feet. Andrew was there immediately to steady him and wipe the sweat from his forehead.

"I'm going to cook for us now, boy. To keep you occupied and horny, I have a little task for you."

He winked at Curtis, who only raised a brow in question. Once they had gotten more used to each other, Curtis would learn what it meant to not give Andrew a verbal response to any of his statements, but not tonight. This was their first scene, and there were more important things to achieve. Driving his boy insane with lust was only one of them.

"Get on your elbows and knees right here." Andrew indicated a spot near the wall, close to the kitchen counter where he would prepare their meal. "Stick your ass out at an angle that will be comfortable for penetration."

"Yours or mine, Master?"

"Yours, boy. I need to work, remember?"

Curtis grunted something before he did as he was told. He looked absolutely delicious on his knees, his ass in the air, his shoulders and neck as red as his asscheeks. Andrew went to his sex toy bag again to retrieve the little help he had brought. It was a dildo of considerable length and girth, not as monstrous as the ones found in porn films, but impressive. It also had a suction pad at the base, with which Andrew secured it on the wall, aligning it with Curtis's hole. He gave it a few tugs to see if it held before he slathered it with lube as well. He walked to Curtis's front to gently guide him backward until his ass met with the tip of the dildo. Andrew pressed a kiss on Curtis's forehead, and then he got up again to get his cell. He swiped over the screen until he found the app he'd been looking for, before he squatted down in front of Curtis again.

"This is an alarm, boy. It will start ringing once every two minutes and decrease until it rings every five seconds. Now, every time you hear it ring, you will move forward until only the tip of the toy remains inside you and then you will go back. I have programmed a longer timespan in the beginning to give you a chance to adjust to the dildo, but when I'm done preparing our food, I want to see you fucking yourself on it like you mean it." He smiled broadly, stroked Curtis's hair. "Needless to say, you're not allowed to come."

"Why on earth did I think having a master would be a good idea?" Curtis had murmured the words just loud enough for Andrew to hear. He knew immediately they weren't meant as a challenge, and knowing that Curtis felt secure enough with him to joke about it made Andrew all warm and tingly inside.

"You love it, and you know it. And since I'm a great master to have, I'll even help you to get the toy in. Now, what do you say?"

Curtis chuckled. "Thank you, Master."

"There. Wasn't so difficult, was it?"

Andrew bent forward over Curtis's upper body to stretch his asscheeks apart. "Now move back. Very good. Can you feel it?"

Curtis grunted. "Yes, Master. It's huge."

"You can do it, boy. Come on, a little more." Curtis did his best and with a little more coaxing and lots of praise from Andrew, he finally had the toy completely inside him. Andrew caressed his back lovingly, pressed little kisses on his spine.

"You're so hot, you have no idea. Seeing you like this, I could come right away. So beautiful."

Andrew took his cell to start the timer. He put it in front of Curtis on the ground, kissed him once more, this time on his lips, and then started cooking.

CHAPTER 16

THE FIRST ring resounded, and Curtis moved his hips forward, felt the drag of the silicone dildo, with its very lifelike veins and bumps, over his prostate. He had now idea how he could manage to not come while riding this evil toy. The way Andrew had dominated him so far had him ready to shoot on the spot. What held him back was the fact that his Dom, his master wanted him to suffer. And he wanted to suffer for him. Wanted to show him what a good boy he could be, how much he appreciated Andrew's affectionate attention. Andrew was giving him so much, making such an effort, it was only fair Curtis did the same for him. The balance between giving and taking they had established seemingly without effort made Curtis giddy with joy. This was what submission should feel like, at least for him: the will to please, the appreciation of what he was offering, the exchange of not only power but also trust and—he hesitated a moment, then dared to think it—love.

The cell rang again, jerking him into motion. Above him, Andrew was putting the kitchen appliances to work, many of them for the very first time. Sometimes Curtis could feel Andrew's gaze on him, full of lust and possessiveness. It felt good to be wanted like that, and he wasn't beneath putting on a little show to turn Andrew on some more. Though the way the dildo was stimulating him, the show was turning more and more into genuine want and despair. Feeling the thick shaft breaching him, filling him, had Curtis yearning for the real thing, for Andrew's thick cock that would feel so much better than this toy.

By the time Andrew put whatever he had prepared in the oven, Curtis was trying desperately to fuck the dildo like he had been instructed while at the same time to hold his orgasm in. It was getting more and more difficult with each thrust, and he honestly didn't know how much longer he would be able to hold out. The ringing was no longer a signal to move but felt like an additional penetration, coming now so rapidly he was panting from his attempts to keep up.

Just when he thought he couldn't take it any longer, Andrew stopped the app and put one hand on Curtis's lower back, keeping him from thrusting again, anchoring him against the orgasmic tide that wanted to crash over him.

"Oh my God, Curtis, if only you could see yourself like I do now. You're the most perfect creature I've ever met, as if you were created only for me."

That Andrew was no longer addressing him as boy was all the proof Curtis needed. Andrew was as gone as he, overwhelmed by the same sense of rightness. He closed his eyes, listened to his Dom, his *partner*.

"I want to fuck you so badly, Curtis, boy. Now. Need you now." Andrew helped Curtis to get off the dildo. He rummaged through the bag with the sex toys until he found a condom and put it on after hastily opening his fly again. Curtis watched him, not bothering to keep his gaze lowered as high protocol demanded. This was their first time having penetrative sex, their first official scene. He had every right to admire his handsome, strong Dom and his impressive cock.

Andrew came back to him, turned him on his back. Curtis winced a bit, because the tiles on the floor were cold. They did warm quickly on his heated back, though.

"Sorry, boy. Can't wait. Need you, want to look at you."

Andrew grabbed Curtis's legs, placed them on his shoulders, and caressed the sides of Curtis's upper body before he aligned his cock with Curtis's twitching hole. When the tip of Andrew's shaft entered him, Curtis couldn't suppress the single tear sliding down his cheek. This felt so right. So good. So perfect. As much as he loved his friends and his life, having a steady partner made it all even better.

His Dom stopped the tear with his finger, licked it off with a soft smile full of love. Then he bent down to kiss Curtis, driving his cock deeper inside in the process. Curtis moaned, accepting both Andrew's cock and tongue, all his dominance. Despite Andrew's obvious need, he did his best to slow things down. He obviously wanted to savor the moment as well, a notion Curtis could get behind. The long, determined thrusts stimulated his prostate to the point where he started to beg.

"Please, Master. Don't stop. Never stop. Let me come, please!"

Andrew smiled against his lips. His tone was slightly teasing. "Have I reduced you to begging already? I thought you'd have more endurance."

Curtis smiled right back. He knew the words weren't meant to hurt. The opposite. "With you, Master? I could beg all the time. I showed great restraint so far. I definitely deserve a reward."

"Do you, now? And what would that reward be, boy?"

Curtis pretended to think about it, while Andrew's divine cock was still forcing him mercilessly toward his release. "Letting me come? Because I'm such a good boy?"

Andrew laughed and bit into his lower lip, just hard enough to make Curtis yelp. "I should redden your ass and forbid you to come for an entire week." He licked over the place he had just bitten. "But you're right. You have been good. An orgasm it is."

Grateful, Curtis slung his arms around Andrew's neck and lifted his hips to change the angle of his master's thrusts. Andrew's movements became more frantic, and the brutal pounding had Curtis's balls tightening while his cock started twitching without being touched. The first spurt was like the literal wave crashing over him, though Curtis usually wasn't one for using stereotypes to describe his sex life. It had been almost a year since he'd last had sex with a partner, and back then it had been a one-night stand, nothing even close to the depth and appreciation he was feeling now.

Andrew's rhythm faltered; his thrusts came faster, more brutal, thus stimulating Curtis into a second orgasm that took Andrew with him over the edge. His master wasn't a screamer. He grunted, his face scrunched up adorably while he grabbed Curtis's hips so hard, it would surely leave bruises. The knowledge that his Dom had marked him had Curtis almost passing out from sheer bliss. Their bodies kept twitching against each other for some time, while a bone-deep relaxation kept them on the ground even though Curtis was starting to feel a little uncomfortable. Cold tiles were okay while in the throes of passion, afterward not so much. He wiggled a bit, which jerked Andrew into action.

Slowly, he pulled out of Curtis's hole and helped him place his feet on the ground. "This was simply great, boy. Do you want to end the scene now or keep going? I'm fine with both."

Curtis groaned and moved his hips tentatively. A pinching in his lower back as well as an uncomfortable pressure around his shoulder blades reminded him that he wasn't as young as he used to be. Though sex on tiles was never advisable in the first place, no matter the age of the participants. "Does keeping the scene going entail you helping me up from the floor and giving me a massage later? If the answer is yes, we have a 'Macarons' situation. If it's no, we're firmly in the 'Degenerate Art' corner."

Andrew smiled and lifted a brow. "Do I sense some topping from the bottom here?"

Curtis huffed. "Hey, you asked! Besides, it's me with my back on the cold, *hard* floor."

Andrew went back on his haunches, grabbed Curtis's wrists and pulled him up with one strong move. "It may have been your back on the floor, but at least for you the weight was evenly distributed. My poor kneecaps, on the other hand, have suffered greatly."

"Then next time we do this in bed? And I was on my knees the entire time you were cooking, so don't go complaining to me about kneecaps!"

They stared at each other for a moment before they started laughing so hard, they had tears in their eyes. Curtis hadn't felt this relaxed and happy in a very long time.

"Okay, I think the scene is done." Andrew leaned in to give Curtis a loving kiss. "But I don't need a scene to give you everything you need. How about I feed you—naked, on my lap—and then give you a massage? You know, because you were such a good boy."

Curtis ignored the teasing tone in the last sentence and snuggled against Andrew's chest with a happy smile on his lips. "Sounds like the perfect aftercare. I wish you could stay the night."

"What makes you think I won't?"

Curtis leaned back in Andrew's arms far enough to look him in the eye. "You have work tomorrow, so I assumed...."

Andrew smiled and kissed him on the top of his nose. "Never assume. I did some preliminary baking this afternoon before I came here. I can afford being late tomorrow. You didn't think I would leave you after our first scene, did you?"

Curtis blushed a little. "Not really. I was hoping you'd stay, but I would have understood if you couldn't. Your business comes first."

"Oh, Curtis, you're so perfect for me. And before you wonder, I do think you are more important than my business. You're my boy, my partner."

They looked at each other in mutual understanding. "I enjoyed our first scene, Andrew. Very much. You're a great Dom."

Andrew grinned. "I know." He winked. "And you're a great sub. The way you yield had me losing control. The scene I had planned was a little different from what we did. But you were so delicious, I couldn't resist."

Curtis tipped his head back in an invitation for another kiss, which he promptly got. "I couldn't tell. And I like that I can make you lose control." He let his hands glide down to Andrew's firm ass. "I also like the scent of whatever you have in the oven."

Andrew hugged Curtis firmly. "It's nothing special, just flaky pastry filled with feta cheese, tomatoes, some bacon, and a few drops of olive oil. I figured you'd be happy if I didn't take forever with my preparations, what with the huge dildo up your ass and the timer app."

"You figured right. It was getting close toward the end."

"You did beautifully, boy. I'm proud." Andrew kissed Curtis on the top of his head.

"Proud enough to feed me? I'm getting hungry."

"Bossy sub. Come on. We need a plate."

Curtis got the plate while Andrew switched off the oven and pulled the griddle with a dozen little flaky pastry squares out. They were a perfect golden brown, filling the air with the scent of butter, cheese, fresh tomatoes, and olive oil. Andrew used a spatula Curtis didn't even know he owned to transfer the food onto the plate. Then he gathered the plate together with a knife and fork, as well as two glasses. "Can you bring some water?"

Curtis filled a glass jug with water and some lemon slices he always had in the fridge because lemon went well with many different teas before he followed his Dom into the dining room. The light breeze around his nether regions reminded him that he was still completely naked with cum drying on his chest and belly. Curtis found he didn't care. It was all proof of the amazing sex he'd had.

Andrew sat down at the table and placed the food there. Curtis filled the two glasses with water. After he put the jug down, Andrew grabbed him around the waist to pull him onto his lap. It felt good to be sitting on strong, cloth-clad thighs, snuggling his naked torso against Andrew's broad chest beneath his shirt. Curtis had always liked the sense of vulnerability he got from being naked while his Dom wore clothes. He also found he loved the fact that Andrew was inclined to keep the scene going on a lighter level even though it was officially over. It showed how much he had enjoyed the scene himself and how much he cared about Curtis's well-being, something Jasper had never really bothered with. Once a scene had been done, his ex had administered the aftercare somewhat grudgingly, as if it were a chore, not a pleasant conclusion of time spent happily together.

Curtis shook his head. He didn't want to think about Jasper or the mistakes he had made in the past. He wanted to concentrate on the bite of steaming flaky pastry with a bit of tomato and crumbs of feta cheese hovering in front of his mouth.

"Careful, boy. It's still hot."

"I can see that, Master. It smells great."

"Thank you. Now try." The fork came closer to his mouth.

Curtis chuckled but opened up obediently. The taste was even better than the smell, rich and fruity with a hint of heaviness from the cheese. He moaned appreciatively, which seemed to inspire Andrew's cock, because it started rising under him, poking him through the fabric of his trousers. Curtis wiggled a bit, just to feel that wonderful shaft hardening even more.

"Curtis!" Andrew dropped the fork to grab Curtis's hips.

"Yes, Andrew?"

"If you keep that up, we're not going to eat. I thought you were hungry."

Curtis grinned. He had almost forgotten how it felt to be desired, to have this kind of power over another man. It was heady and wonderful, gave him the feeling of being fully alive again. He stopped wiggling, took the fork, and scooped up another bite of flaky tastiness, offering it to his struggling Dom. Andrew grinned happily before he opened his mouth. Now the tables were turned. Curtis felt his cock rising at the sound of his Dom's moan.

"What do you think, can we drive each other crazy before the food is gone?" Andrew licked his lips.

Curtis eyed the remaining squares. "You better get another condom."

WITH A content smile, Andrew looked down on his sleeping sub. They were snuggled up in Curtis's bedroom after the longest and most erotic dinner Andrew had ever had. Who would have thought feeding his boy while being buried balls-deep in his ass could be so hot? Afterward they had taken a shower in Curtis's huge bathroom that even had a Jacuzzi bathtub. Andrew found he liked the amenities money could buy. Having the space to suck his boy off under the shower was not to be sneezed upon and despite his earlier reservations, Andrew could see himself spending lots of time at Curtis's home. For reasons he didn't completely understand yet, Andrew no longer felt intimidated by Curtis's wealth. Perhaps it was because of the way his lover didn't make a big deal out of it. Or because Curtis was the least pretentious person he knew. While his boy had suffered so beautifully for him, it hadn't escaped Andrew's attention that all the tools in the kitchen were not simply the most expensive to show off, but from brands known for the longevity of their products. Yes, Curtis obviously spent more money on his home than Andrew would probably ever earn, but it wasn't for show. It was to create something lasting, a sentiment he could fully understand.

Now his sub, his *boyfriend*, was snoring lightly in his arms, which gave Andrew a feeling of contentment. The moon shone through a gap in the curtains, fell on the huge painting across from the bed. His first time in Curtis's home, Andrew had only gotten a glimpse of it. He already knew this was a gift from Collin, and he had to admit it was beyond gorgeous. The weak moonlight obscured many of the details but highlighted the raven soaring toward the sun. Andrew had never been that much into art, though he could appreciate not only the beauty but also the message in this picture. Darkness and light were simply contrasts, there to enhance each other's beauty, not to diminish the other. Andrew found it oddly fitting to his own situation, in bed with the first man he seriously considered a long-term relationship with and who also happened to represent everything his parents had always resented and warned him about.

Andrew pulled Curtis a little closer, pressed a kiss on his temple, and then closed his eyes. Only a fool would reject a gift like the man in his arms, and Andrew was no fool.

CHAPTER 17

THE NEXT morning came too early for Curtis's taste. The sun had just started to cast a weak light on the world when the alarm went off and Andrew got up. He pressed a kiss on Curtis's mouth.

"It's fine, baby. You just close your eyes and sleep. I'll call you later."

Curtis struggled to open his eyes fully. "You stayed the night. I can get up with you." He grabbed Andrew's hand, and Andrew helped him into an upright position. "Just give me a minute."

Andrew chuckled. "Curtis, you really don't have to. You're clearly not made for this time of day. Just go back to sleep. I won't hold it against you."

"Keep that thought in mind, because I surely won't make a habit of it, but this is our first morning together, emphasis on *morning*, and I refuse to stay in bed while you get ready for your day. I'm going to make some tea. Or do you prefer coffee?"

"Tea is fine, boy. And I appreciate it. I can see you're not a morning person."

Curtis huffed. "Mornings are hell. In boarding school we had to get up at five for early exercise. Without breakfast, of course, to build character and stamina."

"Don't worry, darling. The only early morning exercise you'll ever get with me is of the carnal variety. And there will always be breakfast, I promise."

Curtis moaned. "If I hadn't fallen for you already, this would have made me. You're perfect."

Curtis felt Andrew stilling above him and cursed himself inwardly. It was way too early to talk about falling in love. One hot night of great sex did not make a relationship. He opened his mouth to apologize, but Andrew beat him to it.

"I'm so glad. I thought it was only me. I know it's still early and not even twenty-four hours since our first official scene, and now I have to leave you already for work, but Curtis, I feel the same. What we have is something great, something I want to keep no matter what. I think I've never been so happy in my life."

Curtis felt a huge weight lifted from his shoulders. This was good. They had something special together, and they were both willing to explore it further. An entire battalion of butterflies took off in his stomach.

"Thank you, Andrew." He stuck out his chin in determination. "I'm going to make you tea."

Andrew kissed him again. "Promise me you'll go back to sleep once I'm gone. You look horrible."

"And here I thought you felt something for me. Thank you so much, Andrew." Curtis mock-glared at his Dom and pressed a hand on the general area where his heart was. Andrew laughed out loud.

"I didn't mean it in a bad way. You're adorable, even when you look horrible. I'm just concerned. There's so many wonderful things I have planned for you, things you need all your strength for. They won't even be half as much fun if you're tired."

Curtis's cock took a definite interest. "Congratulations. Now I'm horny. Do you really have to go?"

"Unfortunately, yes, boy. You're not allowed to touch yourself, just in case you were wondering."

"That's not fair!" Curtis knew he was whining. It was early, he still felt a delicious sore spot in his ass whenever he moved, Andrew was standing naked in front of him, promising him naughty delights, and he couldn't do anything about his boner, because his Dom had forbidden it. It was perfect.

"You love it. Besides, this gives you added incentive to see me again as soon as possible."

"I don't need added incentive. I don't want you to go." Curtis pouted. He hadn't done that in forever and it felt great.

"Go make me my tea, boy. I'll phone later, when you're fully awake." Another kiss on the tip of his nose, and Andrew vanished into the bathroom.

Sighing, Curtis tried to ignore his hard-on and went into the kitchen. He didn't bother putting on clothes. Andrew should see what he was missing out on.

When Curtis entered the gallery, Patty raised her perfectly shaped brows. "You're floating. The sex must have been good."

Curtis stuck his tongue out. "If you must know, Mrs. Nosy, the sex was great. So great, in fact, that I even got up at the butt crack of dawn to make Andrew some tea."

Patty's face fell. "You mean he was with you till today?"

"Yes. Why? What's going on?"

"Nothing bad, I hope." Patty didn't look happy anymore. "There was a delivery for you this morning, white and red roses with chocolate. I thought it was from Andrew—that's why I signed them off and took them to your office."

Curtis closed his eyes. "I guess there was no return address?"

"No. But the flowers came with a letter."

Patty followed Curtis into his office, where the roses awaited him in a tasteful vase of blue glass. For a moment Curtis nurtured the thought that Andrew was the most thoughtful boyfriend in the world who had ordered those flowers for him before they even had their date. A closer look at the chocolate and the letter destroyed those hopes. It was Island Sea Salt chocolate from Ocelot Chocolate, a brand that was hard to get in the States, and the envelope was of the thick variety that cost an arm and a leg and always made Curtis think of *Misery*. He also recognized the handwriting of his name in bold letters. "Jasper," he murmured.

Patty took her cell phone out, pressed speed dial, and put it on speaker when her wife picked up.

"Patty, darling, is something the matter?"

"Hi, baby. Yes, I'm afraid so. You're on speaker and Curtis is here."

"Curtis, hello, how are you?" Linda sounded pleasant, but Curtis could almost see her furrowed brows.

"Hi, Linda. I was fine until a few minutes ago. How much has Patty told you about my current men situation?"

Linda laughed. "You're dating a hottie who apparently makes macarons so good my dear wife is willing to ignore all her carefully calculated dietary plans for a taste of them."

Patty winked suggestively in Curtis's direction. He decided to ignore her. Andrew was his. So were the macarons. "Yes, that's accurate and actually the good part. Did she tell you about my ex?"

"The sleazebag who visited you unannounced? Yes. Is he causing trouble?" A hint of steel had crept into Linda's voice. She was definitely going into full-on lawyer mode. Curtis stared at the roses.

"I'm not sure if sending roses and pricey chocolate qualifies as 'causing trouble.' Except I don't want presents from him. It creeps me out. I don't want him to contact me at all."

"Can you do something about him, baby?" Patty's voice was stern. She was probably worked up because she had accepted the flowers. A deep sigh through the speaker sent Curtis's stomach plummeting.

"As much as I would love to help, sending flowers is not a criminal act—unless the chocolate is poisoned or there's razors or dead rats in the flowers. Did you find something like that?"

Curtis huffed. "There's a letter."

"Read it to me. If the content is threatening, I have something to work with."

Reluctantly, Curtis opened the letter. He didn't want anything to do with Jasper. Not even through innocent paper that reminded him of one of the creepiest books he had ever read.

"Okay, here's what it says: *Dearest Curtis*—" Curtis shuddered. "Ugh, since when am I his 'dearest'?"

"The letter, Curtis. We'll discuss writing style later. Now I need the content."

"Yeah, yeah." Curtis cleared his throat. "*Dearest Curtis, I wish to apologize for my unannounced visit. It was clearly out of line to simply assume you would want to see your former lover of five years.*"

Patty whistled. "He's laying it on thick."

"Patty, darling, I love you, but I don't need your comments either. Curtis, read."

Patty rolled her eyes while Curtis read the rest of the letter. "*I would really like to talk to you about the topic we discussed at my first visit. To make sure you feel comfortable, I have made reservations at Red, the steak house in South Beach. I remember you like a good piece of meat.*" Curtis put the letter down. "I don't know which is worse, the cheap innuendo or the fact that he just went and made a reservation, expecting me to show up."

An exasperated sigh came through the phone. "The letter, Curtis. Focus."

"Sorry. *Anyway, I expect you on Tuesday, at seven sharp at the restaurant. Then we can hopefully talk like adults. Enjoy the chocolate, Jasper.*"

"Okay, there's no threat in there. No leverage for me. I'm sorry, Curtis. What is this topic he wants to discuss?"

Curtis threw the letter on the desk. "He's broke and wants to borrow money from me."

"What?" Patty's voice climbed about an octave. She was getting seriously pissed, which made Curtis feel all warm inside. It was good to have friends. "Linda, baby, please tell me there's something you can do. Anything."

Linda stayed silent for a few moments. When she spoke, she sounded apologetic. "I'm really sorry, but there isn't much I can do at this point. I'm going to make some inquiries about Jasper's financial status to see if he's lying. Then I could maybe get him for fraud. My advice to you, Curtis, is to document every interaction you have with Jasper. Take pictures of the flowers, the chocolate, the letter. Write down exactly what you felt when receiving them and try to get eyewitnesses to do the same. Patty, darling, that's your job. Be thorough. Even when it seems like overexaggerating, if things go south, even the tiniest bit can help. And if it all just blows over, you can bask in the knowledge that you would have been prepared. Also talk to your scary friends from Whisper, Martin Carmichael and Richard Miller. Mind you, I'm not suggesting they do anything illegal. I just think that, at the moment, they might have the better leverage. And go to that steak house. Take a witness with you, and write everything that was said down afterward. Perhaps you can end this on Tuesday."

"I don't want to." Curtis knew he was whining and didn't care. It had taken him forever to get over Jasper's betrayal, and now he was supposed to talk to him again? The mere thought made him shiver.

"I know." Linda's voice was soothing. "But you want to get rid of him, don't you? This is the fastest way. Hear him out, in front of a witness, and tell him he can go to hell. If he keeps trying to make contact after that, I have something to work with."

"I guess you're right. Thank you, Linda."

"I'm always right, Curtis. Don't let that asshole bring you down. Darling, I'll see you tonight."

"Love you, baby."

The line went dead. Curtis and Patty stared at each other for a moment.

"What do you want me to do with those flowers?"

Curtis shrugged. "Whatever you want. You can take the chocolate as well. It's very good."

"Knowing what a creep that guy is, I'm not sure I should enjoy his chocolate. On the other hand, if he's really broke and went to the trouble of spending that much money on you, he'd probably be livid to find out I benefited from it."

"Yes, definitely. And since I seem to be meeting him tomorrow, I can rub it right in."

They shared a malicious smile. "Now for the fun of telling my new boyfriend that I'm meeting with my ex and not taking him with me."

Patty lifted a brow. Curtis sighed. "I like Andrew a lot, but I don't know him that well yet. I have no way of knowing if he'll be able to keep his cool around Jasper. Hell, I have trouble keeping my cool around Jasper! Plus, I want to get rid of him, and Martin makes his money being intimidating."

Patty whistled. "You're bringing out the big guns. Good idea."

"Yes, from a tactical viewpoint. From a relationship viewpoint, I'm probably digging my grave."

"If he can't understand your reasoning, he's not worth it."

"But the sex is so great!" Curtis winked.

"Great sex is not everything, believe me." Patty winked right back before she gathered the unwanted gifts from Jasper. Once she was out the door, Curtis picked up the phone to call Martin and Andrew. He wasn't looking forward to the second call.

CHAPTER 18

ANDREW HAD just finished restocking the macarons when his phone rang. He smiled when he saw it was Curtis. Their amazing first night together had given him enough energy to get through work despite the lack of sleep. Commuting was definitely off the table, no matter how great Curtis's bed and bathroom were.

"Hello, my sweet boy. How are you this fine late morning almost noon?"

Curtis chuckled through the line. "Somebody's in a great mood."

"You bet. I am, in fact, in such a wonderful mental state, nothing can get to me today. Not even the afternoon rush."

"Hold on to that thought." Curtis sounded very serious all of a sudden, which Andrew didn't like one bit.

"What's the matter, Curtis? Are you all right?"

The deep sigh coming from Curtis did nothing to ease Andrew's worries. "I'm fine. More or less. I got flowers and chocolate today. From Jasper."

Andrew had to grab the counter to keep from falling over in surprise. "I thought you told him to back off?" He knew he sounded accusing but couldn't help it. Curtis was his.

"I did. Unfortunately, he seems intent on meeting me to talk about his financial situation and how I can help him restore it to its former glory, or rather vastness."

"He still wants to borrow money from you?" Andrew almost choked on the words. "After everything he did?"

"I'm not sure if he wants to borrow the money. Knowing Jasper, he wants me to give it to him for old times' sake."

"Is he insane?"

"I wondered that myself, but I can assure you, he's not. Just very entitled and secure in his sense of self-importance."

Andrew grinned when he heard the diplomatic phrase. "In other words, an asshole."

"Yes." Curtis hesitated a moment. "The thing is, he has invited me to dinner tomorrow, and as much as it repulses me, my lawyer thinks it's a good idea to go and hear him out before I tell him to back off. According to her, sending flowers is not a punishable crime, whereas stalking me after I tell him in front of witnesses I want nothing to do with him will give her the leverage to take care of him."

Andrew wasn't an idiot. He could deduce from Curtis's tone that he wasn't about to ask him to be his witness. "You won't take me with you, am I right?"

Again a deep sigh. "I'm sorry, Andrew. My first instinct was to ask you, since you're my Dom and partner, but first of all, we don't know each other that well yet, certainly not well enough to expose you to the madness that is Jasper. Secondly, and no offense meant, I need somebody with me who Jasper knows and who scares the crap out of him. Martin makes a living being intimidating, and he doesn't like Jasper. More importantly, with him around, Jasper won't dare try anything funny—not that I think he would. His bark has always been a lot worse than his bite—if he ever bit. I'm fully aware how this all might look to you, and I swear, my life is usually very boring. What I want to say is, I'm not *not* taking you with me because I think you're incapable of handling the situation. Or because I don't see you as my Dom. To be honest, I'm afraid you're going to dump me because of all the drama that's following me around."

Andrew inhaled deeply. He was hurt by Curtis's decision; there was no denying it. Mostly because he already saw himself in a committed relationship with Curtis, where they supported each other. That didn't mean he couldn't understand Curtis's reasoning, and if he was completely honest, he didn't know if he would be able to control himself around Jasper. Assaulting the man wouldn't help Curtis in the least.

"I can't say I'm thrilled, Curtis. Though it does ease my mind that you're going with Martin. Things between us are moving along pretty fast, and after our fantastic scene last night, I'm determined to do everything to make our relationship permanent. You don't have to be afraid of me dumping you. Little bumps in the road are part of the journey, aren't they? Just promise to call me immediately when you're back home. I don't care about the hour."

"Thank you, Andrew." Curtis sounded so relieved, Andrew wanted to close his shop to race over to his boy and hold him in his arms until all his worries were gone.

"It's fine, Curtis. Everything is going to be fine. Do you want to come over tonight so you don't have to sleep alone?"

"I would love to, Andrew. But I have to work late tonight. I don't know when I'll be done. First, I have a conference call with my other galleries, and after that, Patty and I have an exhibition to plan. Are you free on Wednesday? I'm sure going to need you then."

"Of course I'm free for you, Curtis. Always. And call me tomorrow, when you're done dealing with Jasper. Or before, when you need to hear how incredible you are. And Curtis, I know it's early and everything, but I think I love you. In fact, I'm pretty sure I love you. With all my heart."

Now Curtis was giggling almost hysterically. "You're telling me this now, when I have no way of showing my appreciation."

"You can show me on Wednesday."

"Fine. This will help me through work today and the meeting with Jasper. Thank you. And for the record, Andrew, I love you too."

Andrew felt a silly smile tugging on his lips. "Good to know, boy. See you on Wednesday."

"See you. Bye, Master."

The line went dead. Andrew kept staring at his cell, drunk on his own confession and the fact that Curtis loved him back. He was so lost in his thoughts, he only realized he had a customer when Tim's voice resounded directly in his ear.

"What has that poor cell done to you that you keep staring at it like you want to devour it?"

Andrew flipped Tim off. "Nothing, Mister I'm-all-over-your-business. It just happens to be the medium through which I confessed my love to my boy."

Tim whistled. "You're moving fast."

"I'm too old to take it slow."

Tim raised a brow.

"Fine, Curtis might have told me something I wasn't too happy to hear, one thing led to another, and instead of having a fight with him, I told him I love him. Happy?"

"Not yet. I need to hear the entire story." Tim's eyes gleamed. Andrew knew by now how much his new friend loved juicy gossip, so he told him the whole story about Jasper and the dinner he wouldn't attend. He still wasn't entirely over the fact, something Tim picked up immediately.

"You're not happy."

"Would you be?"

Tim sighed. "Probably not. I get his reasoning, though."

"I do too. Doesn't make it easier to stomach that I can't be there for him. And it isn't even about me being the Dom and him being the sub in this case. I want to be there for the man I hope will be my permanent partner."

"I understand, man." Tim put his hand on Andrew's shoulder. "I think you can be there for him. Call him tomorrow, send him a text before he goes to that dinner. Show him he can rely on you."

"Thank you. I'm going to do just that. Now, why are you here? Not that I'm not happy to see you."

Tim grinned. "Actually, I was in the area on business and decided to get some much-needed sugar into my system." He looked pointedly at the macarons on display. With a roll of his eyes, Andrew took a plate and filled it with the sweets. Tim shoved the first in his mouth, chewed it with half-closed eyes and a happy groan.

"Man, you are a magician. They're delicious."

"Thank you."

Tim ate two more macarons before he started speaking again in a carefully nonchalant tone. "So you said Club Whisper was nice? The people were good?"

"Why, do you want to try it out after all? I'm telling you, Tim, it's an absolute dream, but how are you going to afford it? If I recall correctly, you said you worked from home. Not to offend you, but I don't think that earns you the bucks to get into Whisper."

Tim averted his gaze for a moment. "Uhm, that's not going to be a problem. Not really."

It took a moment for Andrew to understand what his friend was telling him. "You're loaded." His tone was flat. He didn't know what to think about this revelation. "When we first met, you said the people at Whisper weren't your crowd. You let me believe you were close to my financial standing. Why did you lie to me?"

Tim snatched another macaron and stared at it intently before he put it back on the plate. He looked uneasy when he met Andrew's gaze.

"I didn't lie. They aren't my crowd. I fare much better in biker bars, as you should have noticed by now. And I come from a poor background, just like you, so letting you believe we were equals regarding the money wasn't a lie per se." Tim raised his hands. "Semantics, I know. What I want to say is, just like you, I've worked my way out of it. Maybe a bit farther up than you, but those are details. Can you imagine me at any fancy gatherings like that art thing you attended with your boy? I kept away from Whisper because I didn't want to be scrutinized by people for who money is just something you have. Plus, I thought we would be looking for a club together, so I didn't need Whisper. Now you have a boy from there and you said it wasn't that bad. You talked to Richard Miller without even realizing who he was. That speech I gave you about rich people not all being bad? I should have listened to it as well."

Andrew looked at his friend, who put the next macaron in his mouth, looking slightly guilty. He put on his sternest Dom expression, making Tim flinch. "Are you telling me you want to ride on my coattails?" He let his grim gaze linger for a moment before he started grinning.

Tim's head came up sharply. Hastily he swallowed his macaron, stabbing Andrew with his forefinger at the same time. "You bastard!" he yelled as soon as his mouth was empty. "I thought you were going to throw me out! Don't play games like that. I'm not sure my poor heart can take it." Tim put his right hand in the general vicinity of his heart.

"You deserved that. Why didn't you tell me?"

"I don't like to brag. And I don't feel comfortable talking about money. And then you told me your views about the rich, which didn't encourage me to share, if you get my meaning."

"I do. Sorry about that. I'm still learning. Though I have to admit, I don't feel intimidated by you. You're more like an equal to me." Andrew furrowed his brows. "I'd still like to know how you can get rich working from home. That sounds like one of those cheap ads on the web, *How to Make Five Thousands Dollars a Week*!"

Tim grinned. "Well, it was a combination of extraordinary skill and some luck. I started out as a freelance accountant and since I'm very good at my job, I soon had some big clients. Some of the companies I work for do belong to Richard Miller, by the way. As for the stroke of luck, I played around with investing for a bit, and what can I say, right place, right time. A start-up I cofinanced with a bunch of other people shot through the roof, and now it's just a matter of seeing to it that the money keeps growing. I also still do the accounting, but that's for fun."

"Wow." Andrew blinked a few times, trying to match what he had just learned with the man he saw standing in front of him. Then he suddenly shook his head. "Sorry, I just can't see you as some rich snob with a golden spoon up his ass. You're more the Bad Boy with no money but lots of attitude."

Tim barked out a laugh. "As compliments go, I've had worse. Thank you. Now please give me another plate of the same. They're delicious."

Andrew lifted a brow. "You know I'm going to charge you full now that I know you can easily afford it, don't you?"

The broad grin on Tim's face told Andrew their friendship still stood on the same firm footing as in the beginning. "Why do you think that is? Because I freeload whenever I get the chance. The devil's in the details, and saving pennies can make you rich."

"Not on my tab, my friend. Forget it."

They both started laughing and couldn't stop until the next customer came in.

CHAPTER 19

CURTIS TOOK one more look at the text from Andrew while Martin tried to maneuver his monstrosity of a car into a parking space. To the background of muttered curses, he reread the words for the hundredth time. *Good luck tonight, darling. I'm thinking of you. Love, Andrew.* Curtis sighed. They had talked on the phone for over an hour before Martin came to pick him up, and he already missed his Dom. His partner. Tonight couldn't be over soon enough.

"Hey, Curtis, are you done daydreaming?" Martin had finally managed to park the car.

"Yes, of course. Sorry, Martin."

"Don't mention it. This is rather unpleasant business."

Curtis exited the car, head held high. "Let's get it over with."

They entered the restaurant where an impeccably dressed hostess in a black pencil skirt, a crisp white blouse, and killer stilettos greeted them with a cheerful smile. "Good evening, sirs. Do you have a reservation?"

Curtis nodded. "We're here with Jasper O'Malley."

She looked at her list for the evening, brows furrowed. "I'm sorry, sir, there is no reservation in that name."

"Could it be he was only playing with you?" Martin sounded like he was going from annoyed to pissed off in the fast lane. Curtis shook his head.

"No. I got the impression he was rather desperate. He would know that asking me to come here and then not showing would be the single dumbest thing to do. Unless…." Curtis smiled at the hostess. "Unless the reservation was made for Curtis Morris."

She checked the list again. "Yes, here you are. A place for two." She looked between Martin and him. "If the reservation was made for two, who is the gentleman I have already seated there?"

"That would be the asshole who made the reservation in Curtis's name." She gasped at Martin's rudeness, but for once Curtis didn't feel the need to smooth things over. Jasper's gall made him speechless.

"Can you show us to the table, please?" Martin seemed to remember his manners, though it always astounded Curtis how much Martin could get away with in public simply because he was built like a tank and had the aura of a mobster.

"Of course. Please follow me, sirs." She led the way to a secluded part of the restaurant where the tables were shielded by wrought-iron room dividers that were covered in thick brocade of different earth tones. Since Curtis could easily see over the head of their hostess, he had the pure joy of watching Jasper's face going from carefully crafted friendliness to utter shock to a mask of cold politeness when he realized Curtis hadn't come alone.

"Jasper, what a pleasure to meet you." Curtis had no problem laying it on thick. Thankfully, this was America, where his overly cheerful tone would be interpreted as enthusiasm, not as the scolding sarcasm it was meant to be. Jasper flinched. He was aware of all the things Curtis hadn't said out loud.

"What's he doing here? This was meant to be a private meeting, Curtis." Obviously, his shock wasn't too deep.

"After I got your charming invitation, I consulted my lawyer. She advised me to bring a witness to our meeting, just to be on the safe side. Patty says thank you for the chocolate, by the way. I'm sure you remember Martin Carmichael from Whisper?"

Curtis took a step aside to let Martin stand next to him. Martin extended his hand, and out of habit, Jasper took it. If the way he winced was anything to go by, Martin had given him the pissing contest handshake. Jasper could count himself lucky that his hand wasn't broken.

"Hello, Jasper. I can't say it's nice seeing you again." Martin let go of Jasper's hand and pulled out a chair for Curtis while the hostess watched in horrified fascination.

"Could you please bring us an additional place setting?" Curtis knew he was being slightly rude reminding her of her duties like this, but he wanted to get on with this unpleasantness. Once the hostess was gone, he glared at Jasper.

"Thank you for making the reservation in my name, by the way."

Jasper just shrugged. "How else should I have gotten a table on such short notice? Your name carries weight around here, and I wanted the setting to be special."

Curtis sighed. He couldn't even be angry at Jasper for this, because he knew his former lover would never understand how it could be rude to use someone else's name to get a reservation. The hostess came back with an additional table setting and a waiter who brought them the menus and took their drink orders. They spent the time until they got the drinks and could place their food orders in oppressive silence, only interrupted when Martin asked Curtis if he wanted to share a bottle of wine. Once they could be sure they wouldn't be interrupted anytime soon, Curtis cleared his throat. Martin was holding back, as they had decided when they'd talked about how to handle the situation.

"What do you want, Jasper?" Though Curtis already knew. Lydia had called him at lunch, confirming that Jasper was as broke as could be. Apparently he had made some bad investment choices over the years. Combined with a lifestyle that always cost more than he could actually afford, his money had evaporated like spittle on a hot stone.

"If you've talked to your lawyer, you must already know. I'm not stupid, Curtis. I know you told her to do some digging." Jasper sounded more hostile than was good for somebody in his position, but Curtis kept that thought to himself.

"I do know. And it doesn't take a genius to figure out you want money from me, especially since you already dropped some none-too-subtle hints about it." It had been more a case of throwing it directly in Curtis's face, but who was he to be indignant because of it? "What makes me wonder is why you're coming to me. Surely there are other people who would be more inclined to acquiesce to your—wishes." Curtis was deliberately trying to sound condescending and it worked. He wasn't a vindictive man by nature, but Jasper's impertinence rubbed him the wrong way, especially after their ugly breakup.

Jasper's gaze lingered on Martin for a moment before he looked back at Curtis. "None of them wanted to help me. Not even my parents. They said I should learn my lesson."

The indignant tone had Curtis suppressing a smile. Jasper's parents were already over seventy and as miserly as the Scots were often portrayed, even though they were Irish. He could imagine how they had reacted to their son losing so much money. They probably went straight to the family lawyer to change their wills.

"Pity. What about your lover? Couldn't he help you out?"

Jasper's face darkened. "He didn't have money of his own, and he dumped me the moment he realized I was broke. Took all his expensive gifts and ran to another Dom."

Curtis didn't know what to say. On the one hand, he felt a certain satisfaction that Jasper had experienced firsthand what he had done to Curtis. On the other hand, Curtis knew how much it hurt to be dumped and he didn't wish that pain on anybody, not even Jasper.

"I'm sorry to hear that" was all he could come up with.

Jasper shrugged. "It's not like he was the greatest lay I ever had. Anyway, as you can see, I'm in a bit of a pinch and I would appreciate you helping me out."

The waiter chose this moment to bring them their food, which gave Curtis some time to gather his thoughts and formulate his answer. He was still surprised that Jasper hadn't protested more firmly against Martin's presence. Jasper had to be desperate to be so untypically compliant. The man who had once been his Dom would have had no qualms about making a scene in public, knowing Curtis hated nothing more than that. He was either more intimidated by Martin than he let on or even worse off than Curtis had originally assumed. Curtis took a moment to enjoy a few bites of his delicious steak before he spoke again. He glanced at Martin, who seemed completely engrossed in his food. His personal bodyguard and witness for the evening was listening intently, though.

"I'm going to be completely honest, Jasper. I have no idea why you think I would help you. It's not like I have the amount of money you probably need lying around. Most of it is bound in different investments and real estate. And even if I had it and would feel inclined to give it to you, how do you plan on paying me back? You've already proven you can't handle big sums. Why should things be different the second time around?"

For a moment Jasper glared at him. Then his shoulders slumped. "You could sign over your trust fund to me. I know it's not tied up in anything, and the steady money coming from it could help me get back on my feet. It's not like you need it anyway. You have more than enough."

"As did you. My parents set this trust up to secure me for life, not for an ex who didn't even have the decency to end our relationship face-to-face. The answer is no, Jasper. I'm not going to lend you money in any form or amount, and I most certainly won't sign my trust over to you. That idea is beyond ridiculous, which I think you know. I also ask you to never contact me again after tonight." Curtis hesitated a moment. "As a courtesy to your precarious financial status, I'm going to cover the bill for dinner. That's it. That's all the money you're going to get from me."

"Curtis." Jasper had gone deathly pale, a pleading look in his eyes. "You can't do this. I need you. I need your money."

Seeing Jasper like this almost swayed Curtis. Even though the man had put him through hell, he was truly over him, and all he could feel for him was pity and a slight resentment because he had dragged him out here when he could have spent the night with his Dom. Curtis shook his head. Giving Jasper money would only bind them once more, something Curtis wanted to avoid at all costs.

"I'm truly sorry, Jasper. I am. But your parents are right. You are in this place because of your own bad choices. Accept the consequences. Go back to your parents. I'm sure what they have in store for you won't be nice, but they won't abandon you."

For a moment Jasper only stared at Curtis. Then his eyes narrowed to angry slits. "You on your damn high horse! The good, obedient son. What do you think your parents are going to say when they find out their son is a pervert who likes to get on his knees for another man?"

The words were spoken with so much venom, Curtis didn't know how to respond. He didn't have to.

"And we're done here." Martin's voice was as cold as ice. "You just threatened Curtis, who also happens to be an active member of Whisper. I'm sure I don't have to remind you of the NDAs you signed when you were a member. They are still in effect. Exposing Curtis means exposing the club. If I were you, I would think twice about crossing me and Richard. And since you wouldn't be able to pay the financial penalties, you'd end up in jail. Don't think for a second we wouldn't go so far."

Jasper gulped at these words. Like everybody else who had anything to do with Richard and Martin, he knew how ruthless these two could be. Curtis was glad they were on his side. He gestured the waiter to come over, asking for the bill and to wrap the rest of his steak. He had lost his appetite for the moment, but that didn't mean this delicious meat had to go to waste.

Jasper had gotten up. He threw his napkin on the table, his mouth twisted in an angry snarl. "This isn't over, Curtis. Not by a long shot."

With that, he left the restaurant in a hurry. Martin watched him retreat before he turned back to Curtis. "Wow. What a piece of work. Good thing I was here."

"Yes. Thank you. I'm sorry for the drama. I just don't get why he would think even for a minute he could get money from me. And my trust fund to boot!"

"He's desperate. Desperate and delusional. Not the best combination."

The waiter came with the bill and the wrapped food. Martin got his wallet out before Curtis could protest. "No back talk. This is my treat."

Curtis knew better than to argue. He bowed his head in thanks and waited for Martin to pay. They left the restaurant and went back to the car. As soon as they were seated and Martin started the process of getting out of the parking space, Curtis sent Andrew a text.

It's done.

Are you okay?

I guess.

Do you want to come over? Sleep in my arms? A heart emoji accompanied the question.

Gladly. Thank you. I'm on my way.

"Where should I drive you?" Martin looked at him with a knowing smile.

"Can you take me to Andrew? It's a bit of a detour for you, though."

"No problem. He lives above his shop, doesn't he? Collin told me."

Curtis nodded. "Yes. He has to get up early, so it comes in handy."

They drove in silence for some time. Finally, Martin said: "I'm happy for you, Curtis. You deserve a good man, a good Dom in your life, and Andrew seems to be both."

"Thank you, Martin. And thank you for coming with me tonight. You were a real help."

Martin snorted. "I didn't do much. Just sat there and listened to you handling the situation. Which was a new experience for me."

"I wouldn't have been so collected without you. Knowing I had a trained bodyguard in my corner gave me the reassurance I needed." Curtis winked.

"Don't make me tell your master you need a spanking, boy." Martin laughed. They talked a little about the next projects Collin had lined up and about the wedding. Martin was more than pleased that Curtis would be Collin's best man.

"He was so excited when you said yes. It means a lot to him, Curtis."

"It means a lot to me as well. It's nice to have such close friends."

Martin nodded and turned into the parking lot of Sweet Break. Curtis thanked him one more time for his help and for driving him here before he turned to the side entrance, where Andrew was already waiting for him.

ANDREW WATCHED with hungry eyes as his boy left the black Escalade currently parked in front of his back door. He caught a brief glimpse of Martin behind the wheel and thought the other Dom was nodding at him, but he was too focused on Curtis to react. His boy looked delicious in dark gray slacks, a lavender shirt, and those black leather loafers with the white stitching he had seen on him before. The thought that Curtis's ex had had the pleasure of seeing him like this had Andrew's hackles rising. Curtis was his, his alone. He reached out for his boy, drew him close to press a kiss on his mouth. The way Curtis was melting into his arms helped to mollify those unkind thoughts.

"Hello, boy. I've missed you."

Curtis looked up into his eyes, slightly panting.

"And I missed you, Master. Can we go inside?"

Andrew looked around to see Martin's Escalade was already gone. He took Curtis's hands in his to guide him upstairs. When they entered his apartment, he tensed for a moment, remembering how perfect Curtis's home was. He liked his place with the open-plan living/dining area/kitchen, the huge black sofa with the flat-screen TV, and the small white table with the four blue chairs where he usually took his meals. Before he'd moved to Miami, he had started painting the chairs, fully intending to turn the table blue as well; he just hadn't gotten around to it yet. Curtis looked around curiously, with a smile on his lips.

"It's very nice. Very much you."

Andrew raised a brow. "I'm not sure if this is a compliment."

"Believe me, it is, definitely."

Curtis was still staying close to him, as if he didn't want to break the skin contact. It worried Andrew, so he gently pulled Curtis to the sofa and made him sit down next to him. "Are you sure you're okay, boy? You seem—restless."

Curtis sighed, snuggled even closer, his head resting on Andrew's shoulder. "To be honest, I'm not sure what to make of this evening. I expected to feel something profound when meeting Jasper. I mean, that man has hurt me so deeply. After he dumped me, it took me almost two years to get over him. I finally realized that what hurt me so much wasn't the love we had lost, which was never the Shakespearian kind anyway, more a very pragmatic, typically British solution, but how he had done it. My pride was hurt worse than my heart. Once I realized that, it was easier for me to move on and seeing him today, I was surprised at how little I felt. There was no real anger or hatred, just a mild annoyance because he kept me from being with you. And after he told me how badly off he was, I pitied him a bit, but no more than you would any stranger with such a story. Seeing him didn't shake me to the core, like I thought, neither in a good nor in a bad way. I didn't feel triumphant or overly vindictive. All in all, I felt nothing. Which in part is thanks to you. We've only been together for a short time, but you still showed me how much more I can expect from a real Dom. That's nice."

Andrew blushed. He found he liked getting compliments from his boy. "Thank you. I still get the feeling you have a huge 'but' looming over your head."

Curtis started drawing circles on his chest. "There is a but. I'm a bit worried about my lack of reaction. Don't you think it's strange how detached I am?"

Andrew pressed a kiss on Curtis's head. "No, it's not. I think you're truly over him, just like you said, so there's no reason for you to have any lingering feelings for him. I'm aware that practically all TV series live off the opposite, but nobody can accuse TV of being overly realistic. You're through with Jasper, for which I'm grateful. Frees you up for me."

"Oh, I'm very free for you." Curtis chuckled, and Andrew could feel the tension bleeding out of his shoulders.

"Free enough to go snuggle up in bed? I do have to get up tomorrow morning."

"We can do more than snuggle. Just don't expect me to get up with you. Once was enough."

Andrew laughed. "I felt bad the entire drive here. You looked like death warmed over when you served me that tea."

"Yeah, yeah, go make fun of the poor old man who went all out of his way to accommodate his hot Dom."

They both laughed, and Andrew kissed Curtis. "I don't know about old—or poor, come to think of it—but I do know a very distinguished sub who's going to get a little spanking sometime soon." He drew back a little to look at Curtis's flushed cheeks and glazed eyes. It would have been tempting, hadn't he seen the dark circles under his eyes and the tired set of his mouth as well. This meeting with Jasper had shaken his boy more than he wanted to admit. "Not tonight, though. Tonight I'm going to undress you, put you in my bed, and snuggle the hell out of you. No back talk!" Andrew held up his hand when Curtis opened his mouth. "It's part of my job as your Dom to make sure you're well taken care of. You need rest, boy. Rest and love and caresses. I'm going to give you all."

For a moment Andrew thought Curtis would protest. He opened and closed his mouth like a fish out of water. Then he simply collapsed into Andrew's arms with a deep sigh.

"Thank you. Just thank you. You're the best."

With a relieved smile, Andrew guided his boy into his bedroom, where he helped him undress. The last time Curtis had been naked for him, it had been a highly sexual experience, and even though Andrew did feel an expectant twitching in his groin, taking care of his lover, his partner, took precedence over his need to have him. It was a strange, heady feeling, knowing that with Curtis, there were things more important than the fulfillment of sexual desires. He didn't just want to dominate Curtis, to hurt him to their mutual pleasure; he wanted to give him everything else as well. He wanted a life with him. Andrew knew this was big, too big to wrap his head around immediately. He would need time to think about this, to think about all the implications that came with this epiphany. Not now, though. Now he had a boy to pamper.

"Do you want to brush your teeth? Or go to the toilet before we go to sleep?"

Curtis chuckled in his arms. "Both. Do you have a spare toothbrush? I forgot to bring mine. Don't know why."

"Do not worry, sweet boy. As your Dom I am perfectly prepared. When I was at your house, I noticed you use an electric toothbrush, and I bought one that comes close to the performance you're used to without being actually, you know, electric."

"How on earth do I deserve you?"

"You must have done something incredibly kind in a previous life."

Again they laughed, shaking the last bits of tension they both still carried from this evening. Andrew handed Curtis his toothbrush as well as a towel and started to leave the bathroom, when Curtis stopped him.

"Master. Please, stay. We can get ready for bed together."

Andrew smiled. He already knew Curtis well enough to understand what he was offering. Strangely enough, for many people sharing the bathroom was more intimate than having sex or doing a scene. Curtis inviting him to stay was Curtis telling him he was willing to fully embrace the relationship they were building.

"It would be my pleasure."

Preparing for bed together, Andrew learned his sub liked to be thorough when it came to cleaning his teeth and that he preferred warm water to wash his face. He himself was too exhausted most nights to care about water temperature, and he wasn't sensitive to it either. It was good to find out such small things about his partner. This way he felt even more deeply connected to him than after their scene.

When they were both done, Andrew brought his boy back to his bedroom.

"Sorry, my bed isn't as big as yours, I'm afraid."

"As long as it has you in it, you won't see me complaining anytime soon."

Andrew kissed Curtis deeply after that, before he threw the covers back. "Come in."

Curtis did just that. With a deep, content sigh, he snuggled up to Andrew while he pulled the covers back over them.

"This is just what I needed. Thank you, Master."

"You're welcome, boy. Now sleep. I'm here."

CHAPTER 20

ANDREW WAS whistling a crooked tune while artfully stacking the blue macarons. His week had been splendid so far. After his draining meeting with Jasper, Curtis and he had spent the night cuddled close, simply enjoying each other's presence. Since then, Curtis had slept at his place every night. Now it was Friday, and they would head to Whisper in the evening, and after that he would sleep at Curtis's place. Tomorrow, Debbie and Mark would take care of Sweet Break, and if it worked out, which he had little doubt about, he would consider making it a fixture. It was nice having more than one day off every week. Debbie was a more than decent cook, and with the doughs prepared in advance, she shouldn't have any problems getting everything done. She also told him she was glad about the extra money, since she was planning something special for her and her husband's anniversary.

Yes, life was sweet at the moment and he couldn't wait to see his boy tonight. The door bell chimed and a customer walked in, making the hair on Andrew's nape stand up. This man was trouble, plain and simple. Because he was running a bakery/café, Andrew didn't meet as many troublesome customers as if he had a bar, but he had had his fair share of difficult patrons and recognized them immediately. The man moved with the air of somebody who owned the world, or at least thought he should. He was shorter than Andrew but a little broader; his red hair was thinning at the top, though still full at the sides. His sharp eyes scanned the room with obvious disdain before they settled on Andrew with open hatred.

"So you're Curtis's new toy." Jasper. Since they hadn't heard from him in the days after the dinner, Andrew had hoped he was gone for good. Such was his luck that the man had obviously decided to confront him instead of going back to Great Britain.

Andrew sighed. This looked as if it was going to be ugly, and he was just glad no customers were here.

"Yes, I'm Andrew, Curtis's Dom." He knew it was petty, rubbing this special part of their relationship in, but he couldn't help it. Even though Jasper and Curtis had parted ways long ago and Curtis had made it crystal clear what he thought about Jasper, an animalistic part of Andrew still wanted to stake his claim against this rival.

Jasper huffed. "For now. How long do you think Curtis will put up with your vulgar upbringing and low financial status? He's used to better."

Wow. Jasper didn't pull any punches. He was here to draw blood, figuratively speaking—at least Andrew hoped so, because the last thing he wanted or needed was a fight in his bakery.

"Like somebody who lost all his money?" It was a low blow. Very immature. It felt great. Especially when Jasper's eyes lit up in pure rage.

"That was just a stroke of bad luck. Curtis will understand as soon as you stop distracting him. I'm a much better match for him than you. You have to know that."

"Do I?" Andrew raised a brow, which Jasper seemed to interpret as an invitation to go on.

"Why do you think Curtis took Martin to that dinner with me? Because you don't belong, because he knew you wouldn't get the subtleties, and because he didn't trust you to not make a scene. The game is played differently in our circles, and seeing as you have no clue about it, you can never truly have his back."

Andrew grabbed the tongs for the macarons so hard, his knuckles turned white. Jasper spoke like a cheap imitation of a Bond villain, and Andrew knew the man was an entitled, self-important prick, a desperate prick to boot, but he still felt there was a kernel of truth to what he said.

Curtis hadn't taken him to that dinner because he had been afraid of his reaction. If Andrew was honest with himself, he had been afraid of his own reaction as well. And yes, they didn't move in the same social circles. But those were things he would contemplate later, when he had some peace and quiet. Now he had to get rid of a barking dog in his place of work. He put on his best sneer.

"Interesting, hearing this from you, of all people. According to Curtis, you're not running in his circles anymore." When Jasper flinched, Andrew knew he'd found gold. Without giving the man a chance to speak up, he went on. "Face it, Jasper. Curtis is mine now, and you've lost the only thing that might have driven him back to you—your social standing, which seems to be your only redeeming quality. You have nothing to offer him, and you know it."

Jasper opened and closed his mouth a few times before he finally spat out, "Neither do you, toy boy. Curtis will soon grow tired of your inaptitude, and then he'll dump you as soon as you fail to satisfy him in bed. Given how demanding and hard to please he is, I give you till the end of the year, tops. Mark my words when you're all alone again."

With that, Jasper turned on his heel and marched out of Sweet Break. Andrew's only consolation was that he looked a little deflated while doing so. Sighing, Andrew put the tongs down, stared mindlessly at the macarons in front of him. Jasper's words had reminded him of the differences between him and Curtis. Differences he thought he had gotten over. Given how much he was affected, he probably still had some unresolved issues—which he should work through, because he had no intention of ever letting go of Curtis. He was going to need time, though. Time on his own, to take a good, long look at himself and to be brutally honest. Perhaps it would even be a good idea to talk to a therapist if he couldn't figure out how to deal with his problems regarding social status.

Andrew looked at the clock. He and Curtis had planned to go to Whisper tonight to do a scene. A plan he would have to cancel. There was no way he could play with Curtis when his mind was still munching on their differences. Andrew hated himself when he picked up his phone and started dialing Curtis's number. He knew he was going to hurt him with this call, and not in the good way. But there was no way he would hurt his boy even more by doing a scene while he was not in his right headspace.

The phone rang twice before Curtis's happy voice greeted him.

"Hello, Andrew. To what do I owe this call?"

"Hello, Curtis. It's good to hear you. I have bad news, I'm afraid." There was no reason to dance around the subject. If he had to hurt his boy, he wouldn't draw it out unnecessarily.

"What kind of bad news? Is everything all right?" Worry was clear in Curtis's voice.

"Jasper came by Sweet Break today. He blabbed about how I'm not suitable to be your Dom and partner, how you're going to get tired of me and dump me."

"You believed him?" Andrew wasn't sure if it was a question or a statement. Somehow, it sounded a bit like both, and the hurt in Curtis's voice was like a knife to his gut.

"No. Yes. Maybe a bit. I know he was just trying to needle me, to make me insecure. It wasn't hard to look through him. He's angry and lashing out at anybody he can reach."

"But—I sense a but coming." The hurt was now infused with a dose of anger.

"Yes. What he said… there is a kernel of truth to it. Don't get me wrong, Curtis. I definitely have no problem with you being financially more potent than me—and yes, I did choose my words deliberately. What I do seem to have a problem with are the different social circles we're moving in and me potentially ruining something for you because I don't know how to act 'properly'. And yes, I just put in air quotes around 'properly' because I don't think not knowing which fork to use first during dinner should be a criteria of whether somebody is fit for certain company or not. Don't get me wrong, Curtis, *boy*. I want us to be together. I want you, more than I can say. But I also want our relationship to stand on solid ground so that we can grow it from a base of mutual trust. For that to happen, I need to get my shit together. I'm definitely not breaking up with you, Curtis. Do you hear me? I'm just asking you to give me some space to get my thoughts in order. Can you do that for me?" Andrew knew he sounded desperate. He was desperate. There was a long sigh at the other end of the line.

"How long?"

"Just a few days. I—I'll call you as soon as I've thought this through. I swear, Curtis."

"Yes. Yes, I know." Curtis sounded so defeated. So sad. Andrew wanted to tell him to come over so he could comfort him. He had to stay strong, though.

"I'm sorry, Curtis. I really am."

Andrew heard a dry laugh that ended in a snort. "Probably not as sorry as me. Bye, Andrew."

Curtis ended the call, and Andrew couldn't blame him for being so terse. Thanks to his insecurities, everything he had gained with Curtis was up in the air again. Andrew hated it. It also gave him the resolve to clear his head as quickly as possible.

CHAPTER 21

CURTIS STARED at his cell as if it had grown a pair of wings. He couldn't believe the rubbish Andrew had just uttered. Of course it sounded all mature and reasonable, which made Curtis even angrier. Why did the man have to be right in such a spectacularly wrong kind of way? There was no way he would be able to get over this on his own. Curtis needed his friends. After thinking about it shortly, he called Dean, who was the best at organizing things on short notice.

"Hello, Curtis! What's up, man?"

"Hi, Dean. I'm sorry to interrupt. Do you think you have time for me tonight? I could do with some cheering up."

"What happened? Do you need us all?" The cheer had dropped out of Dean's voice. Now he sounded all business.

"Andrew got a visit from Jasper, and now he needs time to think about our relationship. So yes, I do need you all. I feel like eating at least two cartons of ice cream and topping it off with lava cake and chocolate chip cookies." Curtis wasn't prone to whining. He was usually in control of his life and everything happening in it. After the last few days, though, he felt he had earned the right to fully sink into his very own pity party.

"Holy crap! I'm calling the others. Where are you right now?"

"I'm still at the gallery. I was thinking about driving home, though. Can you tell the others to come over?"

"I'm not sure that's a good idea, Curtis. You driving, I mean. Hold on a sec." Curtis heard ringing on the line. Dean was making a conference call.

"Dean? What is it?" Collin sounded a little confused.

"Hello, Collin. Is there a chance you can kick out Martin for the rest of the day? Curtis needs us, and I think it would be best to do this at your house where we can take care of him. He's on the line as well, by the way."

"Oh Curtis, whatever happened? No, don't tell me, I'm sure the others want to know as well and you don't want to rehash it a thousand times, even though we're only what, seven people, no, five, since you and Dean already know, but still, and of course you can come over. I'll just send Martin over to Richard, they can play with Emily and the cats and perhaps Dog wants to go with him, then we don't have to be careful where we put our food, and I just order something sweet, don't I?"

Curtis smiled despite his tumultuous emotions. Collin was simply the sweetest. "That's a great idea, Collin. I'll try to bring some ice cream."

"No, you don't. We'll take care of that." Dean sounded stern. "Collin, I'm hanging up on you now. I still have to call the others."

"Okay, Dean. Bye, Curtis. See you soon."

The line clicked, then started beeping again when Dean called their next friend. "Stay on the line for this, Curtis. I'm trying to reach Leeland."

After five rings, Leeland answered the phone. "Hi, guys, why are we conference calling?"

"Because Curtis's ex is an asshole, and his current boyfriend an idiot." Dean didn't bother sugarcoating things, for which Curtis was grateful.

"Ouch. What do you need, Curtis?" And that was the best thing about their group of friends. They all were willing to drop everything when one of them needed help.

"I want to drown my sorrows in sugar. Are you up for that?"

"Are you kidding me? I'm on my way. Where do we meet?"

"Actually, that's why we're conference-calling you, Leeland." Dean took over again. "You're closest to Curtis's gallery. Can you pick him up and drive to Collin's place? I don't think it's a good idea for Curtis to be driving at the moment."

"I'm not an emotional wreck, you know." Curtis liked the care, though.

"I know. Just let us take care of you like you deserve. I need to stretch my mother hen muscles a bit."

Both Leeland and Curtis chuckled. "No stretching needed, Dean. You're already in full-on mode," Leeland teased.

"Fine. Then you know better than to stop me. Curtis, Leeland is going to pick you up. I'm calling the others. We're going to cheer you right up."

Dean ended the call. Leeland stayed on to tell Curtis he would pick him up in forty minutes, which gave Curtis just enough time to wrap everything up for the day. When Leeland finally came, he was ready to consume his weight in sugar, just to escape the nagging worries and undercurrent of anger.

"HERE, TAKE another cookie. They make for an excellent spoon." Leeland handed Curtis the seventh chocolate chip cookie this evening, along with a freshly opened container of strawberry cheesecake ice cream. Seth was in Collin's kitchen, preparing hot chocolate for the entire group. They were all here, comforting him after he'd told them about Andrew's "suggestion." Peyton had offered to do something horrible to Andrew, though he hadn't gone into details, which was probably for the best. Seth came back from the kitchen with a tray and handed each of them a mug of steaming hot chocolate.

Curtis sighed and took a first sip before he shoved a cookie full of strawberry cheesecake ice cream into his mouth. The combination of hot and cold paired with practically pure sugar was the only thing that kept him from crying. He was more angry than sad, but tears were tears. "I can't tell you how sick and tired I am of being all mature and understanding all the time."

"Then stop it." Dean's voice was firm, his gaze steely. "I'd say you've shown your class more than enough. Now it's time to remind those two Doms who you are and what you're capable of. I'd say you go all high-society bitch on them, get your point across without leaving any room for doubt."

The others cheered, and even Collin waved his spoonful of ice cream around as if he wanted to stab somebody. Curtis smiled, deeply moved by their show of support.

"I guess I have no choice. If I leave it to Jasper and Andrew, this is going to turn into the world's worst soap ever." He closed his eyes for a moment, steeling himself for what he had to do. "First, I need to get rid of Jasper, which means finding out his current address."

"Uhm, about that." Dean smiled broadly, showing all his teeth like a shark. "It could be I heard where he's staying when Richard talked to Martin about that dinner Jasper invited you to."

Curtis lifted a brow. "Could be?"

Dean shrugged. "This seemed like something I wanted to stay on top of. Though I was thinking more along the lines of Leeland and me going there, not you. I wanted it to be a nice surprise for you." He pouted.

Curtis abandoned his ice cream to hug Dean tightly. "Thank you. Thank you very much. But I think I have to do this on my own."

Dean nodded. "I figured as much. Worry not. We're going to watch your ice cream for you."

"So kind of you, my noble friend." They both snickered.

"Personal empowerment aside, I'm going with you." Leeland's tone left no room for arguments, for which Curtis was grateful. Having the MMA fighter by his side was a huge relief.

"Thank you, Leeland. Shall we go?"

Leeland stole one more spoonful of his macadamia nut brittle ice cream before he handed it to Peyton. "Let's do this."

Each of the men gave Curtis a hug and some encouraging words, Peyton's being the most aggressive—"Destroy that asshole and feed his bleeding carcass to the vultures!"—and Collin's the sweetest—"Don't let him get to you, because he's totally not worth it, and once you're done with him, you can stash the memory in one of those rooms you never enter because there's nothing in there worth the trouble."

"You're such a doll, Collin. Don't worry, everything will be fine." Curtis pressed a kiss on his young friend's forehead.

"Oh, I can't not worry about you, Curtis, because you're family to me, but we're all going to wait here and eat the ice cream and watch *Baywatch* because right now we need something light and funny, and you have to tell us the moment you're done, because then we can celebrate, promise?"

"I promise, Collin."

Curtis followed Leeland outside to his Volvo, Dean coming along to give them Jasper's current location. It was a rather cheap motel, something Jasper would have never set foot in when he still had his money. Knowing his snobbish ex had to sleep in a place he probably viewed as a rat-infested shithole made Curtis's steps lighter than it should. Being vindictive was not nice, but it sure felt good.

Leeland started the car as soon as they both had their seat belts securely fastened. "How do you want to do this? Shall I smack him around a bit, just to get his attention?" Leeland sounded more aggressive than usual. Curtis eyed him from the side.

"If possible, I'd like to try and talk some sense into him first. When he doesn't listen, I'm open to more, uh, hands-on measures." He hesitated a moment. "You seem to take this almost personally. Don't get me wrong—I love your support, and I'm more than grateful. I just get the feeling there's more to this?"

Leeland sighed. "You're right. I'm angry on your behalf, of course. I hate irresponsible Doms who hurt their subs out of sheer incompetence."

"You think that's what Andrew's doing? Or do you think another Dom is doing this to someone else you care about, and now you're mixing both situations up?"

Curtis knew he had hit a nerve when Leeland's shoulders slumped. "I actually think Andrew should take a refresher course in 'Being a Suitable Dom 101,' but from everything you told us, he's at least trying to do his best. With Master Garrett, I'm not so sure."

Ah, so that was the problem. Leeland had been chewing on Emilio's relationship with Garrett Kiernan since before he went pro for one year in the UFC. Now he seemed ready to talk about it, which was progress and would keep Curtis from worrying about the impending meeting with Jasper.

"What do you think the problem is? Emilio seems to be thriving."

"On first glance, yes. And every time I ask him, he assures me he only does things he wants to do. Still…."

"Do you think Garrett is abusive?" That would be Curtis's main concern.

"What? No? At least not deliberately." Leeland sighed, set the blinker to turn left. "Which is my problem in a nutshell. I think there is some kind of abuse going on. Call it a hunch. A gut feeling. I'm also pretty sure neither Garrett nor Emilio are aware of it. I mean, Garrett is Mister One Hundred Percent when it comes to consent. Given how he likes to play, he has to be. No, I think there is something deeper going on, and I just can't put my finger on it and it drives me nuts because I want to protect Emilio."

Curtis nodded. He could see where Leeland was coming from. "Now that you mention it, Emilio does seem a bit strange sometimes. I've never thought much of it, though. Could it have to do with his family?"

They both knew Emilio's family had been abusive, even before they kicked him out when he was barely fifteen. Emilio didn't like talking about that time in his life, understandably so, and as far as Curtis knew, he had never had any kind of counseling.

"Could be. He never had it easy." Leeland turned right this time, into the parking lot of the motel. "The problem is, he doesn't want to talk. Every time I try to hint at it, he assures me everything's fine and that he would tell me if he needed help. I know I should let this go. It's just.... He's one of us, you know?"

"I know. And I promise I'll help you any way I can. As soon as I'm done with my own problems."

Curtis looked darkly at the motel. Leeland parked the car, killed the engine. "You can do this, Curtis. I have no doubt."

"Thank you, Leeland. Let's go."

They exited the car and went into the lobby. A teenage girl was playing receptionist, though her attitude would have had her kicked out in any decent hotel. She didn't even pretend to be interested in who they were or why they wanted to know Jasper's room number. She just gave them the information including directions before she went back to playing *Candy Crush* on her cell.

"That was kind of anticlimactic. I thought we would have to at least bribe her into telling us his room number." Leeland sounded disappointed.

"You, my friend, are watching too many bad cop series. And there's going to be enough drama once I confront Jasper."

"Sorry." Leeland didn't sound sorry. "I'm just trying to get into the right headspace."

"We're not going to torture him gang style."

"You're taking the fun out of this. All the fun."

Curtis started chuckling, but it died on his lips when they reached Jasper's room. It was time to get rid of the weeds in his life, metaphorically speaking. He lifted his hand and knocked twice in short succession.

"Who's there?" Jasper sounded anxious and tired.

"Jasper, it's me, Curtis. Can I come in?"

"Curtis?" Something thudded on the other side of the door, followed by hasty footsteps. Then the door opened so violently, the hinges squeaked in protest. Jasper looked terrible. His hair was a mess, his eyes bloodshot and puffy, his shirt wrinkled, and Curtis spotted stains on his slacks. He was barefoot, and the stale odor of cheap alcohol hung in the air.

"It's really you. Come in." Jasper must have overlooked Leeland, because his eyes widened when he entered the room on Curtis's heels. "Who's that?"

"Jasper, this is Leeland, a friend of mine. He's here to make sure our meeting stays civilized."

"Yeah. If you want to get uncivilized, that's when I step in. Believe me, you won't like it." Leeland made his knuckles pop. Jasper stumbled back a few steps, the threat not lost on him. While Curtis admired the beautiful contrast of Leeland's slender body and aggressive aura, Jasper was apparently oblivious to the parallels.

"Leave me alone! I haven't done anything wrong."

Curtis shook his head. "See, this is where you *are* wrong, Jasper. Why did you go to Andrew and confront him with your elitist tosh? What did you hope for? I thought I was crystal clear when we met for dinner."

Jasper glanced nervously at Leeland, who was stretching his arms in preparation of a fight Curtis hoped wouldn't come. "I was angry, Curtis. Furious. Why did you leave me hanging like that? Have you any idea how difficult all this is for me? I mean, look around at what kind of dump I have to stay in these days. Nobody would give me the time of day, not my former friends, no business associates, certainly no subs. You have the power to make all this unpleasantness go away, yet you act like a stubborn mule. I figured it had to be that gold digger you now call Master. He probably doesn't want to share the riches."

Curtis shook his head. "Do you even realize how bigoted that sounds—you calling Andrew a gold digger? So far, he hasn't asked for a single cent, while you expect me to hand over my trust fund to you."

"That's different and you know it! We're the same, from the same class. We have to stick together." The desperate tone in Jasper's voice was getting more aggressive with every minute.

"We don't. In case you haven't noticed, Jasper, we're in America. Theoretically, we're all equal. Which means I don't owe you anything, and you have to stand up for your mistakes. It's as easy as that."

Jasper's eyes narrowed. Curtis saw Leeland tensing in his periphery. "I am standing up for my mistakes. I'm trying to fix them, but you're being stubborn as all fuck. I'm losing my patience, Curtis."

That was it. Curtis was finally done playing nice. He fixed Jasper with a steely glare. "Fine. Since you don't seem to understand the severity of my displeasure with your behavior, let me spell it out for you. I want you to leave me and my Dom alone. Don't phone us, don't text, don't send smoke signals, and most importantly, don't show your face."

Curtis pinned Jasper with his gaze before he played his strongest card. "If you dare to come near us again, I will tell your mother the true reason for our breakup. When she finds out, you're going to wish Leeland would have gotten to you first."

As Curtis had hoped, Jasper blanched. Leeland threw him a quizzical look, which had Curtis mouthing "Later" before he focused on his ex again. Jasper looked as if he was going to keel over.

"You wouldn't dare!"

"Try me!"

Jasper must have seen something in his eyes, because his shoulders slumped. A broken sob spilled from his lips. "That's low, Curtis. Real low."

Curtis shrugged. "Pot, may I introduce you to kettle?"

The only answer he got was a cross between another sob and an angry snarl. Curtis lifted a brow, even though Jasper was still staring at the ground and couldn't see it.

"Do we have an understanding, Jasper?"

Jasper's glare told Curtis he'd won, and that satisfaction would keep him warm on many cold winter nights—should he ever decide to spend a winter in actual *winter*.

"Yes, you son of a bitch. I'm out of town. You won't see me again."

"Splendid. Goodbye, Jasper. This time, the pleasure was all mine." Curtis knew this last little dig was mean, but Dean had been right. Being immature had its perks. For one, his chest felt as if a boulder had been lifted from it. He went to the door, closely followed by Leeland, who didn't spare Jasper a second glance.

As soon as they left the motel, the girl at the reception counter not even noticing them going by, Leeland started with the questioning. "What was that about telling his mother?"

Curtis chuckled. He waited until Leeland had opened his car door and they both were seated inside. "Well, Jasper's parents are... old-fashioned. Deeply conservative and set in their ways. When Jasper came out to them, it was a huge shock. And since Jasper has always been a sneaky, scheming bastard, he waited with announcing his sexuality until he was in a stable relationship with me. His parents were less than thrilled about his 'ungodly tendencies,' but since he had obviously secured one of the most eligible bachelors within their social circle, they couldn't be too mad." Curtis winked.

Leeland snickered.

"Being snobbish does have its merits. Apparently being gay isn't a problem as long as it helps you climb the social ladder. Anyway, when he dumped me, his mother was devastated. So he told her it was because of all my work and that we couldn't maintain a relationship at the moment. I know this because Jasper's mother talked to my mother—at great length, I might add—who then told me everything and congratulated me for having gotten rid of this 'dead social weight,' as she likes to refer to Jasper's family."

Curtis could feel an evil smile blossoming on his face. "Now imagine what his mother would say if she knew how badly he screwed up in addition to losing all his money?"

Leeland burst out in laughter. "You, my friend, are the devil. I love it. Let's drive to Collin's place and tell the boys."

"Uhm, how about you tell the others? I've got the feeling I'm on a roll, and I have a Dom to chastise and then hopefully secure for good."

"You're aiming for victory sex!" Leeland waggled his eyebrows.

"I so am." They looked at each other and started laughing again.

CHAPTER 22

CURTIS STOOD in front of the side door leading to Andrew's apartment, waiting for Andrew to answer. Perhaps it hadn't been the best idea to tell Leeland to leave right away without checking first if Andrew was at home. Curtis blamed the adrenaline from his confrontation with Jasper still coursing through his veins. It somehow seemed to interfere with his higher brain functions, and made him act on a more primal level. He lifted his hand to ring again when the door was suddenly yanked open. Andrew stared at him, his eyes almost comically wide with surprise.

"Curtis, what are you doing here?"

"Setting you straight. Putting my life back in order. Basking in your presence. You can choose one. May I come in?"

Curtis could tell Andrew was overwhelmed by his brusque behavior. He did step aside, though, to let him in.

"Uhm—didn't we agree to take a short break?"

"No, we didn't. *You* told me you wanted one for reasons that are, at least on the surface, valid, but I never agreed. And you refused to hear me out, for reasons I don't understand, since I thought we were partners in this relationship."

A faint pink crept into Andrew's cheeks while he averted his gaze. "I'm sorry. I may have overreacted a bit." Andrew led the way upstairs into his cozy apartment, where he gestured for Curtis to sit on the couch while he took a chair. Seeing his Dom so insecure pulled on Curtis's heartstrings.

"Can we talk about it?"

Andrew sighed. "Yes. Definitely. We have to talk about it. I just seem to fuck up wherever you are concerned, and I'm afraid of making a habit out of it."

"You didn't fuck up. If you had dumped me, that would have been a fuckup. Telling me you need time to think is fine. Though I would have appreciated being consulted on the nature of your concerns first."

A chuckle escaped Andrew. "That would have been the polite thing to do, wouldn't it? I'm sorry. Jasper just caught me completely on the wrong foot. Even though I know he's an idiot."

"An idiot you don't have to worry about anymore. I just visited him, and he's going to leave town. Even the States, if he knows what's good for him." Curtis watched as Andrew's eyes went wide.

"How did you do that?"

"I may have decided to take a really low blow at him, something I'm not entirely proud of, even though the end definitely justifies the means. Seeing as he didn't show signs of leaving us alone, I embraced Dean's advice and let my inner high-society bitch off its leash." Curtis grinned, hoping Andrew understood his attempt at lightening the mood. His Dom's hearty laugh told him he'd been successful.

"Your inner high-society bitch. I like that. And remind me to never get on your bad side. You're a bit scary."

"Me? I'm just a devoted little sub."

Andrew arched a brow. "I don't know about little in any sense of the word, but devoted I can confirm."

"So are we good?" Curtis hated the vulnerability in his voice. He didn't want to show Andrew how much he was hoping for a positive answer, while at the same time he wanted to expose everything to him. It was a weird feeling, one he wanted to shake.

"No, we're not good." Curtis felt his heart plummeting through the floor. "We won't be good until I have shown you in great detail how incredibly sorry I am. This is all on me, Curtis. My own insecurities and shortcomings have made me a prime target for Jasper. I know we've already talked about it, but I still feel strange about the lines of our roles being so blurred. Not bad strange, or break it off strange, just—strange."

Curtis nodded. He fully understood where Andrew was coming from, and he was more than grateful that his Dom was willing to work through his issues instead of just writing Curtis off, which would have been the easy thing to do.

"See it like this, Andrew. Yes, I already have all the material things a Dom might feel the need to provide for his sub, and you *are* self-reliant, which frees us both up to explore our relationship on every possible level without either of us having to fear exploiting the other. All I need to be happy is for my Dom to stay by my side and accept me the way I am—warts and all, just like I'll do with you."

"Neither of us have warts."

"All the better, don't you think?"

Andrew smiled. "I love you, Curtis. So much. I only want what's best for you."

Curtis looked his Dom in the eye. "Do you trust me to know what's best for me?"

"Yes. Of course."

"Then everything's fine, because it's you. You make me happy."

Curtis said the words with all his heart, willing Andrew to understand just how much he meant to him. And Andrew finally got it. He took Curtis's face in his hands, stared at him as if he was seeing him for the first time.

"I'm sorry, Curtis. I get it now. I promise you, from now on, I'll be there for you. Always."

He leaned in to kiss Curtis, and it was the sweetest, best kiss Curtis ever had—because it came from a place of mutual respect and absolute devotion.

"I want to take you to bed, darling. I'm going to make love to you like you deserve it. I'm going to worship you like the treasure you are. And tomorrow, we can go to Whisper and have that scene I've been planning for us."

Andrew held out his hand and Curtis took it with a smile, knowing this was his future, the one he had fought for and won.

CHAPTER 23

ANDREW STEPPED into the private room in Whisper where his boy was waiting for him, waiting for the scene they were going to do. Curtis was naked, as ordered by Andrew, kneeling on a soft cushion a little to the right of the door. After their little adventure in Curtis's kitchen, Andrew had insisted on his boy kneeling on something soft. Kneecaps and age didn't go well together, and he wanted his boy to enjoy this scene without the slightest distraction. Curtis hadn't moved when he'd come through the door; only a slight tensing of his lean back muscles had shown he was aware of Andrew. So perfect, so beautiful. His boy. Andrew gulped. The boy he had almost lost thanks to his own stupidity. He was insanely glad Curtis had come the day before to set him straight. He closed the door before he approached his perfect lover.

"Rise, boy. Let me see you."

Without taking his hands from where they were folded behind his head to showcase his biceps, Curtis rose gracefully, his long, gorgeous cock already filling. Andrew swallowed hard. Such a perfect piece of meat—one he would enjoy thoroughly tonight. He let the tips of his fingers travel along the curve of Curtis's spine, his asscheeks that started trembling under the featherlight touch.

"You're so beautiful, boy. Beautiful and mine."

"Master." Curtis sounded already breathless, his cock now fully erect. Andrew loved that, loved that Curtis was into him enough to get aroused just by the prospect of carnal activities. Before they could get fully started, though, he had a few things to say. Andrew embraced Curtis from behind, his hands resting just above the base of Curtis's cock, teasing, petting. His own breathing became a bit labored from the unfamiliar pressure in his ass, which had him wondering how long he would be able to last. He licked along Curtis's ear shell, breathed into his ear, enjoyed the soft gasp he got.

"Soon, love, we start soon. But I have to tell you something first, my precious boy. Something I haven't dared tell anybody before you. First, I want to thank you for not giving up on me, for giving me a second chance—or is it the third by now? I can't tell you how glad I am you found it in your heart to keep me. Since I met you, I've learned more about myself than in the last ten years combined. I'm not going to lie to you, it was hard, facing my fears and insecurities and preconceived ideas. Apparently it's harder to change things you've been hanging on to for most of your adult life. Though I never regretted it. Even that one day, where I was separated from you—somehow I always knew I would never give up on you. Because you are too precious to me, too perfect to let you slip through my fingers. I do admit it would have taken me longer to come back to you if you hadn't interfered. So thank you again for that."

He pressed a line of kisses on the side of Curtis's neck, listened to the moans his boy gave him.

"You're welcome, Master. Can we…?"

"Not yet, sweet boy. I haven't told you my secret fantasy yet—the one we're going to act out tonight. You know, I've always dreamed of being penetrated. Of using my boy as my own personal dildo. When I first had that fantasy, it scared me, because I'm a Dom, aren't I? We don't get penetrated. We *do* the penetrating. Over the years I found out how wrong that was, that there are plenty of Doms who enjoy using their subs that way. Still, the conditioning remained, and I just never found a sub I trusted enough to even think about broaching the subject. Until I met you. It's not just our insane sexual chemistry. I simply trust you with everything I am because I sincerely believe you were made for me, no matter how corny that sounds. And I want to show you how absolutely I want this thing between us to grow and flourish. What do you think? Can you be my dildo?"

Curtis groaned in his embrace. His arms were trembling, but he held the position like a good sub. "I'd love nothing more than to serve you in that way, Master. Though I think we might have to postpone this until another day. If I understand correctly, this would be your first time and that can be—difficult, as you well know."

"I do. Which is why I've been wearing a plug the entire day."

The whimper coming from Curtis had Andrew's cock leaking like a broken faucet. "When did you put that in? I would have *loved* to see that!"

Andrew hadn't known Curtis could sound so whiney. "Remember when you were groaning obscenely over those éclairs I fed you for breakfast? That's when."

"You distracted me with baked goods!" Curtis was clearly trying for indignant and failing.

"Always works with you, darling. Anyway, I think I'm definitely ready to receive you, especially if there's some rimming beforehand."

"You're killing me, Master."

"That's the plan, sweet boy. Now come on, I want you on your back on the spanking bench. I asked the staff to put a cushioned one in here, since you're going to be on it for some time."

Curtis shuddered in his arms but let himself be led to the bench. It was at exactly the right height for Andrew to position himself over either Curtis's mouth or cock to take his pleasure without turning it into a strenuous workout for his thigh muscles. He helped Curtis lie down and get comfortable before he grabbed his ankles to bring his feet to the ground.

"Is this okay, boy? Nothing hurts?"

"It's fine, Master. Everything feels good."

"I'm going to tie your legs to the bench, boy. I would love seeing you struggle to keep your balance while I'm fucking myself on your cock, but this is a first for both of us, and I don't want it cut short because we fell off the bench."

Curtis started chuckling, which had his cock bouncing merrily on his belly. "Sorry, Master. The visual was just too good."

"It's fine, boy. I can relate." Andrew started securing Curtis's legs with broad leather straps at his ankles and calves. When he was done, he grabbed the leather cock ring he planned on using on his boy. Staring at Curtis like this, naked and bound, waiting to be used in whatever way Andrew wanted, had his cock straining against his leathers. After a short internal debate, Andrew decided to strip first, to relieve some of the pressure on his poor shaft before binding Curtis. His chest was already bare, so all he had to get rid of were his leather boots and the trousers. Curtis watched with narrowed eyes when his cock sprang free of its confines, pointing directly at Curtis's mouth.

That pink tongue licking over those plush lips almost put a serious delay on their scene. Andrew managed to pull himself together. He tossed his trousers in the general direction of the bed, then placed the leather cock ring on Curtis's belly, right under his navel to tease his boy. Curtis was breathing heavily, his chest flushed in a lovely shade of red, his eyes glued to the ring that would go around his cock.

"Master?"

"Yes, darling?"

"Can I… can I see it? The plug, I mean?"

Andrew smiled. "Before or after I put the ring on you?"

Curtis groaned. "After. I want to be as full as possible for you."

"My perfect boy." Andrew bent down to give Curtis a deep kiss before he turned around. He bent slightly, put his hands on his asscheeks, and exposed his hole. His plugged hole. It felt strange, but in a good way. Andrew had anticipated being at least a bit shy or hesitant, not with Curtis, though. It was as if Curtis's presence alone put all his insecurities to rest.

"Master. You're beautiful. I want to serve you." It sounded so breathless, so eager. Andrew straightened and turned around.

"Soon, boy. First, though, we need to bind that sweet cock of yours."

Andrew made quick work of slinging the strap of leather around the base of Curtis's shaft and balls, securing it so that it was just this side of painful. "Is it okay, boy? Not too tight?"

"Perfect, Master."

"Wonderful. Now let me get that plug out so you can take care of my hole."

The moan he got for that was porn film worthy. Andrew made sure to pull the plug out at an angle that would allow Curtis to see every last tiny detail. When he cleaned the remaining lube with a wet wipe—because nothing tasted worse than lube, no matter what it said on the package—he made a big show of it, wanting his boy to know exactly what was coming. When he turned around again, Curtis's pupils were blown so wide, they had swallowed the irises almost completely. There was a small puddle of precum on his belly, with a thin thread back to his cockhead, which had already turned an angry red. Somebody was eager. Andrew grinned. Somebody was not alone in that sentiment.

He leaned down to place another kiss on Curtis's mouth. "Ready to eat me out, boy?"

"Yes, Master. Whatever you wish."

"Good boy." Andrew swung his right leg over the bench and Curtis, positioning his ass right over Curtis's mouth. He lowered himself slowly, until he felt Curtis's nose against his crack.

"You can use your hands to hold me open, boy. That way, you can also control my weight. If I become too heavy, just shove me up."

"Yes, Master. Thank you."

"Always, boy."

Curtis raised his hands and Andrew planted his on both sides of Curtis's hips. He felt the warmth of Curtis's palms massaging his cheeks for a moment before the grip tightened and his boy spread him open. There was a tentative lick, as if Curtis wanted to test the waters before he dove in fully. Andrew learned quickly that his boy was a connoisseur who took his time getting acquainted with Andrew's most private parts. Curtis started with long, sure strokes from his balls to his hole, again and again, until Andrew heard himself groaning from pleasure. When the tip of Curtis's tongue breached his rim for the first time, he thought he was going to pass out. For a moment he considered giving Curtis a blow job, edging his boy a bit to distract himself from the pleasure building inside him, but he decided against it. First, in his current state he wasn't sure if he'd be able to determine when it got too much for Curtis, and second, this was his first time being rimmed, his first time using his sub like he'd been dreaming for years. He wanted the full experience, and he knew Curtis didn't mind being used. Not when it was for Andrew's pleasure. So he enjoyed the stabbing and licking and gentle bites in, on, and around his hole until he knew he wouldn't be able to hold it in anymore. He lifted his hips, pulling away from Curtis's heavenly mouth. The disappointed whine from his boy made his cock jerk wildly.

Andrew stepped away from Curtis for a moment to grab the lube. "Do you want to watch, boy?"

Curtis whimpered. His lips were swollen and red, his hair a tousled mess. Gorgeous. Andrew squirted a generous amount of lube on his fingers, bent over in Curtis's direct line of sight, and started applying the cool gel. Even though he had stretched himself the entire day, he was surprised how easily he could slip three fingers in. Curtis's tongue had worked wonders. He made sure the lube was well spread before he took the condom he had already prepared. Rolling it onto Curtis's rock-hard shaft was a joy, seeing the blissed-out look on his lover's face, knowing the thick meat would soon penetrate him, his boy giving him the pleasure he wanted and needed. As soon as the condom was rolled down, Andrew poured some more lube onto his palm, pumping his boy's cock a few times with it. Andrew wiped his hands clean on a towel he had put on the small table next to the spanking bench where he had also placed the lube, the plug, the condom, and the wet wipes.

"Ready to be ridden by me, boy?"

Curtis squirmed under him, licked his lips, fisted his hands. "Yes, Master."

"Don't forget, no coming before I tell you to. Though with the ring, you should have a hard time." Andrew grinned at his own pun.

"Yes, Master." Curtis didn't sound amused but rather desperate.

Slowly, savoring every second of it, Andrew lowered himself on Curtis's cock, held himself open with both hands, which did put a strain on his thighs, but he refused to do this with a crane. He wasn't that old yet, dammit. The cockhead bumped against his hole, which twitched in anticipation. Andrew took a deep breath, lowered himself farther, let gravity help. It felt great. Better than anything he would have dreamed of. Combined with Curtis's desperate moans, it was already among the top five sexual experiences Andrew had ever had. Sleeping with Curtis for the first time being number one. A slight burn started in his rim, reminding him that this was his first time, but it was more pleasurable than anything else. He stilled for a moment to get used to the stretch before he let himself sink down to the hilt. The leather from the cock ring tickled his asscheeks while he moved his hips around a bit to get comfortable. Curtis's deep moans only made the experience that much better, the feel of Curtis's hands on his thighs almost unbearably sweet.

"You're so beautiful, boy. So perfect. So deep inside me."

"Please, Master. I won't last even with the cock ring if you keep saying things like that."

"If you don't last, I have to punish you, boy. You know that."

"Not helping, Master." Curtis whimpered.

"No coming, boy." Andrew used his sternest Dom voice. "I want to enjoy my first ride with you."

"Yes, Master. For you."

"For me. For us. Forever." Andrew bent down to kiss Curtis, which did enjoyable things to his filled ass. He straightened again, determined to find out what else he had been missing all those years.

First he went up again, until Curtis's cock almost slipped out, then down again, reveling in how full he felt. He did that for quite some time, increasing the pace, enjoying the feeling in his ass as much as the groans spilling from his boy's lips. His thighs started to tremble from the strain, making his movements a bit shaky, which led to a twist of his hips that had him seeing stars. *Prostate* was all he could think before his body made the same movement again, all on its own. Andrew knew immediately he wouldn't last much longer. This was simply too good. He looked down on his boy, who was staring at him with wide eyes, clearly fighting for control himself. Andrew stilled for a moment to reach for the cock ring and open it. Then he started gyrating again, rubbing his prostate on Curtis's cockhead in a quick rhythm. All too soon he felt the tingling of his oncoming orgasm in his spine. He barely managed to shout, "Now, boy. Come now!" before his own seed shot from him in wild spurts. Curtis screamed his name, dug his fingers into Andrew's thighs, and arched his back, following him over the edge.

It took several minutes before Andrew got his breathing back under control. It was then he realized he was lying heavily on Curtis's upper body, most probably making it difficult for his boy to breathe. Groaning, he got upright, which caused an interesting sensation in his ass, where Curtis's cock was still buried.

"Wow, Master. That was… I don't have words for it."

"It was incredible. Amazing. Perfect. Thank you, boy. You made my first time something I will never forget."

"You never forget the first." A smug grin played around Curtis's lips. Andrew kissed it, drunk on orgasm and general happiness.

"I can't ever forget you, since I very much hope you'll also be my only one from here on out until you are also my last."

"You're so sweet. I love you, Master Andrew. With all my heart."

"And I love you, Curtis. More than anything."

He groaned. "I think it's time to get cleaned up. We're a mess."

"A true romantic, just how I like my men." Curtis giggled, then made a face. "It is a little sticky, though. Shower?"

"Definitely. And perhaps…." Andrew hesitated. "Perhaps we should get tested sooner than later. Next time we do this, I want to feel your cum inside me."

"It would be my pleasure." Curtis grinned. Andrew bent down to open the straps on his legs before helping him up.

They dealt with the condom and took the best shower ever, as far as Andrew was concerned.

EPILOGUE

"I'M SO nervous, Curtis. What if something goes wrong? What if Martin decides at the last minute he doesn't want me? These things happen, you know, all the time, and in millions of parallel universes, Martin does exactly that: he dumps me at the altar, washes his hands of me, and takes somebody else, though in millions of alternate universes, we never meet, or don't get together, or die before we even reach adulthood, or marry somebody else, or...." Collin had finally run out of breath, which gave Curtis the chance to pull his young friend into a firm hug. He felt the lean body tremble against his.

"It's fine, Collin. Martin is already waiting for you under the oak tree out in the garden, together with the officiant and all our friends. Isn't that so, Andrew?" Curtis looked at Andrew, who was on guard duty at the huge window of Collin and Martin's bedroom.

"Yes, Collin. In fact, I think Martin looks a bit anxious. Maybe it's time for you to get down there before he starts crying?"

Curtis knew Andrew had meant it as a joke, a way to distract Collin from his panic attack. His Dom had still a lot to learn.

"You think he starts crying? That's not right, Curtis. Nobody should cry at a wedding, unless it's a forced one, but we don't do those, and not this one, surely, and did you know it hasn't been that long that people married for money and status, not love, and sometimes they didn't even know their partners before the wedding, though I think that might have been better sometimes, like a surprise and all people like surprises, though when your surprise is the person you're going to spend the rest of your life with, then perhaps it's not so good, unless you met somebody you totally clicked with, like Martin and me and I really think we should be going now or I'm going to lose my mind."

"A wonderful idea, Collin." Curtis took Collin's hand to guide him out of the bedroom, down the stairs into the garden, where all their friends were waiting under the beautiful, minimalist decorations with paper lanterns in the colors of the rainbow, garlands made from silk flowers, because Collin didn't want to kill something living simply for aesthetic pleasure, and two rows of burning garden torches, through which Curtis led Collin toward the old oak tree on Martin's property, where Martin was already waiting with Richard as his best man, and the older lady who would be their officiant. The sun had almost completely set, the last deep red rays in perfect harmony with the flickering glow from the torches. Collin had wanted to have his wedding in the evening, when all the insects in the garden could be their orchestra. Curtis had to admit it was a charming idea, especially since the insects were definitely cooperating. It felt like a perfect evening outside after a long, leisurely day spent among friends. Emily joined them with Dog at her side. The guard dog was carrying a little basket with the rings in it, while Emily held a similar basket with little paper balls she and her friends in kindergarten had colored and squished.

When they reached Martin, he took Collin's hand with a smile, his eyes glinting suspiciously. Curtis took his position next to Collin. A quick glance assured him Andrew had followed them down and was now watching the proceedings from his seat next to Leeland and Jonathan. The officiant started talking about love and commitment, which transported Curtis back almost seven months, before he met Andrew and thought he was doomed to spend the rest of his life alone. So much had changed in those few months, and Curtis couldn't have been happier if he had scripted his love story himself. He and Andrew were growing closer every day, getting acquainted with each other's quirks and peculiarities, learning their bodies, their lives. They had found their rhythm, in the bedroom or out of it, and Curtis couldn't wait to get his Dom home tonight. Or perhaps tomorrow. Tonight, they would celebrate with their friends.

XENIA MELZER was born and raised in a small village in the South of Bavaria. As one of nature's true chocoholics, she's always in search of the perfect chocolate experience. So far, she's had about a dozen truly remarkable ones. Despite having been in close proximity to the mountains all her life, she has never understood why so many people think snow sports are fun. There are neither chocolate nor horses involved and it's cold by definition, so where's the sense? She does not like beer either and has never been to the Oktoberfest—no quality chocolate there.

Even though her mind is preoccupied with various stories most of the time, Xenia has managed to get through school and university with surprisingly good grades. Right after school she met her one true love who showed her that reality is capable of producing some truly amazing love stories itself.

While she was having her two children, she started writing down the most persistent stories in her head as a way of relieving mommy-related stress symptoms. As it turned out, the stress relief has now become a source of the same, albeit a positive one.

When she's not writing, she translates other authors' manuscripts to German, enjoys riding and running, spending time with her kids, and dancing with her husband.

Website: www.xeniamelzer.com
Email: info@xeniamelzer.com

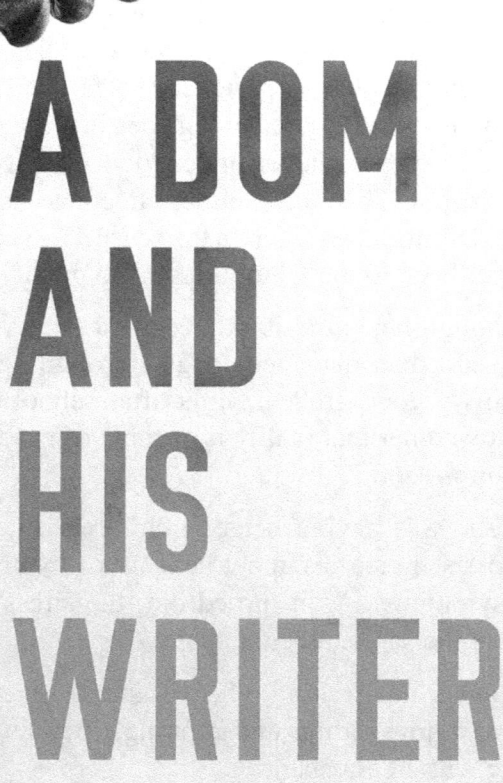

A DOM AND HIS WRITER

XENIA MELZER

CLUB WHISPER

A Club Whisper Novel

Life is perfect for Richard and Dean. Richard is a wealthy and successful businessman who also owns a BDSM club, and Dean is a best-selling author and sub to Richard. They're young, happy, and in love. The future is bright….

Until tragedy strikes and an accident claims Dean's beloved sister. Dean finds himself the guardian of a three-month-old infant, and soon he's trading in his leather fetish gear for diapers and drool bibs. But little Emily is all that remains of his family, so how can he abandon her?

It's not what Richard signed up for. As much as he tries to be supportive, he never wanted kids and misses having his partner to himself. Suddenly the life he imagined for them is gone, and he's not sure their relationship can survive the upheaval. But fate isn't through with Dean, and when misfortune strikes again, will he be able to turn to the man he loves? A final crisis will determine if they can pull together as a family or must face facts and part ways.

www.dreamspinnerpress.com

A DOM AND HIS ARTIST

XENIA MELZER

CLUB WHISPER

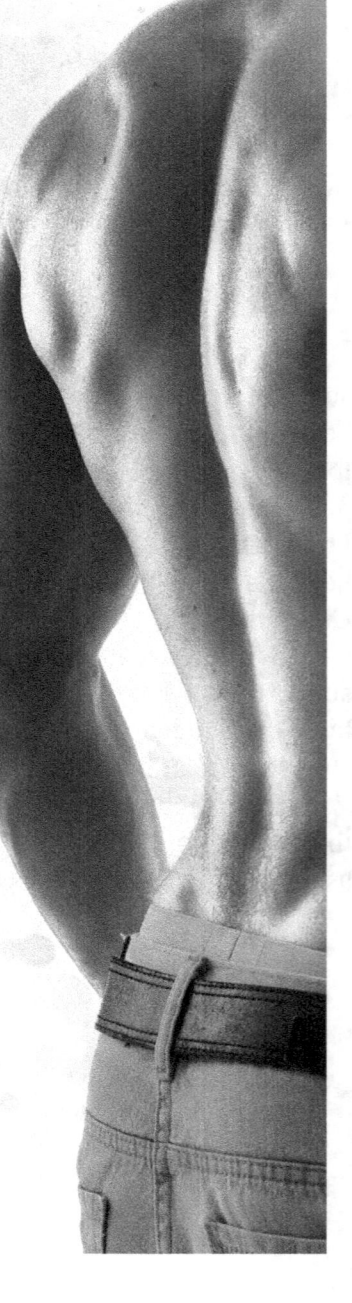

A Club Whisper Novel

Sometimes the perfect man can be found in the most unexpected place….

Martin Carmichael owns a security firm and is part owner of Club Whisper. He's a Dom in search of the right guy, and when his car breaks down on a lonely stretch of road, he thinks he might have found him.

Artist Collin Malloy is talented, easygoing, but somewhat insecure. Still, he has a big heart and is quick to offer help when he sees Martin in need. To thank him, Martin invites Collin to dinner, where the attraction between them becomes harder to resist.

But what will become of their budding relationship when Martin reveals that he likes his men bound, submissive, and in pain? Is it something Collin can accept… and possibly enjoy exploring? Even if he can, Collin has a secret of his own—a secret he doesn't even realize he's keeping.

www.dreamspinnerpress.com

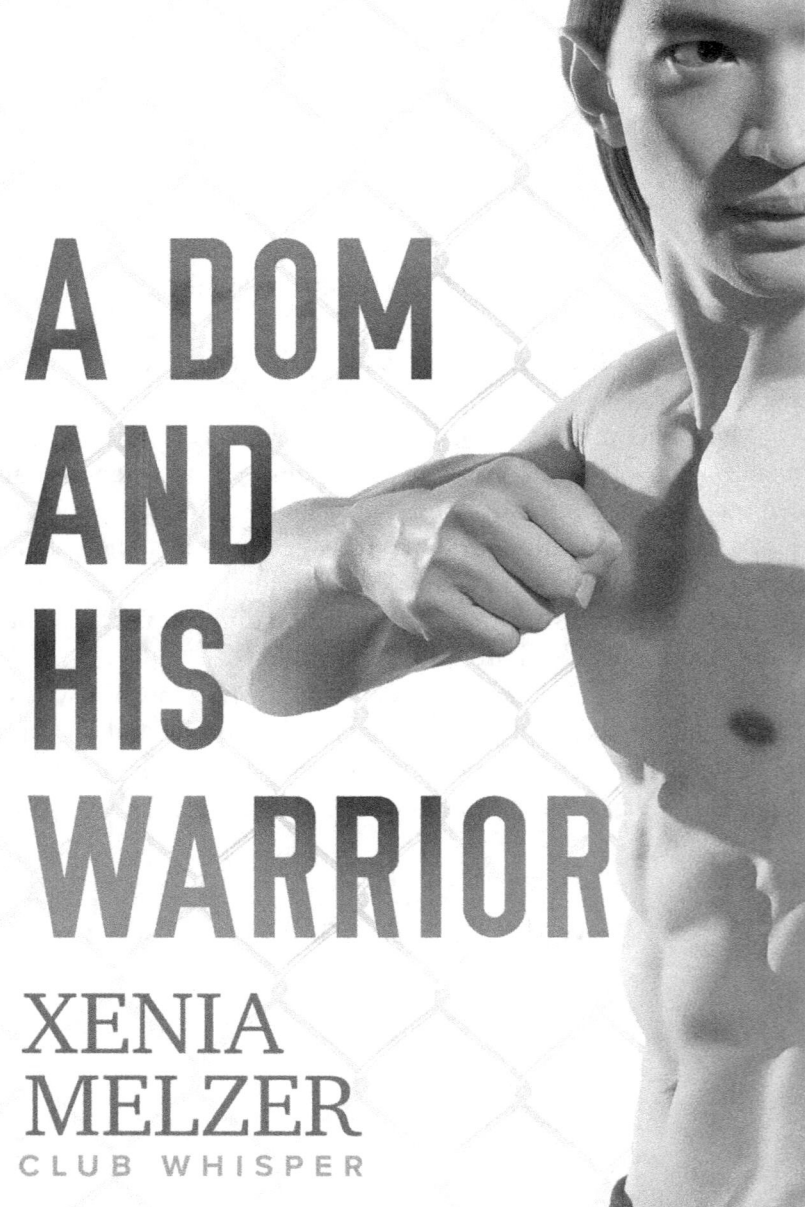

A DOM
AND
HIS
WARRIOR

XENIA
MELZER

CLUB WHISPER

A Club Whisper Novel

Leeland Drake and Jonathan White are a committed BDSM couple and have just moved in together. Leeland has only one year left in college, and everything seems perfect… until Leeland's uncle asks him to stand in for an injured UFC fighter.

Leeland wants to help his uncle, but he remembers all too well from his years competing in martial arts how strenuous life as an athlete can be. He doesn't want to risk his relationship with Jonathan. After some discussion, they decide Leeland will go pro for a year.

As if the training and strict diet weren't bad enough, the pressure skyrockets when Leeland encounters homophobic fighter Noah Adams—especially when they end up facing each other in the championship.

Between the bigoted rants of his opponent, the scrutiny of the media, the pressure from his sponsor, and a fire in his uncle's gym, Leeland is close to breaking down. Only Jonathan's support and love keep him focused enough to set foot in the octagon once more—and maybe even walk away a winner.

www.dreamspinnerpress.com

Also from Dreamspinner Press

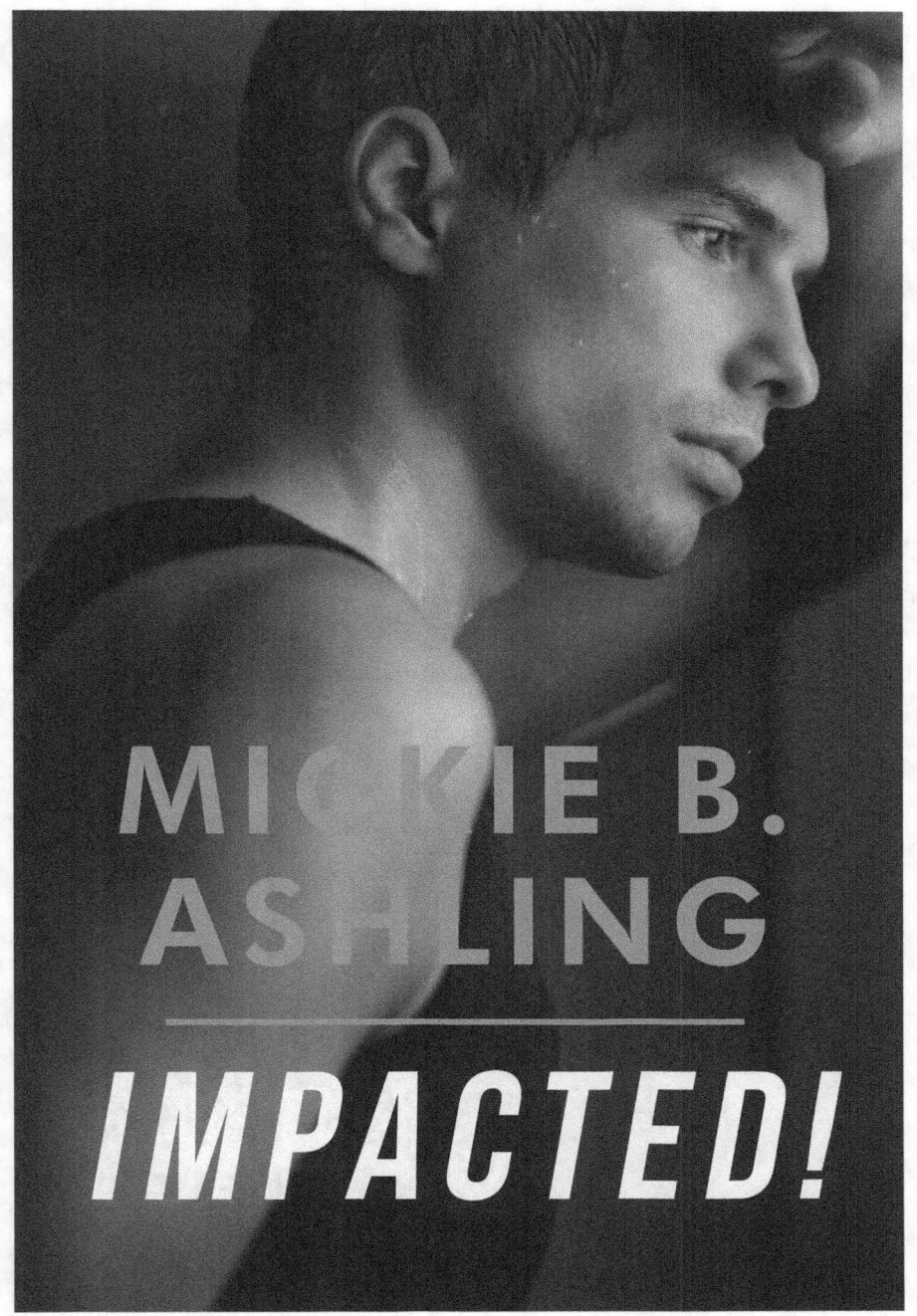

MICKIE B. ASHLING

IMPACTED!

www.dreamspinnerpress.com

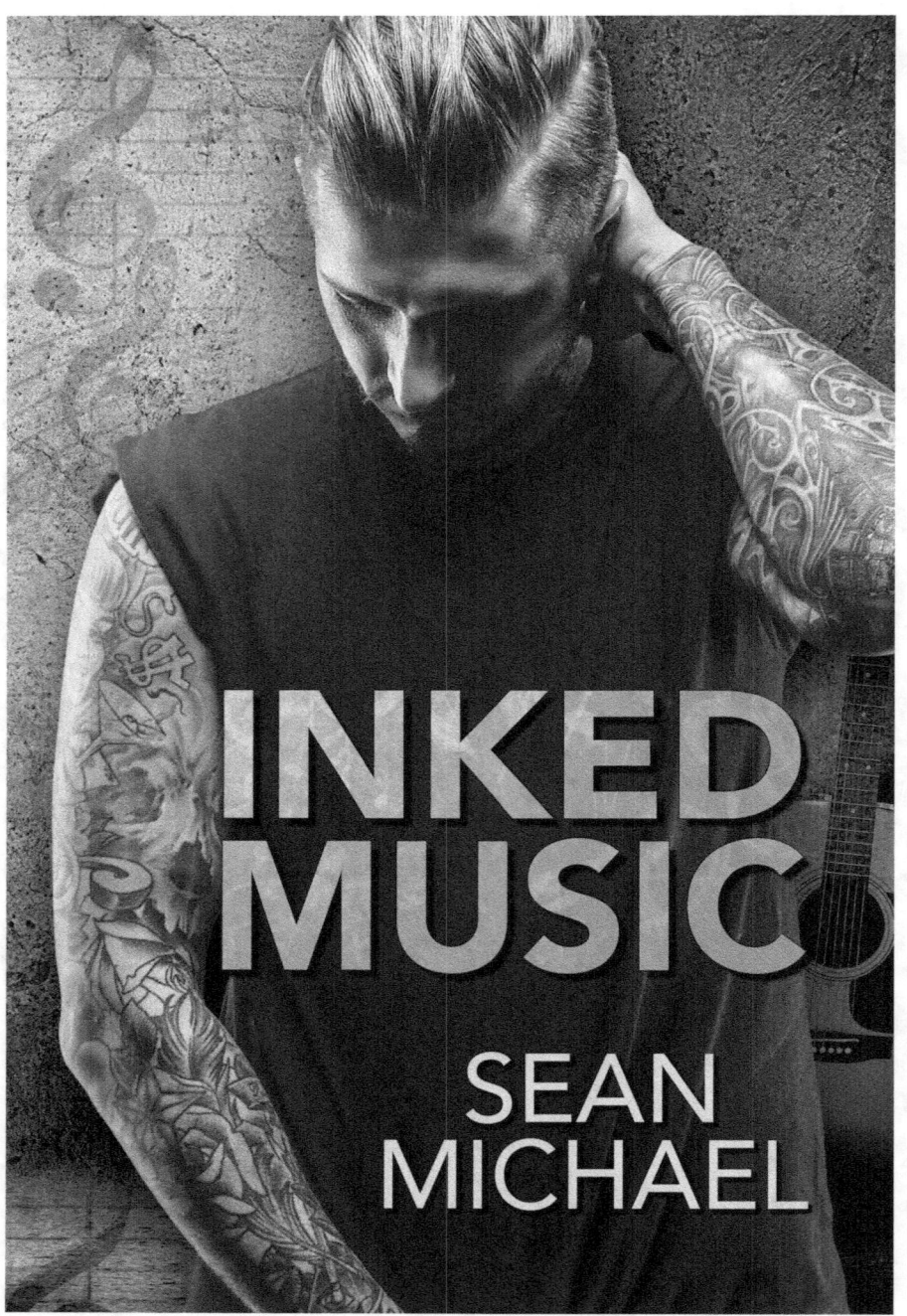

Also from Dreamspinner Press

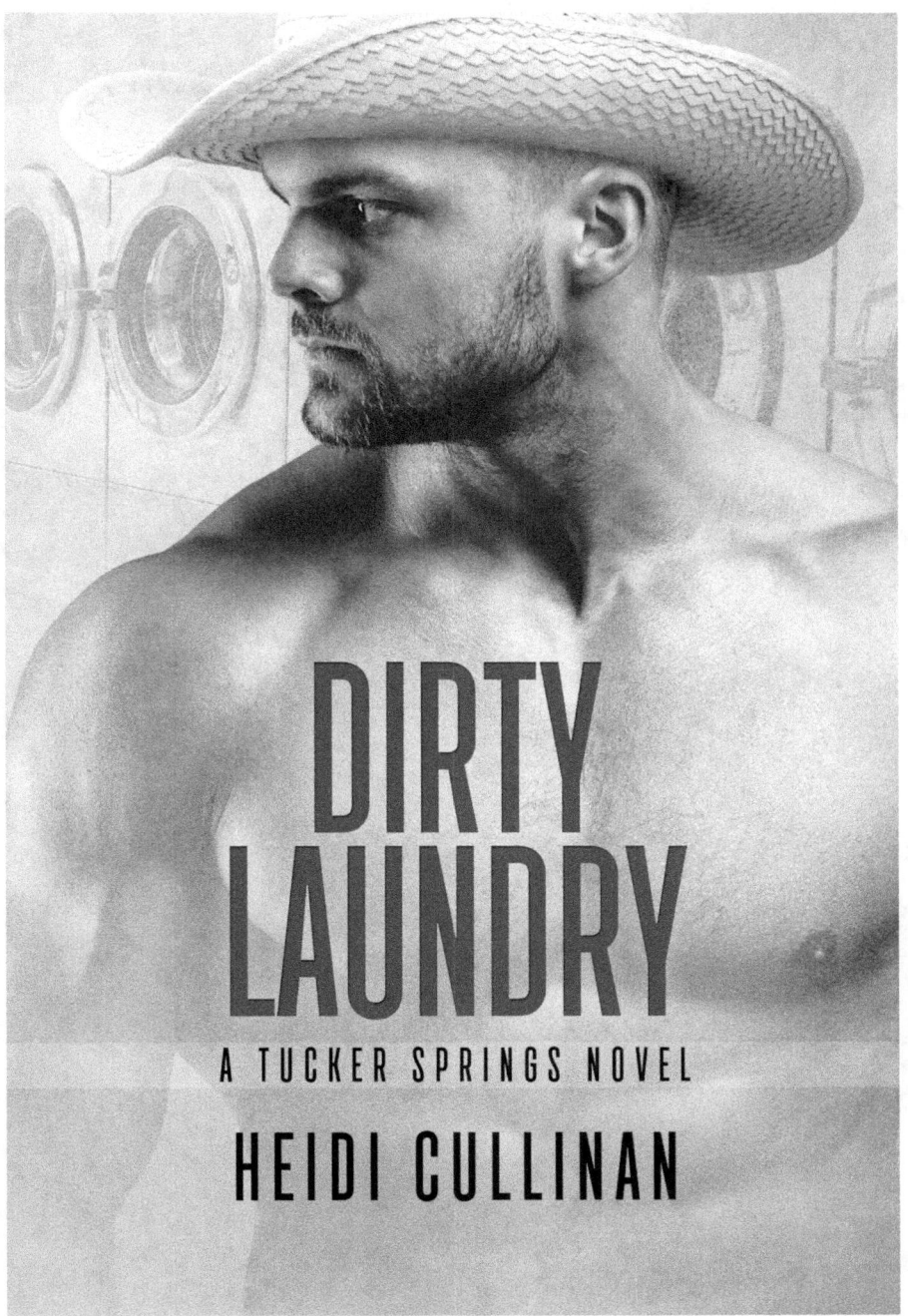

DIRTY LAUNDRY

A TUCKER SPRINGS NOVEL

HEIDI CULLINAN

www.dreamspinnerpress.com

EXPLORING

Exploring Limits: Book One

LIMITS

NICKI BENNETT

ARIEL TACHNA